MW01256539

BLUE APOCALYPSE

End Days

BOOK 1

Fighting to Get Home

BY E.E. ISHERWOOD & CRAIG MARTELLE

Connect With Craig Martelle

Website & Newsletter:
http://www.craigmartelle.com

BookBub –
https://www.bookbub.com/authors/craig-martelle

Facebook:

https://www.facebook.com/AuthorCraigMartelle/

Connect With E.E. Isherwood

Website & Newsletter:
http://www.sincethesirens.com

Facebook:

https://www.facebook.com/SinceTheSirens/

Cover Illustration © Heather Hamilton-Senter

Editing services provided by LKJ Bookmakers – www.lkjbooks.com

We couldn't do what we do without the support of great people around us. We thank our spouses and our families for giving us time alone to think, write, and review. We thank our editor (LKJbooks), cover artist (Heather), and insider team of beta readers (Micky Cocker, Kelly O'Donnell, Dr. James Caplan, and John Ashmore). It's not who we are as authors, but who we are surrounded by that makes this all happen. Enjoy the story.

TABLE OF CONTENTS

CHAPTER 1

11 am PST, August 1ˢᵗ, 2020. Modesto, CA

"Writing a letter to your girlfriend?"

Buck smiled at the young server working him for a better tip before he'd even ordered. "No, ma'am. I wish." He chuckled and shook his head. "I'm just doodling in my comic book."

"Looks like a trucker's federal logbook." Her bright eyes sparkled with her smile. Buck was old enough to be her father, but he understood. It was part of the game, and she was a master player. He bowed out of the contest early.

"How about a burger and fries?" She nodded. "And a Doctor Schnee."

"We don't have anything like that, unless you mean a Doctor Pepper." She wrote 'DP' without waiting for his answer. "That stuff will kill you."

"Eventually. It's a guilty pleasure, but everything in moderation." Buck had been driving semis for almost ten years. On one of his first solo trips, he stopped at a truck stop on a pull between Indianapolis and Kansas City and had a Doctor Schnee. He'd never heard of it before, and he hadn't found it since. Still, he wasn't one to give up on a good beverage, so he kept up his search.

She tucked her order pad in her apron and walked to another table.

It was the same dance he'd fumbled through at countless other diners and bars over the years. For the millionth time, he cursed his luck at being blessed with his father's good looks but socked with his mother's introversion. Sometimes he wished it had been the opposite.

He sighed and shut his logbook. With plenty of sleep under his belt, he was stoked to get on the road and head back east. Under Uncle Sam's rules, he could drive for eleven hours today. If he put the hammer down, he'd make it to Salt Lake City before he ran out the clock.

Buck fingered the edges of his road atlas, even though he already knew the route, so he pulled out his phone instead. The shiny black device sported a tiny slide-out keyboard and an even smaller viewscreen. His son's face beamed out, which caused him to get lost in thought for a few minutes.

"Ooh, he's a cutie," the server said in a bubbly voice while sliding a burger in front of him.

Buck slowly shook his head. "They need to put a bell on you."

She harrumphed and put the Dr. Pepper on the other side of the table from his logbook. She pulled a ketchup bottle from the next table and plopped it next to the plate with the burger.

Buck closed his eyes and fully inhaled the burger's aroma. It made his mouth water. Schnees weren't his only guilty pleasure. He wondered if it tasted as good as it smelled.

When he opened his eyes, he found the young woman's face too close as she peered at his phone. "Your brother?" she ventured.

The dance.

"Here you go." He handed her a twenty on a fifteen dollar bill. "Keep the change."

She shrugged and strolled away, the twenty disappearing as if by magic.

"I'm coming for you, Garth," Buck told the picture. "I need to tell you I'm sorry, and then I need to take you camping, fish for our dinner. All that good stuff that I don't get to do enough of with you."

2pm EST. La Guardia Airport, New York City, NY

"I dare you to call that number."

"Dude? Are you crazy?" Garth elbowed his best friend Sam. They sat in the back of a New York City Transit bus, studiously examining the scrawl penned into the seatback in front of them. Someone had etched "Call Mona for god tim" in the leather.

"I bet it's a smokin' hot girl," Sam asserted, "probably Puerto Rican with mamma mia legs."

Garth knew his buddy wasn't going to let it go. They'd spent most of the morning living inside a running joke with cologne, so a prank call would only continue his friend's fun. It was his job to talk him down from taking things too far. "It is more likely a four-hundred-pound shut-in named Claus. Who wants to have a 'god tim' anyway?"

"Ha! Then how did he get all the way out here to write this?" Sam elbowed him back.

Garth slowly shook his head. It was an affectation he'd picked up from his father. The fifteen-year-old had needed the gesture many times over the years when he was around his wiry best friend. He lived with Sam and his parents while Garth's dad was on the road.

"Just call it then."

Sam seemed surprised. "No, I dared you to call it."

They'd come off the subway line near the airport, but for some reason, they had to take a regular bus the last two miles. It gave them plenty of time to stir up trouble.

He had his friend trapped. "I'll read the number, you put it in your phone." Sam already had his phone in his hands, so Garth read off the numbers.

"You don't think I will," Sam said with bravado. "I swear I'm not afraid to do it."

Sam put the number in his phone, but Garth didn't really want him to call it, so he backed off.

"We're almost there. Put your phone away. For now."

Sam hesitated.

"Seriously," Garth pressed.

"Fine." Sam shoved the phone in his pocket like he'd been given the worst news in the world. "But I have the number for when we're ready to talk to Mona." He said the name with a suitable moan.

Garth laughed at his friend. He had no doubt in his mind the call would get made. Sam was fearless when it came to girls. Even fake ones who put their numbers on random seats.

The two of them scrambled down the steps of the bus and trotted into the main terminal. Sam was evidently a veteran traveler because he knew exactly where to go. At least until they reached the baggage screening area.

Garth led them up to a bored-looking security woman guarding a little podium.

"Need to see ID and your tickets, boys."

"I, uh, we're fifteen. We don't have ID." Garth felt stupid for not knowing there would be paperwork involved at the airport.

"Do you at least have tickets?" She turned up her nose like he was an unwashed vagrant.

Garth shrugged and motioned to Sam. "We're here to see his parents."

He turned around to get Sam to back him up, but the asshole had fast-walked to a distant corner where he tried to blend in with his fellow travelers.

"Looks like your friend ditched you," the TSA worker said dryly. "You might want to take a shower. Next!"

Garth marched to his friend and clocked him in the shoulder with a right hook. "You are such an ass shovel."

Sam feigned pain at the shot, but snort-laughed while trying to hold it back. "You looked like such a tool in front of all those people. How do you not know about the TSA gestapo? You can't flush a urinal at the airport without your papers."

Garth and Sam traveled all over the city on their outings, but he didn't want to admit it was his first time at an airport, if Sam hadn't already figured it out. "I thought all we had to do was prove we were there to pick someone up."

After brushing his blond bangs from his eyes, Sam turned to what was important. "Did she get a whiff of your cost-cutter perfume?" He snickered some more.

Garth nodded heavily. "Yeah, this stuff is starting to make me sick."

"I saw her squinch up her nose like you'd dropped a deuce right in front of her. That was an added bonus."

Sam waited to see if Garth was going to reply, but then kept talking.

"All right. We'll have to wait. I like to watch planes land until Mom and Dad show up. They should be landing right now." He strode off but glanced over his shoulder. "Come on, newb."

"I'm not a newb," Garth answered. There were few insults greater than being told you weren't an expert at something. They used it a lot when they played video games, but it never rose to the level of bother he felt at that moment. He prided himself on being prepared for the real world and knowing what was going on around him. Sam had used that pride to play up his joke. They knew each other too well.

Sam rushed to the waiting area and plopped into a seat. The floor-to-ceiling windows along the terminal wall gave them a perfect view of the runways. It would have been a great place to wait in peace, except for their never-ending joke with the cologne.

"You had to sit there?" Garth pointed nearby because his buddy sat in the middle seat of a three-chair row. There were no other chairs in the vicinity.

"Where else would I go?" Sam said matter-of-factly. "This window has these nice, comfy chairs. We're lucky no one was here."

"Yeah, I see that. But why did you sit in the middle? Take one of the ends, you jackass, so I don't have to sit next to your nasty cologne." Today, they both doused themselves with the cheapest, most off-brand colognes they could buy while in the city. Not to impress girls, but to stink each other out. Garth's reminded him of a flower that had been tossed into a port-o-potty. Sam's was worse. They played dumb when people acted like someone farted on the subway, but they laughed uproariously once they were clear. It was probably why no one sat near them on the bus, too.

Sam slid over to the end. "Yeah, good point. I don't want to smell you for another second, either."

Garth got in the seat, slid up against the back, and finally relaxed. After a long weekend of being alone with Sam, he was ready for his friend's parents to get back from Chicago. If there was one thing he'd learned in the experience, it was that he couldn't leave Sam alone for any length of time or he'd get into some kind of trouble. Having his parents back would finally give Garth a break from keeping an eye on him.

I wonder when my dad is coming home, he thought, repeating the question that was always at the back of his mind. They'd been angry when he last drove off. There was no reason for it. He opened his phone, thought about sending a text, but stopped when he caught Sam watching him.

The airport was super busy. In the few moments they watched, numerous planes maneuvered on the runways and tarmacs around the terminals. It fascinated him to see the different colors and sizes of planes. A jumbo jet sat not far away, almost blocking his view. The Korean logo made it seem exotic even as the plane blended into its bland surroundings.

"We shouldn't have long to wait. My parents will run right over here when they get to this terminal. They've probably been worried sick about me." He paused and looked over to Garth with his trademark smirk. "And you, I suppose."

He could appreciate their concern. If anything, his parents had been irresponsible to leave Sam by himself, although Garth wondered if they counted on him to be their kid's babysitter. If so, the joke was on them. Pouring whole bottles of craptastic colognes on themselves was anything but responsible.

"Yeah, I—" Garth tried to respond, but a brilliant flash of blue light caught his eye. It traveled from one side of the skyline to the other with the speed of lightning, from west to east. In a flash, it was gone.

"Holy shit!" Sam pointed outside.

"Yeah. Holy shit." Garth replied with wonder.

Modesto, CA

Lunch was exactly what Buck thought it would be. The burger didn't taste as good as it smelled. The fries had been under the heat lamp for too long. Salt shakers and ketchup bottles that looked like they'd served hard time in an elementary school cafeteria. Buzzing flies added that extra ambiance he always looked for in eateries.

At least it was cheap and fast. He wasn't getting any closer to home waiting for his food to digest.

Buck gathered his things and went out the door the instant he got the text that said his load was ready. The fresh California air made him a bit light-headed after being in the stuffy diner.

The sound of trucks greeted him. A hundred tractor trailers working the low gears nearby signaled his return to the job he loved and the world he understood. It paid the bills and allowed him to see the country.

He strode across the parking lot of the giant shipping company, careful to avoid the many rigs pulling in and out. The atlas and logbook were under his left arm, and he carried the Dr. Pepper cup like it was precious cargo. It was so hot on the short walk, he'd already taken a few swigs, but he'd intended to save it, so he'd have something to suck back while on the road.

A gleam of silver caught his eye on the dark asphalt ahead. When he got close, he couldn't believe his luck.

"Bingo, Buck," he said to himself.

He squatted down to pick up the quarter.

A centennial. Must be my lucky day.

The 1976 quarter wasn't worth much more than 25 cents, but he collected the special quarters because they meant something to him. Since he did so much travel and spent tons of cash in eateries across America, he figured he'd collected hundreds of them.

On a whim, he flicked the quarter up in the air like the coin toss at a football game.

"Heads, I win. Tails, you lose!"

While the coin was mid-air, a sapphire blue wave of light darted across the sky from out of the east. It was impossible to miss, even in the bright light of the morning.

"What the fuck?"

The coin flipped through the air, forgotten, as Buck blinked the flash from his eyes.

CHAPTER 2

AirBlue flight 586 flying at 8,000 feet over La Guardia Airport.

"What is that?" Captain Cody Alderbrook watched as a blue light shot across the sky above their Bombardier CRJ1000 aircraft.

Charles, his co-pilot, strained to see the phenomenon out his side window. "No idea. Hoo-boy, is it moving like a gunshot."

"Call it in," the pilot ordered calmly. They were already holding at 8000 feet over La Guardia's air traffic control tower, waiting for a runway to open up, so he needed to know if a meteorological condition was going to screw with his arrival time.

"Aye." Charles flicked on the VHF transmitter. "Tower, this is AirBlue 586."

The La Guardia tower replied immediately. "Go ahead, 586."

"Hey, we're seeing some weird weather up here. Can you confirm?"

He didn't see where the blue wave of light had come from, but it headed out over the distant horizon of the Atlantic Ocean. Cody guessed it moved at several times the speed of sound. He thought it might have been a shockwave from a meteor.

"586, we have no unusual activity on our end. Wait one."

A blue arc of electricity erupted from the plane's dashboard and past the aircrew.

"Tower, this is 586—" Cody tried to say.

The plane nosed downward like the aircraft had fallen off a cliff. The airframe rattled so violently, he thought his teeth would shatter. His harness held him to the back of his chair while the rest of the plane went vertical. While his heart tried to jettison from his chest, he remained steady on the outside. 98 passengers depended on what he did next.

Cody jammed the throttles forward while pulling the yoke back. "Power up!"

The twin-engines responded with a roar, and the nose of the plane reluctantly lifted. The shaking stopped somewhere along the thousand-foot descent. The control board shimmered with blue energy. They stared at it, expecting a catastrophic failure.

"Tell me that was turbulence," Cody croaked when the worst didn't materialize.

Charles' hat had flown from his head and was wedged against the front window. That was a first.

"I don't know," the co-pilot responded in a deliberate voice.

"And that blue crap?" Cody added.

"I don't know. These are fried, though." The co-pilot pointed to the altimeter and air speed dials in the middle of the dashboard; both dials were frozen in place.

Cody watched the controls while mentally running through the oft-drilled emergency flight procedures. He decided what needed his attention when they were once again flying level. He picked up the mic to speak to the back.

"This is Captain Cody. We've hit a bit of turbulence." He forced a chuckle because it was proven to calm the nerves of the customers, but more importantly, it soothed his flight crew. "But it looks like we're in the clear."

He got off the line just as multiple audible alarms came on.

"What now?" he mumbled.

The captain was ready to play the part of the hero, but his blood froze in his veins when all the noises and lights went out.

"What the?" he blurted.

The alarms were off, but so was everything else. The entire plane had lost power. For one surreal moment, Cody and his co-pilot sat in perfect silence.

Then the screams began.

La Guardia Airport, New York City, NY

Garth jumped out of his chair and pointed outside. "Did you see that?"

The blue light had already faded, so he pointed up into the empty skies.

"Sure I did. Must have been a supersonic plane, or whatever. I've seen videos of fighter jets breaking the sound barrier."

Garth turned back and brushed through his unkempt hair. "I didn't see a plane."

Sam snickered. "You're at an airport, dude. Look around!"

He briefly thought of fishing trips with his father. They used to spend a lot of weekends out in the country, sitting in their jon boat, with two lines over the side. His dad would point to the sky and pick out cool planes. He'd never seen anything like the blue light on any of those trips.

"Well, I don't think it was a plane. It was...weird."

"Yeah, okay, Nancy. Don't be scared."

"I'm not scared!" Garth shot back, not sure why he took such offense.

Sam seemed to study him before speaking. "Look, I know just what can fix you." He hopped up and began walking. He didn't even look back.

"Fine."

Garth caught up to Sam, who started talking. "It was probably just moon dust or sun rays or whatever bullshit they taught us in Roper's science class."

"That's your answer?" Garth laughed. "You didn't pay much attention to Roper, did you?"

"Who needs science when you have a whole world to explore?" Sam seemed lost for a few seconds, but then adjusted his course toward a less-crowded portion of the busy terminal.

"That's kind of the point of science," Garth said in a conciliatory voice.

They soon stood at the sealed doors of an elevator.

"Why are we here? Aren't we going to miss your parents?"

Sam pressed the button and the door opened a few seconds later. He walked in like it was part of his plan. Garth hated to be led around not knowing what was going to happen next, but that was how Sam lived his life.

"Entrare," Sam said with a fake French accent.

When the doors shut, someone started to sneeze, and it wasn't either of them.

Garth leaned around Sam to see a gray-haired man and woman standing way back in the corner. He'd been so busy managing Sam, he failed to notice them.

He smiled at the couple to be polite.

"Going up," Sam said nonchalantly.

It was a fifteen-second ride, but the woman sneezed a few more times on the way.

When the doors opened, they all moved forward, but the woman shoved Garth to push past him.

Sam cracked up laughing at full volume as the boys got some distance from the older people. "You needed a good laugh," he said in a not-so-quiet voice.

"My wife is very allergic to perfume," the old guy said over his shoulder.

"Oh shit," Garth said as he realized they'd just trapped the couple inside the enclosed space with their smelly colognes. Between the blue light and becoming mostly immune to the stinky cloud they carried everywhere, he didn't realize how bad it would smell in there.

"Sorry!" Garth yelled back. "Really."

Sam was still laughing when they reached the ticketing area of the terminal.

"That was a dick move, Sam."

His friend's shoulders slumped. "Yeah, maybe. I didn't mean to hurt anybody. How was I supposed to know they'd be allergic?"

"Look, we shouldn't be screwing around. I want to find your parents and get out of here."

"Ah, yeah. That's why I brought you up here. See?" Sam started toward a giant billboard showing hundreds of arrival and departure times.

Garth was happy to be moving in the right direction, but he soon stopped in his tracks.

"Whoa! That's amazing!"

It was Garth's turn to indulge as he zig-zagged through slow-moving travelers and around the ticket counters until he stood at another set of windows. With an elevated view, they saw over the landing strips to the large island in the middle of the East River.

"Yeah, that's Riker's Island, I think," Sam said with little interest. "A huge jail is out there."

Squat gray buildings and numerous parking lots dotted the island, making it easy to believe as a correctional facility.

"That's pretty sweet," Garth went on "A prison. Right here in the city."

"Yep, a real happenin' place. Everyone wants to live there. Maybe they can move the entire city inside and we'd have one big, happy party. Come on, let's go. You're the one who said we shouldn't screw around."

"Yeah, okay," Garth answered distantly. Could the whole city's population fit on an island that small? That was the type of science and math he enjoyed, but it wasn't what they taught in school. Maybe it was worth looking up on his phone while Sam's parents drove them back home.

He was going to follow Sam, but he caught sight of a black dot in the air. It fell straight down like it had been dropped from miles above.

"Hey, there's a..." He quickly glanced toward Sam, but he was already halfway to the billboard.

By the time he looked up again, the winged dot was almost to the runway.

Modesto, CA

Buck jogged into the shipping terminal, expecting the place to be going crazy with talk about the blue light, but when he got inside, there was only the normal hustle of truckers and shippers trying to get product to market.

Maybe I'm overreacting.

Rows of garage doors along the outer wall of the stadium-sized facility gave the dock workers access to trailers. Pallet loaders and forklifts skidded back and forth to fill them up. His own rig was about two hundred yards away. Not even halfway to the other end.

All of it was exceedingly ordinary.

Definitely overreacting.

Still, he wanted to check on Garth before hitting the trail, so he pulled out his phone and opened his contacts. There were only a few numbers programmed into it, so it was a snap for him to get to the one he wanted.

He mashed the device against his head to drown out the noise of the warehouse.

"Come on, son, pick it up," he said under his breath.

They had an agreement about using phones. Buck insisted that no matter what else was going on, Garth had to pick up anytime he got a call from his dad. Buck thought that was reasonable. Naturally, teenaged Garth believed it was a death sentence of inconvenience.

His son's number rang with a hollow echo in the line that made it sound distant. After about five rings, the noise changed to a series of clicks, like someone was dialing using a rotary phone. The connection died after a few seconds of that.

"What the hell?"

Something IS wrong.

He called again, and the ringing was normal.

Damn. I'm being stupid.

"Pick up." He tried to imagine where Garth was at that moment. His boy had sent a text saying he and Sam were almost at the airport, but he provided no updates. They should have collected Sam's parents and been heading home already.

Garth didn't pick up, but it did go to his voicemail.

"Yo, this is Garth. Drop those digits and I'll get back to you." Buck hated how fake he sounded, but it had been "explained" to him that it was how the kids talked these days.

He took a deep, mind-clearing breath. His anxiety had gone back and forth in the last few minutes. The blue light might have been a nothingburger, but he needed to hear his son's voice. However, he couldn't sound panicky and uncertain, especially on voicemail, or he could inject fear where none belonged.

"Hello, son. I'm, uh, almost loaded here in Modesto, California, and I'll be mobile within the hour. I just got done eating another crappy meal." He chuckled. "You would have hated it. Lots of pickles involved, and the patty was as dry as tree bark."

Buck considered whether to mention the blue light, but in that brief decision loop, he decided against it. Whatever it was in the sky, it only lasted a couple of seconds and nothing had come of it. The dock workers doing their normal routines proved that.

"Anyway, I'm looking forward to seeing you at the end of the week. I know we haven't been fishing in a while. What do you say we pull the old boat out of storage and find a quiet lake? I would really like that."

Even thinking about it made him happy.

"Love ya, kid. Be home soon."

He hung up and felt much better.

NORAD, Cheyenne Mountain, Colorado

"What the fuck just happened?" General Obadias "Obi-Wan" Smith had spilled coffee on his leg, but that was only a small part of what made him angry. The lights were not supposed to go out in the bunker. Ever.

He'd personally witnessed a total power shutdown for a full second. Every light. Every computer screen. Every phone charger. Out.

"Checking!" several subordinates shouted from the control room.

"I better have a goddamned answer in sixty seconds or heads are going to roll!"

His mind rubber-banded to a series of impossibilities.

A nuke could have gone off nearby. If it was big enough, that might shut us down.

Hackers could have found a way in.

I'm not saying it was aliens...but...

Nothing could touch NORAD and not leave evidence. He had to know what it was, no matter how impossible. The life of every American citizen could depend on the answer he got in the next 52 seconds.

"Warm up the red phone," he said without a hint of mirth in his voice.

CHAPTER 3

5 am local time. Wollemi National Park, New South Wales, Australia

For an instant, a flash of light filled the Australian night sky.

Destiny Sinclair woke from a deep sleep, thinking someone had taken her picture.

"Real mature, mates."

It wouldn't be the first time she'd been the butt of someone's joke. It was the kind of childish prank animal researchers pulled on each other after reaching the bottom of Tequila bottles, and several were emptied at camp last night. She was up and ready to chew out whoever did it, but her anger changed to concern for her mates when she smelled smoke.

"Bugger me," she coughed.

By E.E. Isherwood & Craig Martelle

She tossed off her wool blanket and fell sideways out of her hammock. It was winter in New South Wales, and the overnight temps sometimes dropped all the way to ten degrees Celsius. That worked in her favor, however, because she slept with her clothes and boots on. Once those boots hit the dirt, she was on duty.

In addition to surprising her with the bright flash, the prankster made it harder to see anything in the tiny glade where she'd made camp. Her night vision was ruined by a blue afterimage. "Who's out there? Come on, this is serious!"

No one fessed up.

A thunderous crash echoed up the small valley. There had been no rain in the forecast, so she was pretty sure what it wasn't. Thick smoke gave her a clue what it was: a tree had toppled over.

Forest fire.

Ironically, her own campfire had gone out hours ago, so she had almost no light until she pulled a tiny flashlight from her nylon hiking pants. That helped her get to the rope bag hanging from a nearby tree. It was up there to keep it away from critters, but it also gave her an easy landmark to find.

She coughed from the exertion of those few steps.

"Shit!"

There was no way to know how close the fire had come, or how large it was, but if the smoke was thick enough to affect her, she needed to move.

The first thing she pulled out of the bag was her radio.

"Base Camp, this is Dez, come in. I've got a problem."

Static crackled for several seconds before she tried again.

"Come in! This is Dez. There's a forest fire nearby. One of the team might also be over there. Possibly lost." All anger about the prank was gone. That person might have been affected by the smoke, too.

A groggy man answered. "Hey, Dez. This is Pat. Where are you?"

"I told you last night, I'm just over the hill. Is the fire on your side?"

It took him a whole five seconds to answer. When he finally came back, his words were slightly slurred. "Oh, right. You wanted to get away from us drunkards. Nothing going on here. You okay?"

"No, I'm not okay, thanks for asking," she sassed. "Is anyone missing from camp?"

Patrick hesitated again. "You are."

"Shit! Is anyone else gone? I thought someone was just here. I need to know, Pat. Look around!"

There was a sound that might have been the microphone tipping over, but then the line went silent. She prayed he was checking on the team to be sure they were all there. She also begged fate to give her the one night in history where none of the students paired off.

Another loud crack belted out from the valley. She would bet anything the fire was already engulfing hectares of scrub.

It surprised her how fast Patrick came back on. "All good here. No empties. Everyone is here but you."

She let out a sigh of relief. Tracking down a drunk university student inside a burning national park was not her idea of animal research.

"Good. Now listen. I'm coming over the top. You might need to call triple zero to get some firefighters in here. Get a drone in the sky to see how big it is."

The man on the other end snickered. "How big what is?"

"Are you still pissed drunk?"

"How dare you!" Patrick sounded like he'd put the radio mic in his mouth.

"Get someone sober on the line!"

I'll have to do this myself.

The base camp was just over the hundred-meter-high ridge at her back. She left the uni kids as well as the other profs because she didn't like to swim in alcohol each night, but she didn't hold it against them. It gave her a chance to get out alone and sleep with nature, which was the true love of her life.

A large burning leaf floated down as she grabbed her backpack and shoved her arms through the straps. A thick column of smoke followed.

She eyed the hammock and little camp chair she had carried in last night, but there was no more time.

"Cut your losses, woman."

She started up the rocky escarpment between her and the team.

European Laboratory for Particle Physics (CERN), Switzerland

"Will someone please tell me what the bloody hell is happening?" Dr. Tomas Eli, team leader at the Large Hadron Collider, demanded. It was the assignment of a lifetime, and his team's experiment had been going swimmingly until moments ago.

A soft-spoken Italian physicist typed code into a black monitor not far away. "Experiment 7HC is still running, sir. The power is feeding in, but nothing is coming around the loop."

"That's impossible."

"I thought so, too," she agreed.

Dr. Eli spoke evenly into the microphone. "Anyone else? Cambridge unit? I need to know if we should stop it."

He looked toward his fellow scientist from the Home Island. She and her team worked at a computer station across the gymnasium-sized control center. The dark-haired woman was named Claire, he thought.

The spectacled physicist looked up at him, then back to her terminal.

"Claire? I need an answer."

"It's Clarice, actually."

He wanted to smack his forehead. "Just talk!"

"Sir, we're getting the same thing on this end. Power is dumping into the loop and feeding the experiment, but nothing is coming out the other side. Take a look for yourself."

The giant screen on the biggest wall of the room lit up. Clarice projected her monitor so the other scientists could see her data.

"Right here." Her screen showed a perfect circle that represented the collider loop. "The beam shoots down the magnets until it reaches this point. Then the energy disappears."

He felt a faint rumble under his loafers, much like a heavily-laden lorry driving on a street nearby. That was impossible, though, because they were far underground.

"People!" he shouted. "Energy doesn't just disappear. The collider loop is no more complex than a sewer, for cripes' sake. You piss in one end of the pipe and it comes out the other. If we lose connection or alignment, the power gets shut off. We have ten different safety programs with that one simple task. So. Tell me where that energy is going!" He pointed to the giant image on the wall.

The people who would most likely know were currently out.

"Where the holy hell is Dr. Johnson?" he asked the room. There was some good-natured competition among the twenty-two nations who shared research time at the collider, but he was man enough to admit the American scientist from MIT was near the top in terms of intellect.

But the shaggy-haired brainiac was gone.

The American team, including Dr. Johnson, had run out of the control room a few minutes before the power spikes and lags. The Americans left a few grad students at their desk, but he didn't trust them to take out the trash. It wasn't a knock on the Yanks, either. He didn't trust any grad student with complex problems.

When one of the young men spoke up, he almost scoffed.

"Sir! I think we have the answer!"

"Just tell me," Tomas droned.

The grad student took a deep breath before continuing. "It's not us. It's—"

A blue light on Dr. Eli's computer keyboard caught his eye.

Then it filled the room.

The Large Hadron Collider finally returned all that energy.

Wollemi National Park, New South Wales, Australia

Destiny shouted into her radio, desperate to know where to go. "Base, come in. Base!"

The fire came in with cyclone-force winds and instant summertime heat. She'd seen fire move at over a hundred kilometers per hour, but only from the safety of a spotter plane. Never from the ground.

It's not even forest fire season.

The blaze came up the valley so fast, she appreciated she might have died if someone hadn't flashed that light in her eyes. It was a mystery how they got back to camp so fast, but she was going to kiss them once she was safe on the other side of the hill.

For the first few minutes of her escape, she dealt with Patrick and his slurred words, but finally someone else got to the radio who wasn't sloshed.

"I'm here, Dez. I've got ya," the female voice reassured her. Taiga Skyler was another animal researcher from Brisbane. She studied birds, but Destiny wasn't going to hold it against her. At least she knew how to work a radio. "We're still trying to figure out what that blue light was. BBC says it was a worldwide event."

"Blue light?" she asked.

That's what woke me up.

She didn't have time for trivial things.

"I'm halfway up. I need to know if the fire is up top." She thanked her luck that her big sister had taught her how to rock-climb and scramble. Those lessons were two decades old, but they'd kept her alive the last fifteen minutes as she hopped from rock to rock up the exposed hillside. Her footing felt sure, even in the shaky beam of her weak flashlight.

"The drone is already up in the air. You're mostly clear, Dez. Go to your right one more time, then go up again. You'll be fine. We're chucking in the tents and already have the trucks started to get us out of here the moment you arrive."

"K. Out." She hung the radio off her belt and continued to hop from rock to rock. Somewhere up above, a small four-prop drone carried a video camera over the sandstone ridge. That eye-in-the-sky gave her a huge advantage over the surging fire. Several times on her climb, flare-ups began above her, and she asked Taiga where to go to avoid them.

The hillside brightened as she climbed higher than the forest in the valley. The dancing flames engulfed tree crowns like giant torches and cast plenty of light on her. She made better time once she didn't need to hold the flashlight.

But fire likes to go up too, so she couldn't take a rest at any point on the hill.

Push it, girl!

As she neared the top of the steep climb, her radio crackled with Taiga's excited voice.

"This thing's a whopper! It's spreading through the park. It's hopping all over your valley, Dez. You have to get up to the top before you get boxed in."

She didn't ask any questions. She shook off her backpack and shoved it behind a rock. A tense situation had just become life or death.

"I'm going to make it," she said into the black walkie before securing it to her belt one last time.

She looked up at the last thirty feet of the steep terrain with grim determination, but a black shape scurried by her feet and made her lose focus. For a couple of seconds, she teetered between standing there and falling backward down the rocks.

"Sweet Jesus!"

She recognized the compact shape and cute waddle of a wombat. The little thing was about the size of a cattle dog with the gray fur of a roo. She'd never seen one move that fast, but it headed back down the escarpment instead of up. It wouldn't find sanctuary down there unless it had survival skills she didn't know about.

"Good luck, little guy," she said sadly.

Destiny grabbed onto the rock with both hands and pulled herself up. She used her feet as supports and kicked her legs to give momentum to mount the next big ledge. Her long pants scraped the sharp edges, and her legs banged against the rocks, but she ignored the pain.

"Up, up, up!"

The heat of the fire made her sweat like mad, but she continued to climb. The inferno also roared like a freight train behind her back. There was probably some formula regarding how much smoke a person could suck in and still operate like she was, but she didn't want to know when she'd reach the limit.

She grabbed onto another ledge and repeated the process to climb another six feet.

Her radio interrupted her climb. "Dez. You are beating the fire, but it is coming around the hill toward us, so don't stop."

There was no time to respond, but she did catch sight of the flashing blue and red running lights on the tiny drone's undercarriage as she headed up the last pitch of the rockface. The whole camp was undoubtedly watching her on the data collection laptop.

Her palms puddled up from all the anxiety. She wiped them on her hips before stepping off. "Slow and steady," she said to herself. None of her sister's training ever covered fast evacuations from fire zones.

Destiny hopped to the next boulder, then reached for another shelf edge. It would be a simple up and over to the top. However, when she grabbed onto the rock, the soft sandstone lip broke off.

She hit the ground ten feet below before she knew she was in the air.

Southern Cross Logistics, Shipping Terminal. Modesto, CA

"We've got you all hooked up." The dock hand shoved a clipboard at him, so Buck pulled a pen from his shirt to sign off. He'd already done a walkaround to confirm the service lines were solid, the fifth wheel was locked, and the tires on the trailer had some tread left.

He checked the boxes on the clipboard to affirm to king and country he had indeed looked those things over.

While he had a captive audience, he tried to strike up some small talk.

"Did you see that blue light about ten minutes ago?"

"No, but you are the third driver to ask me about it."

"You know our type," he said dramatically. "Get a few miles behind us and we start to see ghosts, aliens, and bears. Sometimes all at once."

He laughed and signed his name, but when he went to hand off his masterpiece, the other guy was punching keys on his phone. The dock worker continued typing for a few seconds before taking the offered clipboard.

The man lazily ripped the top sheet off the stack of duplicates and whipped it back to Buck. He turned around without saying a word, returning his attention to the phone.

"Thanks," Buck said to the man's back.

"Yeah," the man replied.

"There's those California manners," Buck said to himself.

Only eleven states between him and Garth, but at least he had his paperwork done.

CHAPTER 4

Three Mile Island Nuclear Generating Station, Pennsylvania

Carl Junker glanced at the tired gray phone. It rang every hour, on the hour, when the safety team called him in the main control room. He was the day manager of the TMI-1 reactor, and he detested the prospect of endlessly picking up that phone for the rest of his career.

Everything at the nuclear plant ran on schedules, especially maintenance and safety. He peeked at the big analog clock hanging from the wall to confirm the hour of yet another safety check.

It's not time!

Carl scrambled to get the phone up to his ear. He said "Hello?" before the base reached his mouth.

"Holy shit!" the tech screeched into the phone. "We just had a radiation spike that was off the charts! Fuck, we didn't have our suits on! We have to run!"

"I don't show any issues," Carl replied in a businesslike voice. "Just talk to me. Stay calm." There were lots of reasons for calls to come in at the wrong time. In one instance, a safety inspector's watch battery died, and he was ten minutes late with check-in. That almost shut the whole plant down.

The man on the phone let out a string of cussing that was hard to decipher because of his hammering shouts. The tirade ended with "and we have to clear out, you stupid asshole!"

The crew counted on him to be the voice of calm and reason, and in this case, he had plenty of evidence on his side. Carl's control board showed clear. No radiation. No alarms. Nothing. The designers worked in five layers of redundancy for almost every piece of equipment, and the detection sensors were linked together on the sprawling campus, so even a radiation spike as faint as a dental x-ray would engage alarms throughout the plant.

"Don't run. We're still good up here. I need you to stay calm."

"No way!" the tech shouted. "Calm? I'm dead! We have to go!"

Carl shifted on his feet as if bracing himself for something unsavory. Sending men and women to die was a potential part of his job. He'd never had to do it before, but if the plant was in danger, he'd send everyone to their doom to prevent a bigger catastrophe. But his board was still green.

"I need you to stay there and tell me how I can make this right. We all have to fix this, or people outside the plant are going to die." It was what he would say if the emergency was real.

"Lots of people are going to die," the man blubbered.

He didn't believe anything serious was happening, but he couldn't ignore the call. The eggheads had told them there was a one-in-88 quadrillion chance that all of the sensors could fail at the same time, which he took to mean there was always a tiny bit of chance left in the system. To figure out if all the sensors were wrong, he needed the tech to give him actual information.

"Who's this on the line?" he asked in an even tone. Techs moved around, and the tinny phones made every man's voice sound the same, so it was hard to know.

The man didn't reply right away, which led him to suspect the guy had dropped the phone and made a run for it, but he answered after ten or fifteen seconds. "Pete. Pete Boddington. I took an extra shift. I shouldn't be here."

Fuck. Not Pete. I didn't even recognize his voice.

Manpower always drove him crazy. Pennsylvania Power figured anyone could be slapped into a chair to physically watch some dials and switches and walk around the cooling tower every forty-five minutes. It was easy money for college kids and recent retirees like Pete, but it was about as exciting as watching already-dried paint. Some people couldn't handle it.

However, Pete had worked at the plant for almost four decades. He'd been in the middle of every emergency procedure they'd had during that time, including the Big One. The man retired and came back for more, so he couldn't write him off as being overly dramatic.

A pang of anxiousness repeatedly kicked him in the gut.

"Hey, Pete," he replied. This time, he fought to keep his voice steady. "I didn't recognize you."

Without realizing he did it, Carl's hand touched his radiation badge. He found its silence very comforting.

"Boss," Pete sobbed. "I need to go."

He considered that he could have run out the door and down the long hallway and been at the containment area in the time it took him to get the other man talking.

"Listen, Pete. Just a second. We're gonna walk through this nice and slow. Tell me what you saw."

The veteran plant worker breathed heavily into the handset. "Blue light. Everywhere. It shot out of containment and went up into the sky."

A mental alarm finally went off in his brain. He'd read an eyewitness account of one of the survivors of Chernobyl. In the middle of the night, he witnessed blue light bursting out of the damaged containment building. He described it as a laser-like beam shooting up into infinity. For some reason, that man's words had always stuck with him.

Carl still didn't think the old man could be right when all his instruments said otherwise, but he trusted him enough to hit the warning claxon.

"How about a shutdown drill?" he said to the Pennsylvania Power crew in the room.

His team snapped into action, as he expected.

It wasn't part of the exercise, but he figured he'd go pay a visit to Mr. Boddington anyway. See what would make him say something so out of character that he threatened to break and run away.

"I'll be right back."

Wollemi National Park, New South Wales, Australia

Destiny woke up where she had fallen.

"That was a real dumper," she remarked.

She tilted her head to see what was on her chest.

"What the?" Her friends had parked the little white drone smack in the middle of her body. She picked it up and looked into the black dome camera. "Did you guys lose power?"

When she sat up, her eyes became blurry and the back of her head painfully pulsed with every heartbeat. She gingerly touched a small cut under her hair and felt blood.

"Ouch."

She set the drone aside and used the wall of the escarpment to help her stand. She looked around, trying to figure out how long she'd been out. The sky was still mostly black, save a lighter blue on the eastern horizon. The fire continued to lap at the rocks below her.

"Guys, I hope I wasn't out long." She felt silly talking to the futuristic device. "Take off and get out of here. I'm fine, now. Go!"

The four-prop camera platform still had its lights on, but the fans weren't spinning. She figured her friends landed it on her chest to rouse her from her fall, but she couldn't fathom why the operator wasn't getting it into the air again.

"Up!" She extended her arms and held it out like it was baby Simba, expecting it to gloriously turn on and lift off, but nothing happened.

It was an expensive item, but she was more than happy to leave it behind, just like her bed, blanket, chair, and all the personal items in her backpack. Nothing was more important than escaping with her life, so she placed it on the ledge by her feet.

The smell of the fire was pungent, and it felt like breathing in air from a smokestack, but she forced herself to stand there for a few moments and regain her wits.

"I'm— I'm—"

A tongue of fire appeared on a bush a few feet away, so she hopped up to the first rock she could grab. Her brain swooned inside her head, but she held on until it cleared up.

"I'm fine," she told nobody.

Her arms were almost spent, but the heat below gave her the motivation to pull herself back up. Then she grabbed onto the next ledge, to the left of where the rock had split off before.

With one last grunt that would have made any tennis diva proud, she pulled herself up to the very top. The flat summit of the scrub-covered ridge was ten feet ahead of her, but she also saw the open air of the next valley. Unlike the conflagration on her side, there was no smoke or sparks floating in the air over there. The base camp, and her research team, were in the clear.

By E.E. Isherwood & Craig Martelle

She turned around for a second to look at what she'd escaped. The forest fire had reached near the top of the escarpment, but it hadn't yet jumped to the summit. The steeper wall of rock near the top didn't have anything to burn, which was why her friends with the drone had guided her there. Now it was calm around her, relative to the furies of Hell burning in the rest of the valley.

"Good god." She pulled out her walkie, concerned the drone was still on the ground below. "Guys, get that thing out of there. We don't want to lose it."

She wiped her dry lips and laughed at what she was thinking.

I could scale back down there and rescue the stupid drone.

It was fifteen feet below, and she'd already made it once.

"Don't be a hero after the battle is won," she whispered. It was something her sister had taught her. "I know where it is, guys. We'll come back after the fire, if we can. Right now, I'm coming down. I'll take a couple of long necks if you don't mind." She laughed with relief.

While she secured the walkie talkie to her belt, she noticed the leaves rustle in some brush about twenty feet away. An animal stepped into the unnatural light cast by the mammoth fire.

Her breath caught in her throat, but this time, it wasn't caused by the oxygen-sucking fire or the stench of the smoke.

"Oi."

Southern Cross Logistics, Shipping Terminal. Modesto, CA

Buck drove his tractor-trailer around the lot with the windows open while waiting for the air conditioner to spit out some relief. He waved at another driver coming into the terminal because he piloted the same model of Peterbilt sleeper as his. He was happy to indulge that bit of camaraderie, but the second he was out of the tight parking lot and on the main road, he turned on the radio to search for information.

"And the media continues to complain about fake news—"

He clicked to the next station.

"My brothers and sisters, the church is at a crossroads—"

Click.

"—like we saw with the Fukushima reactor."

Buck listened for a moment to confirm it was actual news, but soon had to concentrate on making a left turn. One of the clueless drivers waiting at the light had stopped too close to the intersection, so he had to swing wide to avoid clipping a bumper.

He wanted to glare at the driver, but the woman didn't look up while he drove by. He was used to four-wheelers lost in their own worlds, so he decided to ignore it. However, she disappeared from his awareness entirely when he spotted the sign pointing the way to the interstate.

"Freddy? You got your ears on?" He talked to the GPS route-finder bolted to the top of his dash. It earned the nickname Freddy, after Freddy Kruger, because a previous version of the software had a knack for jolting him awake in the middle of the night to tell him where he was. It was a real nightmare on every street. "Come on, boy. Get me to Interstate 5."

He'd programmed the route before he ate lunch, so it should have been calling out every turn. Despite giving the computer a stern look, it remained silent.

"Come on! Just freakin' work!" He felt the temptation to bang on it to get it to talk, like they did in the movies, but in his experience, that never worked with anything technological. That was why when he went home, he preferred the company of big-block carbureted engines in his hot rods, rather than the modern electrical monstrosities they put in vehicles these days.

The news caught his ear again. "And who do we believe? People around the world report seeing a blue light, but no one is able to say what it was." The male voice handed off the question to his partner, a woman.

"So far, officials at NASA have been unwilling to commit to an answer. Privately, off the record, some insiders with the agency suggest it was a big meteor that bounced off the outer atmosphere. Another theory is that it burned up or struck the ocean somewhere. If the latter, we may expect tsunami warnings to be issued very soon."

The man spoke as if their dialogue was well-rehearsed. "Would that cause some of the electrical disturbances we've seen here on the East Coast?"

"It would indeed. These EMP-like fluctuations—"

"EMP?" the man inquired with a practiced interruption.

"Electro-Magnetic Pulse. It means there was a disruption in the upper atmosphere that could result in the sorts of interference we are seeing here on the ground."

"I've always heard that was associated with nuclear weapons."

The woman let out a tense chuckle. "Yes, that is the most common threat in fiction. However, EMPs could be caused by benign sources, relatively speaking, like solar ejections or meteor strikes, as we've been discussing."

Buck knew a little about EMPs from his books on tape. The narrated stories gave him something to do during the long hours behind the wheel, but he didn't listen just for recreation. Each of them taught something new about prepping and survival. In his view, there was no tougher challenge than facing a world stripped of modern technology, devoid of electricity. Deep down, he always wondered if he could survive such a catastrophe.

An EMP would explain the blue light high up in the atmosphere.

He rolled up the windows as he approached the highway on-ramp, because the air coming out of the vents was finally cool.

"Would it knock a plane out of the air, like it did at La Guardia?" the male host asked his companion.

Buck almost pulled his truck over because they mentioned the airport where Garth was this morning.

"Possibly. Planes are hardened to the effects of electromagnetism since they spend a lot of time plying the skies through thunderstorms. If it was close enough to the source of an E-M pulse, the energy might overwhelm its defenses. The problem is that military grade EMPs are designed to explode twenty or thirty miles in the air. Meteor strikes against the atmosphere might cause spikes much higher than that. Say sixty miles."

"So they weren't close to the aircraft."

"Not that anyone can confirm."

The pair went back and forth with their discussion but never returned to the briefly-mentioned crash.

He'd had enough. "Tell me about effin' La Guardia!"

"Could it have been a UFO?" the radio man asked.

Buck hammered the dial to get it to another station.

"...we're still waiting for a statement from our European correspondent regarding the disaster at CERN."

He hit the button again and spoke in a terse voice. "What about the plane crash?"

"...the St. Louis Rams lost this weekend."

"Sports? Come on!"

He hit every pre-set button on his radio, but none of the stations mentioned a plane accident.

Buck reached into his pocket and pulled out his phone. He hit the redial button and listened to the ringing on the other end of the line as he merged into the traffic of the interstate.

"Pick up, Garth. Be okay."

The phone went to voicemail, same as last time.

"Yo, this is Garth. Drop those digits…"

He hung up. Adding another voicemail to the one he'd left before wouldn't get his son to call back any faster. His boy wasn't on a plane, so there was no reason to think he'd been injured in the crash. Overreacting was something Garth's mother was famous for. He didn't want to follow her example.

The familiar green of the highway sign caught his eye.

"Ten miles to I-5, then seventy miles until Sacramento and I-80. From there, we turn east for the rest of the trip," he said in an upbeat tone.

Buck glanced over his shoulder to the little dog crate sitting on his bed. Big Mac had been asleep when he'd started the truck and hadn't stirred since. The little monster would sleep all day if Buck allowed it, but today he was tempted to find some potholes to shake him awake. He enjoyed having someone to talk to on the long trip.

Especially when he was nervous.

He wouldn't admit it to Big Mac, but all the talk of EMPs, plane crashes, and the blue light had him thinking about how far he was from his son. All his years of planning for the end of the world as we know it would count for nothing if he was on the wrong side of the country when it all kicked off. His mind raced in that direction as if summoned by a higher power.

He didn't know why, but too much time behind the wheel allowed for a fertile imagination.

His heavily-laden truck was already up to 75. He had no plans to slow down until he reached White Plains, New York.

"I just need everything to hold together for four days," he joked to himself. "Just four days."

CHAPTER 5

La Guardia Airport, New York City, NY

The black shape fell from the sky and revealed itself to be a tumbling, out-of-control jetliner. Garth recognized the twirling silhouette a fraction of a second before it crumpled into the runway and exploded.

"Whoa!" he mouthed.

The tendrils of the blast reached out in every direction, and bits of hot debris shot off with it. One piece of flaming metal ricocheted against the tail fin of the big Korean airliner, then tumbled through the glass of the terminal about fifty feet to his right.

"Garth! Shit! Move!" Sam ran up from behind and pulled him away from the windows. Smaller pieces of the downed plane tore through panes of glass, some close to his head.

The inside of the terminal went from zero to chaos in two seconds flat. Men and women squealed as they panicked and stampeded toward the far side of the building. Many looked back as if seeing the next deadly projectile would give them a chance to dodge it. If Garth were running with them, he knew better than to look back. His dad taught him to never be at the end of a fleeing crowd.

Why am I not running with them?

He became aware of Sam tugging at his t-shirt, so he would follow.

Garth went with him because he was temporarily on autopilot. "Did you see that thing crash?"

Sam snorted. "The whole world did. I saw it the second it hit. I hope someone survived."

Garth didn't bother offering his opinion that no one could have walked away from such a wreck. The doomed jet hit with its nose pointed right at the pavement.

He followed his friend for several seconds as he mulled over what he'd witnessed. How many people were on that plane? How many did he watch die, right in front of him? This was foremost on his mind until he stepped on broken glass.

"Hey, where are we going?" he finally thought to ask.

Sam released him, so he was free to go where he wanted, but his buddy kept walking toward the giant billboard at the end of the terminal. "We came up here to see where my parents are, and I'm going to do that. If that was their plane, I'm going to fuckin' lose it."

Garth looked at the wreckage. He expected to see fire rescue trucks and ambulances out there, but he realized it had only been thirty seconds since the impact. There was no way anyone could get to the crash site that fast.

"I really don't think that was their plane," he offered, knowing he was just making things up. However, he thought of something positive for his friend's benefit. "They are probably already on the ground, like you said."

"Yeah, well, we'll know in a second." Sam hopped over more glass and continued on his way. Garth also jumped over the shards, but he purposefully ignored a little smudge of red on the tiled floor.

"Cool."

By the time they reached the big board, the terminal was mostly clear of personnel on the half facing the accident. Even the ticket agents and baggage handlers stood on the far side.

A police officer yelled the second he came up a nearby escalator. "Hey, you two!"

Sam ignored him and studied the billboard. There had to be five hundred cities listed in a dozen columns. Some names blinked. Some changed colors. Fortunately, they were in alphabetical order, so they weren't hopelessly lost.

"Chicago. Chicago. There are ten flights from Chicago today. Which one were they on?" Sam stuck his hand in his pants pocket and began to dig for something.

"Get the hell out of here, you two." The officer strode right over to them. Another cop ran up the escalator, looked at the boys and the attending policeman, then took off in another direction.

"Just a damned second," Garth snapped.

"You aren't safe, kid. Get moving before I drag you out of here." The bearded officer reminded him of a Marine drill instructor. His dad taught him to always respect officers of the law because of the uniform, but this guy demanded respect because he already was a badass.

"We're going," Garth responded with trepidation.

He turned to Sam. "Come on. He says we have to leave."

"Not yet," Sam deadpanned.

The policeman pressed the button on his shoulder radio. "I'm up on two. Minor damage. We've got the north side of ticketing. It's pretty clear already, except for a couple of kids at the kino board."

That struck a nerve, because Garth didn't see himself as a kid.

"We're moving," Garth assured the guy. He took several steps away from the board and hoped Sam got the message.

"Almost have it!" Sam shouted.

Instead of walking away, his buddy got closer to the column containing the ten Chicagos. He'd pulled out the flight information from his pocket and compared it to the names on the board. He read them aloud until he found the one he wanted.

"5-8-6. On time. That's it!" Sam looked at the officer and acted surprised to see him. Garth knew that was part of his act with authority figures. He wasn't exactly lying, but he did know how to play dumb like nobody's business. "Sorry, Officer. We didn't know this was going to be evacuated."

"You didn't see that plane come down and break these windows?" The officer's sarcasm was highly refined, like he used it all the time. "It's your lucky day I was here to warn you about it then. Go on!"

Sam bowed and held out his hands as if begging for forgiveness. "Sorry. We're going."

Garth also bent his head out of respect for the officer.

They both took a few steps, but the big flight board started beeping. When he glanced back at it, each line in the columns changed to show the flight was delayed. Hundreds of cities flipped as he watched.

"586?" Garth inquired.

Sam looked at the board. Every flight was affected, including the one he'd just confirmed. He shook his head before storming off.

"Scram!" the uniformed man insisted to Garth.

He had been playing it cool for Sam's sake. He really wanted him to check on his parents' flight, but it felt unnatural to not run away with all the others. He wondered if Sam was in shock. Is that how he fought that initial urge to run?

Could I be in shock, too?

Seeing that plane crash and explode was a lot to process. Once he and Sam began to trot toward all the other frightened passengers in the terminal, their mood infected him like a deadly virus.

I could have been killed back there.

Wollemi National Park, New South Wales, Australia

Destiny's head was already scrambled from her fall and inhaling too much smoke, so she didn't react as fast as she might any other day. When the sleek predator came out of the bushes, she didn't even think to run. Instead, she tried talking to it.

"Hey, girl, what's up?"

At first, she thought it was a dingo, because a few had recently been spotted in the park. It was about the size of a large dog with orange-colored fur and a long tail, but there was something wrong with the head. If it was a dog, or even a dingo, it was a breed she'd never seen in the wild.

"And what are you, cutie?" she added with a clumsy snap of her fingers.

The animal answered with a snarl, and all thought of taxonomic assignments took a back seat. She was frightened, but still laboring under the effects of oxygen deprivation. She giggled, and it surprised her.

"Ha! I make it to the top only to be attacked by a feral dog."

No self-respecting Aussie outdoorswoman traveled alone in the woods without a knife, so she reached for hers.

"Oh, fuck." Her knife was in her pack, which was probably burning bright somewhere below. Destiny slapped herself across the cheek to force herself to focus. "Pour yourself a glass of concrete, girl. Toughen up."

The dingo-like creature stalked a few paces forward, where she got a good look at the whole body. It had weird stripes on its hindquarters, like someone thought it would be funny to draw black tiger stripes over that part of its body.

It growled and squared its shoulders as if getting ready to pounce.

"Good doggie!" The fire had stressed every animal in the vicinity. The clinical researcher part of her brain didn't hold it against the visitor for being scared. At the same time, she tried to subdue the growing spiral of fear swirling through her gut.

Should she puff out her chest to make herself larger? Play dead? In the heat of the fire, she couldn't say for sure. She was pretty certain she wasn't supposed to turn and run away, lest it give chase, but she wasn't going to stand there and do nothing, either.

Her body poured out the adrenaline as she realized the animal was going to strike.

When the beast lunged, she was already moving. She side-stepped as best she could and tried to get one of her boots to land on the dog's face, but all she managed to do was knock herself off balance.

"Shit!"

The dog wasn't fooled. It skidded on its front paws and twisted its body toward her. It let out a strange bark-yap that sounded more wolf than dog.

There was no way to outrun the four-legged beast on the narrow ridge, so she swung herself toward the edge of the rocks and tried to flop on her bottom. Her intention was to slide off the side but catch herself at the last second, like sliding down the pitch of a roof and hooking yourself on the gutter.

The dog got its teeth into her long, curly hair, which yanked at her already-sore scalp.

She screamed as she went over the side, desperately searching for something to grip.

The dog breathed in her ear the whole way.

10 miles north of Modesto, CA

Part of Buck's duty as a truck driver was calling into the headquarters of his trucking company each time he dropped or picked up cargo. That allowed the bean counters to keep track of their fleet. It was usually a time-waster for him, but Buck was glad to make the call once he settled into his drive. At least they hadn't installed the auto-tracking GPS like the newest rigs were getting. He only tolerated so much of big brother's oversight, even if it was his employer.

They picked up on the first ring. "Hey, Blake, how are you doing?"

The owner of the company refused to use his nickname like everyone else. It was one of those details that got under his skin, but it was a minor act compared to some of the weapons' grade assholes he'd worked for throughout his career.

"Hey, Mr. Williams. I'm fine. I'm carrying enough pallets of chili to stink up the entire East Coast. Heading for the Vickers hub in West Plains. I wiped up all the paper about fifteen minutes ago."

"Great," the owner replied in a friendly but concerned voice. "You planning on going the distance for me?"

"Sure. Why wouldn't I?"

"I've had two good drivers call in the last half-hour to tell me they were dumping their loads and bobtailing it home. Can you believe that shit? Dumping! Anyway, I was beginning to think this was some kind of stealth walkout or something."

Mr. Williams was middle-of-the-road as bosses went. On the one hand, he didn't stop his business for any holiday on the calendar. On the other, he threw as much work at Buck as he could stand.

Buck had big plans for his life and wanted to do right by his son. He already owned his own truck, so all he needed to do was work for a good shipping company and drive off with the dollars.

"Uh, sir, can you tell me if you've heard anything about a crash in La Guardia? My son was in the area, and I want to make sure he's okay."

The other guy had several kids, too, so he hoped that would work in his favor.

"Yes, I'm watching the news right now, in fact. I wanted to know if something was going on to make these guys cut and run. I still don't see anything big, but one of the channels has been broadcasting about that plane crash. There is a helicopter getting shots from the air, but the transit police are keeping them far away."

That was only part of what he wanted to know. "Can you see if the crash happened in the airport itself? Do you think anyone on the inside could get hurt?" His heart leaned up against his ribs with a plastic cup to listen for the answer.

"Let me see..."

Buck imagined his Peterbilt was on self-drive while on the straight stretch of highway. The number of cars and trucks had been growing, but that wasn't unusual for California's Central Valley, even around midday.

Buck couldn't stand it anymore. "Well?"

"Hmm. It looks like the fire trucks and police are all out on the runway. I do see some other flashing lights at the entrance to the airport, but I'd bet those are to evacuate people. Lots of passengers are walking out the front doors."

That sounded like good news.

"Anything else you can see? Does it say anything about survivors inside the airport?"

Mr. Williams' laugh was a bit on the condescending side. "Just because they were there when it happened doesn't make them survivors. Based on what I see on the TV, there were no survivors on the plane. It is just a black pile of debris."

"All right, thanks, Mr. Williams. I really needed to hear that."

"Yeah, anytime. I know your boy is in that area. I'll watch the news and make sure nothing changes at the airport. I'll give you a call if it does."

"Thanks. I really—"

"Hold on. Another driver is calling in. If I get another one quitting on me, I'm going to be very upset." He paused for a second. "Just to confirm, you aren't quitting on me, are you, Blake?"

"No, sir. I'm in it to win it. I'm going to New York if it kills me."

"Good. I mean, I hope it doesn't." He laughed it off. "But I'm glad you're still with me."

Buck hung up the phone.

"Hey, Mac, the boss wishes us well." He laughed to unload some of his stress. "Garth is just fine, too. I'm sure of it."

He said the words aloud to make them more solid, more believable. Why wasn't Garth calling back?

NORAD, Cheyenne Mountain, Colorado

"General!" a lieutenant called from among the dozen workstations in the secure room. "We have a video."

After all of General Smith's bluster about wanting an answer to the mysterious power outage, demanding an answer in under a minute, they were fifteen minutes in and still in the proverbial dark. During that time, he briefly talked to the president and read five seismic reports confirming there were no ground impacts near his bunker. But he'd also been advised about a wave of blue energy that had passed around the globe. It was his job to assess its threat to the heartland of the United States.

The general hurried over to the lieutenant's computer display.

"What am I looking at?"

"DARPA and Boeing have a joint project called Sun Diver. It's a solar-powered aircraft that can stay fifty-five thousand feet in the air for years at a time."

"Yes, and?" the general replied impatiently.

"They have an onboard reconnaissance package that records around the clock. It's nighttime there, but it caught the blue rip as it went by." The junior officer pushed a button to start a video. The perspective was from high in the atmosphere, and even though it was dark below, the bright curvature of the Earth made him feel like the camera was close to outer space.

"Here it comes," the lieutenant said dramatically.

On cue, a long line of blue appeared from over the round bulge of the horizon and approached the camera like a wave at the beach.

"How fast is it moving?" the general asked.

"Based on how fast it reached the camera after our power went out, the back of the napkin math is about a hundred and fifteen thousand kilometers per hour."

"Damn. And where is this camera?"

"It is currently parked over the border between Pakistan and Afghanistan."

"And how long after our power went out did this light show up over there?"

"About eight minutes."

What could cause this thing to go around the whole planet?

CHAPTER 6

Search for Nuclear, Astrophysics, and Kronometric Extremes (SNAKE). Red Mesa, Colorado

Dr. Faith Sinclair had the room to herself. Her assistant cleared out the others, so she could gather her thoughts in relative silence. After the disaster she'd just witnessed, that calm reflection time quickly devolved into silent head-banging on the solid wooden table.

"That sucked," she groaned.

As managing director of the University of Colorado's SNAKE lab, it was her job to ensure the corporate partners got enough time to run their scenarios through the mainframe. For the better part of the past week, their largest donor had been running a test, but moments before its scheduled end, an apparent hardware glitch forced an early termination. Her final moment of silence was appropriate, considering her career was about to be terminated, too.

Azurasia Heavy Industries was not known for their patience. Their Izanagi Project was a huge investment in research and development for the foreign firm.

After a minute of indulging in self-pity, she raised her head to see what could be done to salvage the worst day of her life. With arms outstretched, her chin rested on the table while she built up her usual confidence. Things were bad, sure, but she'd seen failure before. The only way to overcome a setback was to get back in the game.

Faith was going to stand up and take her own advice, but she caught sight of some words etched into the tabletop near her fingertips.

'Prof Sinclair's bosons will super charge your neutrinos!'

She huffed. "Oh, come on. Neutrinos don't even have a charge."

Is that really the point here?

"Dammit," she said under her breath before checking the door behind her. It was still closed, so she took one of her car keys and scratched at the uneven words etched in the wood.

Admitting it was a pointless task, she nonetheless went at it with fervor. Cleaning one little mocking phrase was something she could control. Once she got up from the table and walked back to her collapsing world, it would be dog-eat-dog. As director, she hated the feeling of helplessness.

Faith sawed into the table like it was a thick steak, but before she could do more than blot out her name, someone knocked on the door.

She shuffled a few papers over the imperfection. "Yeah, come in."

Mindy Paulus appeared in the opening. Faith's assistant, and friend, the woman was fifteen years her junior and twenty pounds heavier, but she reminded the professor of her best friend back home, so they got along well. "Dr. Sinclair. You aren't going to believe this."

"What is it? My reassignment to research snowdrifts in Fairbanks?"

"No, just the opposite!" She held out a fax sheet. "Look."

Faith stood up and snatched the printout. "This is from the president's National Science Advisor."

Mindy flashed a conspiratorial grin.

She started to read the words aloud but stopped after a few sentences. The first part was nothing more than a bunch of glad-handing and thanking various departments and scientists in the government. However, when she got to the third paragraph, she had to read it to her friend.

"At 2:01 pm Eastern Standard Time today, we believe a heretofore unknown meteor made contact with the Earth's upper atmosphere. An electromagnetic wave was created during this event and it continues to interfere with commercial and private power consumption throughout North America. We are still trying to ascertain—"

Faith looked up like she'd been commuted from a death sentence. "It wasn't my fault!"

"No, it wasn't," Mindy agreed.

Dr. Sinclair took a deep breath and finally allowed herself a smile. The fine print of the two-story-tall stack of legal documents she signed prior to the experiment probably had something to protect Azurasia from an Act of God, but at least they couldn't blame her, personally. "Still, it's a good thing we didn't allow that reporter to watch the conclusion of this experiment. A failure is still a failure, even if it was no one's fault."

"Should I give this sheet to Mr. Shinano?" Mindy pointed to the fax.

"No. I want to give it to him myself."

She walked out the door, confident her career had been saved.

I-5 North of Modesto, CA

Buck drove for several miles half-listening to the radio. He was concerned for Garth, but that was the same as any other day. His boy lived in a city of six million residents, and minor disasters happened all the time. A lone plane crash at a busy airport wasn't something that could get him to abandon his wagon, like the guys Mr. Williams mentioned.

I could fly home if I dropped out.

That was something new. He'd not considered flying home, but that would be the fastest way to get back to Garth if he was sure the world was coming to an end.

He guffawed. "Yeah, right! Like that's going to happen."

His time listening to books gave him some insight on what to expect if the world ended. They were filled with clueless characters who never saw the obvious signs. He used those lessons to run his own mental checklist.

"Mac, do you see any medical labs with zombies running out of them?"

He looked back to the monster in the cage.

"No, me neither." He tapped the steering wheel. "And the Peterbilt is still running smooth as the day I bought her. No EMP blast knocked her out, right?"

Buck wasn't certain Mac was awake, but he continued.

"I study this shit for a living. That blue light might have been military testing or solar interference, but it wasn't a nuke EMP. If it was, the story would be all over the news, or there'd be no stations left on the air, like in the books we listen to."

As if to prove the point to himself, he switched the station again. The sports guys still talked about sports. The preacher on the religious channel still yakked about church. Even the talk radio guys babbled on about politics, same as any other day.

"See, Mac-daddy, we're good to go. And, if anyone uses a blue light as an excuse to make trouble with us, well, I've got a nice surprise for them. It's chambered in nine-millimeter." He eyed the vinyl wall panel where he kept a few of his supplies stowed away.

He gripped the wheel as his attention returned to the road where it belonged. Brake lights in the sea of cars and trucks ahead signaled a slowdown.

"There's our real enemy, right? It ain't EMPs or viruses or any of that end-days crap. It's G-D traffic!"

He engaged the Jake brakes and slowed down with everyone else.

"What now?"

La Guardia Airport, New York City, NY

Garth and Sam ran away from the policeman and joined the rest of the herd waiting at the far side of the terminal. They took a few minutes to catch their breath and shake off their misgivings about sticking around, but Garth couldn't stay quiet for long.

"Thanks for pulling me away from that window, dude. I don't know why I didn't run."

Sam laughed. "That's what friends are for. I saw you standing there with your jaw on the ground and figured you weren't going anywhere."

Garth laughed it off because he hated losing control like that. "I thought you were nuts for going to that board, but I'm glad you got the info on your parents. Did you see if the plane landed before all those lines changed out?"

"No, but good point. If they weren't already on the ground, then it could still be their plane that blew up out there."

He noticed his friend nervously tapping his pant leg. "Come on, Sammy, I know exactly how we can figure it out."

Now Garth pulled at Sam to get him to come along. His friend willingly walked with him once it was clear where they were headed.

"Let me see that slip of paper," Garth demanded.

Sam handed it to him and he noted the airline. He then looked around the giant terminal for the ticket counter to match. He found it right away, but when he realized it was on the cleared-out side of the building, he slowed and then stopped.

Sam saw the empty service counters as well. "Shit. Good thought, but what do we do now?"

Garth understood what his friend needed. In those first few minutes since the accident, many of the passengers took the escalators down, but most of the airport workers still milled about near the ticket counters. His parents flew on one of the biggest airlines, so all he had to do was find the biggest group of employees loitering nearby.

"These folks will know. Come on." Garth led him to a gathering of twenty or thirty men and women in dark blue uniforms. Once they got close, he confirmed the airline logo on their nametags.

"Excuse me. Can anyone tell me if that airplane was one of yours?"

Garth expected it would be a straightforward question with a simple answer. If it wasn't theirs, they'd be ready to disown it. However, when none of them gave the response he sought, he prepared himself to keep digging.

"My parents are on an AirBlue flight. It would really help to know the burning plane isn't yours." He let himself sound vulnerable and pointed outside at the wreck. "I want to make sure my parents aren't out there."

A young redhead with a smart-looking pair of glasses stepped near him. "We are all trying to find that out. I promise."

"When will you know?" he replied.

"No idea. We've never had something like this happen before. They'll probably have to call every plane of ours currently airborne and ensure they are where they should be."

Sam stepped up. "Why is this so hard? That plane had to be on the radar, or whatever, with a little number by it. How could something crash in front of your tower and nobody knows who it was?"

The woman turned on the empathy. "I'm so sorry, you guys. We really are trying to answer that question for you. If the airport doesn't tell us all very soon, we will be swamped with questions like yours." She touched Sam's arm, then recoiled a tiny bit. "I, uh, promise you we'll know soon."

"Thanks," Sam replied. "I know. I stink."

The woman's smile was uncertain, but her professional demeanor came roaring back. "Why don't you two stand right over there and we'll let you know the second we do, okay?"

That seemed reasonable.

He poked Sam in the ribs. "That time, she thought you were the one who filled your drawers."

They laughed together, but it was forced.

Three Mile Island Nuclear Generating Station, Pennsylvania

Carl hurried to the end of the corridor and went outside into the heat and humidity of central Pennsylvania. It was a shortcut that saved him a few seconds as opposed to walking the winding hallways. He sped up when he heard shouting from the containment safety office ahead of him.

He burst through the swinging door, expecting trouble, but when he charged into the classroom-sized office, he encountered nothing but cool air.

"What the hell? Pete? You here?" He first checked the safety inspector's phone attached to the leftmost wall; the detached handset twirled near the floor at the end of the spiral cord. His eyes were drawn downward toward a pair of feet sticking out from behind a desk.

Carl pawed his radiation badge. It remained silent on his breast pocket.

After a few moments of indecision, he ran over to the boots, sure it had to be Pete. Right as he turned the corner on the desk, his badge chirped.

"Fuck!"

He took a few steps back but managed to get a better view of the downed man. He was face up with closed eyes, and there was no movement in his chest. Carl's first thought was heart attack, which might also explain Pete's crazy talk on the phone. However, the other guy's rad badge told a different story.

Pete and the safety guys had a different style of badge than the audible electronic versions plant operators like Carl used. Pete's was the older photographic film type. Pennsylvania Power probably figured there were so many sensors around the plant that it didn't pay to suit up guys like Pete with the more sensitive, and expensive, version of radiation badges. If the badge was white, you were safe. If it darkened, there was radiation in the area.

He leaned in to confirm what he thought he spotted on the dead man's chest.

The badge's film was solid black.

CHAPTER 7

Wollemi National Park, New South Wales, Australia

Destiny and the feral dog went over the side together, but she managed to grip the ledge at the last second. The dog's momentum and lack of hands made it impossible to stay attached to her, and she heard a satisfying yelp from below when it struck the rocks. Her knees and boots smashed into the rock face. An instant later, her scalp blossomed with pain, like tape had been pulled off, ripping her hair out.

"Ow!" she grunted through gritted teeth.

Smoke swirled around her head, indifferent to her pain.

Beads of salty sweat stung her eyes as she struggled to pull herself back to the top. She wasn't a weakling, but it had been a while since she'd done any strenuous exercise, and her lungs were choked with smoke dust, making it harder to get oxygen to her tortured muscles.

She didn't even grunt as she slid herself up and over the top of the ledge. All she could do was roll to her side and put her hand to the pain on her head.

Holy shit, Destiny thought. The dog's bite had yanked out a tuft of her hair, leaving a bloody puddle in its place. It hurt like a bitch. She wanted to know that her attacker was dead. She held the wound as best she could while peeking over the edge.

"Not good."

The feral hadn't gone down as far as she expected. Instead of falling a long way and dying, the dog only fell about six feet onto a wide boulder. It looked stunned, but otherwise unhurt.

"Good doggy," she said, mostly to herself.

The fire blazed bright, as if it wanted to get all its energy out before dawn broke over the horizon. For a few crucial moments, she got a good look at the animal. It was on its feet and appeared to be searching for a way back up the steep hillside.

Dingoes were like domesticated dogs, but their heads were a bit wider and longer than the average mutt. Their bodies were long and sleek, like they were built for the wild, rather than man's hearth. The animal below was no dingo, nor was it a dog, but the animal professional in her remembered seeing the odd duckling in a book a long time ago.

"No freaking way," she wheezed before taking a few shallow breaths.

The wobbly four-legged beastie could have made her rich a few years ago. There were bounties offered by wealthy benefactors, including Ted Turner, for anyone who found one of the endangered animals. The creature looked a lot like the sleek dingo breed, with an even larger and more wolf-like head, but the stripes on its back and hips were the real clue to its heritage.

She pulled her phone from her back pocket and took several blurry photographs while it paced below. As she suspected, the fire drove out all kinds of animals from their hiding places, but this one was a real gem. No one in modern times had ever found one in the wild, despite many rumors of sightings on mainland Australia. The last one in captivity died in the 1930s.

"Tasmanian Tiger," she said with pride. "Gotcha!"

She pocketed the camera, hoping she'd be able to produce evidence for wildlife researchers. Destiny got back on her feet and reached for the walkie to tell her team she was coming in, but the animal became frantic.

"Stay there, pup," she said in a soothing voice.

It jumped from its rock to another ledge on the steep incline.

"Oi. Shit." The walkie talkie was no longer so important.

She took several steps back from the edge, but knew she had waited too long. The smart tiger figured out how to use the uneven rock ledges to head back for the top. Some of the gaps were wide, but the animal was desperate, same as her.

Destiny scanned the scrubby ridgeline for a weapon, though there was great conflict inside while she did. Almost without thinking, she'd managed to get the attacking animal away from her by lunging for the edge. She probably couldn't do that twice. If the Tasmanian Tiger attacked again, she might have to hurt the last living specimen on the continent. Probably in the whole world.

"Don't come up. Don't come up." She repeated the words over and over as she searched for a weapon to defend herself. A few sticks lying in the brush might have sufficed, but she wanted something with more heft. She tried to scoop up a large stone, but she couldn't lift it any higher than her waist.

Not high enough.

The tiger came over the edge as she threw down the rock. They locked eyes for a second until she remembered her training to avoid such combative postures. It was too late, though, and the beast came right for her with a series of high-pitched barks.

She reached for a stick she'd spotted earlier in the shadows nearby. She thought it would make a decent-sized poker, but when it came out of the weeds, it was more like a thick staff.

It came right for her. There was no time to do anything more sophisticated than take a swing.

"Ompf," she gasped as the wood struck the side of the tiger. The animal yelped and recoiled, the end of the staff breaking off, leaving her with nothing more than a weak billy club.

She tried to get better footing while the tiger kicked up dust and debris to get its paws beneath it. Once balanced, it snarled and came at her again. She felt the hyper-awareness from a surge of adrenaline. The world started to slow down.

It arrived before she was ready. The busted staff moved too slowly. She watched, almost like a spectator. Her swing clumsy and late. The endangered monster closed.

"Back off!" The club glanced off the tiger's neck. It made straight for her leg, past her club, and with a snap, locked its jaws onto her long pants, burying a fang into her calf.

"Holy ass!" Destiny howled, jumping back and trying to kick it away. Of the innumerable bites she'd suffered at the hands of the animals she'd worked with, the tiger's wasn't so bad. The teeth caught part of her boot, so they were less damaging than they could have been.

"Don't make me hurt you, you little bitch." Destiny shifted her grip as she backed away from the animal.

The tiger paid no heed to her human words. It slunk from side to side as she held out her broken staff, and for a moment, they seemed to find a mutual understanding. However, more smoke blew up from below and cloaked them both in its gray confusion.

The tiger lunged.

She swung with about seventy-five percent power but whiffed it. As she did, the exertion made her take a stumble-step to her right, and the animal bounced harmlessly off her knee.

"Oh, god." Her breathing was labored, like she was fighting on a high fourteener with thin mountain air as her only fuel. Even the act of dodging was consuming all she had left.

The tiger's ribcage heaved in and out, too, but it hadn't slowed the beast. The creature paced the dirt for a few seconds, then reached a decision. As soon as her staff moved slightly to the side, it charged straight toward her.

There was no time for complicated attacks on her part, either. The Tasmanian tiger didn't know it was special or nearly extinct. It was just fighting to stay alive in the face of the fire engulfing the forest around them. Her sister would personally rip her a new one if she died because she went easy on a member of an endangered species.

She swung the three-foot club with everything she had left.

"Die!" she screamed.

La Guardia Airport, New York City, NY

Garth and Sam waited impatiently for the airline to update them about the downed flight. They paced around and stayed quiet, but only made it about ten minutes before they lost their cool.

"How friggin' hard is it to walk out there and check?" Sam asked.

"Maybe they don't want anyone to know," Garth replied, channeling his dad's tendency to go right to conspiracies.

"What the hell good would that do? We can all see it out there. Surely there's a YouTube of the crash already."

"Yeah, probably," he agreed. He couldn't think of a reason they'd hold anything back, but he was getting bored and needed to talk about anything that came to mind. "We should—"

Before he could finish his thought, the power in the terminal went out. The signs above the ticket counters went dark and caused a stir among the loitering employees. Garth thought the complaints were stupid since giant windows surrounded the outer edge of the terminal and provided plenty of daylight.

He had more sympathy for the riders of the escalators. When the power went off, several riders were thrown forward. A man in a gray suit was still on his knees at the top of the nearest.

"Now why do you think they did that?" Sam asked. "Wait! Don't tell me. They shut down the entire power grid so we couldn't watch the news. Then they shut off the phone system, so we wouldn't give any reports from inside the airport."

The two boys looked at each other like they'd been let in on the secret. Each of them pulled out their phones and tapped feverishly. Garth pulled up his dad's avatar and clicked off a simple message: 'Yo.'

He stared at the word like it was a bobber at the fishing hole.

"Come on, Dad. Answer."

"Fuck," Sam whispered. "Network is down."

"Mine doesn't say that. Oh, wait. Now it does."

"So, is this all part of the plan? Crash a plane. Shut off the power. What's next? Line us up against the wall and shoot us?"

Garth rolled his eyes. "Leave that dark helicopter stuff to me. I think the most likely problem is they wanted the power off at the airport to prevent further damage from the fires and shit. We watched a video in science class about the fire department."

"Where was I when you saw it? It doesn't ring any bells."

Garth laughed. "You don't remember? Maybe you were in the bathroom playing kissy-face with Trish Todd?"

"Damn. You're never going to let me live that down, are you? I only went out with her twice."

He nodded with excitement. "Yeah, but you went out in a blaze of glory." Garth didn't hold it against his friend for trying to date; he hoped to stir up the courage to do the same someday soon. Sam freely admitted he got into the dating scene way too early, but sometimes his lack of maturity resulted in hilariously disastrous failures.

"Hey! You two." The feminine voice of the airline ticket agent brought them back to the moment.

The boys jogged over to her.

"I have some good news. The downed plane wasn't one of ours. We've contacted all of our flights scheduled to land at this airport today, and none of them are missing. Most diverted to other airports or headed back to their point of origin." She said it in a loud voice, so the dozens of other airport visitors heard the news.

"Please feel free to go home. Don't worry. Once the airport re-opens, I'm sure those diverted flights will resume service to our beautiful New York hub here at La Guardia International."

Several people shouted out questions about lodging vouchers, local transportation, and traveler information he didn't need to know. It did make him appreciate how many people were affected by that one plane crash, even beyond the poor souls who died on the flight.

Garth placed his attention back on his friend by doing their mutual told-you-so gesture: a firm punch to the meaty part of Sam's upper arm.

"Ouch! What the fuck, dude?" Without parents around, they both reveled in wielding the words of adulthood.

He laughed. "I told you there was nothing to worry about. Your parents are fine. They are probably back in Chi-town."

Sam rubbed his arm but made no effort to conceal his grin. Garth privately wondered if his arm was as sore and bruised as his own, but neither boy would ever admit it hurt as much as it did. "Yeah, I guess you know some stuff, jackass."

"So, what do we do now?" Garth replied. He wondered about very basic life questions that didn't seem important when he thought he'd be taken care of by Sam's folks today. His dad always reminded him that survival depended on finding food, water, and shelter, even if you were just going to spend the day in the city.

"I'm not one to let a crisis go to waste," Sam said matter-of-factly, "but I'd like to point out to my esteemed colleague that it looks like we have the day to ourselves. And probably one more night."

His buddy saw the same facts but came to a totally different conclusion. While he was worried about what to eat and where to go, Sam seemed to focus on the freedom they would enjoy. They did just dodge a bullet, almost literally in his case with the flying debris, so he assumed his mind went right to worst-case because of that. Maybe he needed to let this one go.

He exhaled. "Indubitably, Master Sam." He used a British voice to amp up his fake sophistication.

The crisis was over. They could go back to acting like two teens turned loose on the city.

Sam pointed to the powerless down escalator that would take them to the exit. "Let's get to the subway in case they think about shutting it down, too. On the way, I'll tell you about Tammy again. I know you like that one."

"Yeah, I could use a good laugh."

The boys headed for the exit without a care in the world.

I-5 North of Modesto, CA

Freddy the GPS helped Buck get to I-5, but it wasn't the high-speed Mecca he'd expected. He threw the shifter back and forth as he worked up and down the gears. For a trucker, there was almost nothing worse than stop and go traffic.

A charcoal-colored sedan sped in front of him. "Make up your mind, dammit!" There was always that one asshole who weaved back and forth between lanes to try to jockey himself to the front of the pack. Those mentally-deficient drivers loved to pull ahead of his truck, since he always left a wide gap between himself and the next vehicle. His motor-assisted Jake brake relieved some of the mechanical wear on his pads, but it didn't reduce his stress.

He did have one advantage that helped dull the pain of traffic. Buck's height allowed him to see over the tops of the four-wheelers ahead of him. "Hell yeah, Big Mac, we're getting ready to open up again."

His pup whined when he heard his name.

"Ah, you're up. Great!" Buck smiled, glad to have his little friend awake. After he delivered the pup to Garth, he was probably going to get a dog pal for himself, because he'd come to love having someone to talk to on the long hauls.

A few minutes later, as expected, the traffic jam busted open. He mashed the pedals and twisted the gears just like all the other vehicles, but his heavy payload took a lot longer to get up to speed. Eventually, he matched the pace of most of the others, and the wide expanse of endless fruit orchards of the central California valley started to roll by.

His blood pressure was almost back to normal when a cherry-red Mustang convertible caught his eye in his side mirror. The silver running pony in the front grille twinkled as it approached, but the driver's blowing blonde hair made it so he couldn't look away.

"Well, hello," he said in a practiced "cool-guy" voice.

His blood pressure spiked once again, but it had nothing to do with traffic.

The young woman looked up and flashed a smile that seemed meant only for Buck. Her long blonde locks blew wildly, which made her seem like the water nymph attached to the prow of a Viking ship.

"Nice '65," he mouthed to her. He knew every muscle car from the 60s and early 70s, to which he included the mustangs, although others did not. That was when America knew how to build shit. Not that he expected the young thing to know such facts.

By E.E. Isherwood & Craig Martelle

He felt self-conscious looking down on her, because she wore a shapely lime-green dress that barely covered her thighs. She floated her left arm in the wind out her window and sat right up against the door, so the rest of the white vinyl bench seat appeared as a huge, empty snowfield.

"Mind if I drop into that seat?" he said to himself.

He tried to be cool and wave to her, but in the excitement, he misjudged the distance and surprised himself when his hand struck the glass.

Fuck. Real smooth.

The young woman laughed and let her foot off the gas for a moment, maybe to let him have his look, but then she sped up without a glance back.

"Even has the historical plates. That thing is pristine, lady. You need to take good care of her." He couldn't speed up to pursue her like Chevy Chase in *Vacation*, but that was just as well.

"That 'stang would be a hell of a ride," he said to Mac. "But no time for distractions like that until we get back to Garth, right?"

CHAPTER 8

Search for Nuclear, Astrophysics, and Kronometric Extremes (SNAKE). Red Mesa, Colorado

Faith's meeting with Mr. Shinano was a brief affair. She showed him the fax as if it were her Get-Out-Of-Jail-Free card. He accepted it but demanded to know what she was going to do to prevent another external event from shutting them down again.

She assured him they would work around the clock to figure out how the blue wave affected the test equipment.

They shook hands and parted ways.

Get the momentum of the day under control.

More faxes came in before she could address her staff. She put out the call for her team to once again assemble in the large conference room.

The computer geniuses arrived with the particle team and quickly filled all available chairs. The facilities and engineering department heads sat at the twelve-person table, with their associates spread around the outer wall of the underground chamber. As soon as her watch said 2pm, she shut the door.

"Thank you all for coming. I'm jumping right into it. As I'm sure you've heard, there has been an event." She used air quotes around the word *event*. "Mr. Shinano's simulation was halted, as were several lesser programs running on the mainframe. I got this fax from the United States Federal Science Administration, which mentions a meteorite and electromagnetic interference, but in the thirty minutes since this came in, I've seen and heard of no less than three additional theories as to what caused us to go offline. All of them sound plausible, so I need you guys to help me figure this out."

"You shut us down too soon," a male voice said just loud enough to be heard but not loud enough for her to see who said it. A few sympathetic chuckles came like spears out of the forest, suggesting some members of her team weren't solidly behind her.

She sighed heavily and tried to pretend she didn't care about dissent. Her natural inclination was to search for consensus, but she'd found that nearly impossible with such a diverse team of intellectuals. Normally, when she understood the science, she could wrangle everyone to her way of thinking no matter what opinions were shared. Today, she was working with limited data and had to walk on eggshells around an important client. She had to share the risk on figuring out what caused the problems.

"A burst of energy was seen in the skies from California to New York with other sightings around the world. Some news sources say it was a meteor. Some news channels claim there was a release of radiation at Three Mile Island that made the sky glow. And still other channels are saying it was a North Korean nuke that caused an EMP."

She shook her head. "Any of those are terrible, but that isn't the end of it. My social media feed is crammed with people who swear the blue light erupted when an alien spaceship penetrated our atmosphere with giant thrusters. Of course, no one has seen the actual ship."

Her team shared some uncertain laughter.

One of her computer guys responded. "Doctor Stafford and I didn't see shit in the sky. We took a smoke break up in the treehouse when this mythical blue light supposably went by."

Mindy handed her another fax, but she didn't look at it right away because she wanted to give a good comeback.

She nodded to the computer scientist, letting his mispronunciation of 'supposedly' go by without comment. She prided herself on good verbal skills, including minimizing her childhood accent, for the sake of science. The man somehow got through his whole life without anyone correcting his mistake.

"Were you two looking up?" she asked sarcastically. "The treehouse is in a lot of cover."

Her skills were more on the theoretical side of physics, so she didn't socialize much with the computer guys, even though they all took breaks in what everyone called the treehouse. It was an emergency exit for the underground science lab but was no more than a corrugated metal outbuilding with lots of windows and a few vending machines.

"Everyone else saw it, so I don't know how we could have missed it. We always stand and watch nature. You know that as well as anyone, because Dr. Stafford and you—"

"Yeah, sure. Let's stay focused, people. The other thing I didn't tell you all is that we've lost our data feed from the CERN Large Hadron Collider."

The room became instantly quiet. The SNAKE lab was closely attached to the University of Colorado system, especially for distributed computing and data collection, but it also had all kinds of parallel projects going with labs around the globe. The CERN supercollider was so important to SNAKE research, they kept an American science group on-site in Switzerland to handle the back and forth.

Dr. Bob Stafford seemed as surprised as anyone. "Have you called Dr. Johnson's team?"

She gave Bob a steady look, doing her best not to feel threatened by him.

"Yes, Dr. Stafford," she replied tentatively, "once we lost the feed, we tried everything. At first, I thought our power issues might have cut off the link..."

She finally glanced down at the fax sheet Mindy brought in. The CERN logo caught her eye and she scanned a few lines.

One half of her brain absorbed the message while the other half kept her talking. "...but the power is fine now and I still can't get the line back. He isn't picking up his mobile phone, either."

She shifted all her concentration to line after line of bad news.

"Faith," Bob whispered before she finished the whole sheet. "Is everything all right?" She was almost as shocked at his sympathetic tone as she was with the content of the fax.

"Yeah, I'm fine." She remembered where she was. "I'm sorry. I was reading this communique from the European News Agency."

She held up the fax like it had a communicable disease.

"It isn't just us. Apparently all of Europe has lost contact with CERN."

I-5 North of Modesto

The big Peterbilt's engine brake brought the rolling monster to a full halt. Buck was conditioned to hate traffic on the interstate, but this one time, he was okay with it. As soon as the wheels stopped, he jumped out of his chair and opened Big Mac's cage.

"Come on out of there, Mac," he said in a soothing voice.

The six-month-old Golden Retriever sprang out of the small kennel like a fifty-pound bullet. He hopped off the sleeper bed and jumped onto the passenger seat in one fluid motion.

"You can't get out, yet, so don't get any ideas about doing your business, okay?"

The pup's tongue lolled out the side of his mouth as he panted with innocence, but Buck figured that was his usual ruse. Taking a leak was always on the little guy's mind.

Buck got back into the driver's position, buckled up, then glanced over to Mac.

"Don't you do it. We're stopped, but there isn't enough time to get out." He pointed ahead, even though the dog couldn't see over the dashboard. "See? The cars are moving up there. We're next."

Mac sat upright with canine attention, and even tried to look where Buck pointed, but then he held out a paw to signal he wanted something.

"I know. Here you go." Buck had traveled with the dog for the past week, so they'd gotten to know each other pretty well. He reached out and gave Mac a good scratch behind an ear.

Mac voiced a low grumble, which meant he was loving it.

"All good? I have to put my hands on the wheel, now. Sorry."

He halfway expected the excitable dog to get down off his seat and put his head on Buck's leg, but his words seemed to calm him. Mac walked around his perch for a moment then plopped down and curled up into a ball.

"I wish I could lay there and sleep. This traffic is for the—"

Two fighter jets screamed overhead.

"Holy shit!" he yelled.

The roar of their engines shook his ribcage because the aircraft weren't flying much higher than his roof. They came up from behind and zoomed along the highway mere feet above the stopped traffic. He marveled at the military precision as the two jets shot off toward the horizon in front of him.

"Sheesh. What the hell is going on today, eh, Mac?"

The planes stayed low to the deck as far as he could see, but he lost them when they reached a bank of low clouds several miles ahead.

"What now?" he asked his little partner. Buck wondered if the noise had scared him.

It had. The evidence was already soaking into the seat cushion.

"Well, at least I don't have to take you outside, now."

Traffic was about to move once more, so there was no time to clean up. He did his best to grab one of the beach towels he kept for puppy emergencies, but soon got busy driving.

"There's nothing to worry about, buddy. I promise."

In the distance, angry lightning danced among the dark clouds.

Nothing to worry about, he told himself.

Search for Nuclear, Astrophysics, and Kronometric Extremes (SNAKE). Red Mesa, Colorado

Faith walked out of the conference room after everyone else had left. She would have slipped out first if she could, because she wanted to escape her ex. However, the staff had the usual backlog of questions for her. Some related to the loss of contact with CERN. Some asking about their own canceled experiments. Others, just the normal day-to-day questions related to life in a science lab. If she got lucky, he might have tired of waiting for her.

Fuck, she thought when she saw him.

"Hello, Dr. Stafford," she said preemptively to the figure leaning against the metal wall.

"We're back to formalities while in private?" he responded in a tired voice.

"I never left the formalities, Bob," she said with barely-controlled anger. "And thanks for ganking me over in there. I'm sure that was you trying to undermine me."

"Oh, come on," he complained. "Just because I broke it off doesn't mean I'm out to get revenge."

She gave him a withering look. He seemed to realize he'd gone too far.

"What I meant was, we ended things in what I thought was a good place. I have no reason to want to hurt you. But, listen, this is some serious shit. Whatever happened with the experiment, you have to be the one to take responsibility. I can't let our history get in the way of accountability. We both have careers on the line."

Bob was directly below her on the org chart. He was in charge of the computer team, but he reported to her. As much as it pained her to admit, he was correct. The shutdown had tested his relationship with Mr. Shinano, as it did hers. Both of their careers hinged on figuring out who to blame.

She softened a little, but a passerby would need a microscope to see it. "You and your damned career. Something is happening out there, and you're worried about being the leader of this facility, aren't you?"

Bob's eyes narrowed like an owl homing in on prey. "I promise you, if this job opens up, I'm going to grab it. However, I'm not going to have to lift a finger to remove you from this position. You're doing that all by yourself. Two mistakes in one week. People are going to notice."

"Two?" she replied.

The man casually stood up straight. "Yuh huh. You failed to anticipate the power fluctuations in Mr. Shinano's experiment. That's an easy one. But then you told the whole team you failed to keep contact with our assets inside the CERN campus. That simple communication could have given us a clue as to their fate. Maybe Dr. Johnson could have told us how our place got shut down. Instead, you were running around micromanaging everyone."

It was too much. "That's bullshit, and you know it! I was running the shutdown protocol. You helped write it, for god's sake."

"So I did," he said easily. "That's how I'm so sure you've got two marks against you. One more and maybe your job becomes vacant."

Her skin bubbled with anger just under the surface, but she fought for control of it. They'd spent many years together, romantically, so he knew her better than almost anyone. He'd always been good at drilling through her professional exterior and laying waste to her emotions. Most of the time it was to get her to do what he wanted, but she was convinced sometimes he did it simply to be an asshole.

This time, it was a little of both.

Queens, New York

"That was some messed up shizz." Sam slapped Garth on the back, but not with much force.

"Yeah, I hope my dad doesn't hear about the plane wreck. He'll call me every five minutes if he thinks I'm in danger." His father had burned up the phone lines when there was a stabbing near the Staten Island Ferry. Garth wasn't near the ferry when it happened, nor did he have plans to go near the ferry that day, but his dad wanted to make absolutely sure he stayed away. That was about six months ago, so it was still fresh in his mind.

Sam seemed to think for a few moments as they walked to the bus stop. "My parents didn't call, either."

"I'm sure they will once they get back to their airport. You can't call on a plane."

"Yeah, you can. They always travel first class. They've called me from the air before."

Garth had never been on a plane. He had no idea what was possible beyond what he saw in the movies.

"Hey," he said in a way that was meant to distract his friend, "before we get on that crowded bus, let's try to wipe off some of this god-awful cologne."

Fifty or sixty people stood in line at the open-air bus stop. Those were the smart ones—they had cleared out of the airport immediately after the disaster instead of waiting around to see what happened.

Sam stopped without hesitation. "Brilliant idea. I've got a headache from hell because of this shit. How do you figure we'll get it off?"

Garth stood for a moment, then pointed to a small patch of residential grass next to the sidewalk. "You ever been deer hunting?"

"You know I haven't," Sam replied. "My parents are scared of guns."

"Right. Well, my dad taught me this one simple trick to fool deer. You roll around in the dirt and grass." He fell to the lawn and began to wiggle like a snake. "I think it gets the smells of the forest on you, but it also wipes off the detergent and fabric softener smells of your clothing."

Sam didn't need to be invited. He dropped and rolled the same as Garth.

"Of course, if you really want to hide your smell, you can pour special chemicals on you."

"Or douse yourself in deer whizz," Sam said during a brief pause. "I saw that in the movies."

Garth paused next to him. "Uh, Jester, that's not right. You use urine to attract deer to come to your stand. If you wear the stuff, they'll probably climb your tree to get to you."

They both cracked up laughing at the imagery.

"What do I know?" Sam continued rolling. "I don't leave the city. You're the pro when it comes to this sort of stuff."

Garth chuckled at the thought of being the professional at anything, because his dad would have another opinion about that. If he asked him about removing cologne the way he'd thought up, Dad would undoubtedly bitch about putting on the cologne in the first place. Then he'd say they were rolling the wrong way.

He sighed heavily as he watched Sam roll back and forth. He wasn't going to mention any of his adventure when his dad finally called. As far as his father knew, he and Sam were late getting to the airport, so they missed all the excitement.

What his dad didn't know wouldn't kill him.

CHAPTER 9

I-5 Between Stockton and Sacramento, CA

Buck caught the attention of the panting Golden in his passenger seat. "What do you think those planes were doing?" The last time he'd seen jets hug the deck like that, they were chopping up insurgents in the sandbox.

"Aw, it's probably nothing." It was uncomfortable to remember his past, so he chose to look ahead. "At least traffic is moving again, huh?"

He glanced over to Big Mac, because that furry face always cheered him up.

"Let's see if the news has anything for us." He turned up the volume on the radio, but he also did the same for his CB. He seldom used the squawk box because it was easier and faster to get road updates from the GPS route-finder on the dashboard. Channel 19 was considered the Romper Room of the citizens band, filled with every type of handle, often stepping over each other as they tried to chat. That was exactly what they were doing when he tuned in, so he turned it down a little.

"...definitely a freak storm." Buck turned up his FM radio to hear the man on the news. "The monster weather system exploded out of an existing storm, like energy was fed into it. It is now moving at surprising speeds."

Buck warily eyed the dark wall of clouds ahead. *No shit.*

A woman replied, "Does the national weather service have warnings posted?"

"Of course, Dianne, but the storm is growing so large, it would take a long time to list all the counties affected. Even the number of states is considerable."

He reached over and scratched Mac's head. "That chick in the Mustang is going to get soaked, isn't she?"

The news report changed to talk about other storms around the country, which held no interest for him. The only thing that mattered was the growing darkness between him and Sacramento. If he reached I-80 before entering those clouds, he would turn east and leave it behind. He'd be on easy street, because the 80 would take him all 2800 miles to White Plains, New York, and his boy.

A powerful signal came through his CB. "Break 19. This is Tenstepn riding the I-5 at marker 508. Can anyone near Sacramento tell me about that sheet of pain up ahead? Switching to channel 4."

Buck listened for a moment and noted the green mile-indicator coming up on his right. The small rectangular signs were like postal addresses for truckers on the move. He went by the 497 marker, which meant he was eleven miles behind Tenstepn.

He flicked the controls on the CB to channel 4. When no other drivers hopped on, he decided to introduce himself. "Heya, Tenstepn, this is Buck Rogers. I'm about ten behind your back door but heading for the same storm. Did you see where those two F-16s went?"

"No, sir. They went into the soup, and I never saw them again."

"I don't like the sound of that," he replied. It was stupid to think the storm ate up the sophisticated aircraft, but his attitude reflected his mood.

A wild bolt of lightning shot out of the dark wall far in the distance. It bounced like a nimble cat between several outlying clouds before it petered out.

"Holy shit!" Tenstepn cried out. "My hair is standing straight up."

"Did that lightning hit you?" Buck asked with urgency. "Come back?"

The other man keyed his mic but didn't speak for a moment. When he did, he sounded panicked. "Negative, but four-wheelers are pulling over everywhere. Somethin' ain't right."

"What is it?" Buck felt odd being the only person responding to the guy, but he wasn't going to complain. Normally, there would be ten truckers stomping all over each other on the radio.

"Hang on, Bucky, I'll get back to you."

"10-4," Buck replied.

He let his foot drift off the gas pedal, like he was hesitant to reach the next mile marker. Ahead, the wall of storm clouds went thousands of feet into the sky and stretched miles to his left and right. He was all ears for even a hint of news.

"The following states are affected." Buck tapped the volume on the radio because it sounded like they were going to announce how big the storm was. "South Carolina. North Carolina. Virginia. Mary—"

They went through ten more states.

Buck yelled at the radio. "Those are on the East Coast!"

"Summer Storm Audrey is extremely powerful right now, but its core is also unsettled. As of this time, our best guess is that it will track toward Washington D.C., then turn right and continue overland through New York and into New England."

Garth.

More lightning crackled ahead. Buck waited for Tenstepn to send back his live report about what to expect at mile 508. Leading clouds blocked out the sun, lending a dark aura to the green fields and row-filled orchards on both sides of the highway.

He cast his eyes to the southbound lanes. Every vehicle that went by was far over the speed limit. Even the big guys. "That's jacked up, Mac. They're flying."

His foot let off the gas a little more.

NORAD, Cheyenne Mountain, Colorado

"General, we have more on the blue light. This is the first official report."

Obadias took it from his lieutenant. "This came from the top?"

"The president's team issued this one minute ago. I got it here as fast as I could."

"Thank you, son." He dismissed the junior officer with a wave.

The entire staff of NORAD shuffled papers, banged keyboards, and talked on phones inside the secure room, but his attention was devoted to the one piece of intel that came from the outside.

"Let's see what this is all about," he mumbled.

He scanned the lines until he found the one he needed. "Not a meteor strike. NASA confirms no near-Earth object has struck atmosphere."

A few more lines were dedicated to the staff at NASA, he assumed so that he would have faith in their findings. But finally, he read the next point. "No unusual solar activity reported. National Oceanic and Atmospheric Administration confirms."

"Well, that's two things it isn't."

He kept reading until he found the next piece of news. "Not an intercontinental launch vehicle. Multiple confirmations."

His command sent that piece of intel up the chain. NORAD's data confirmed no solid-fuel rockets had come off the ground anywhere in the world.

"That's what it wasn't. Tell me what it was!"

He eyed the rest of the briefing without getting the satisfaction he sought. Despite the certainty it wasn't a ground-based launch from somewhere across the world, he still couldn't rule out a high-altitude fixed-wing delivery vehicle of a powerful EMP nuclear device. It was the not knowing that kept him uneasy. The Joint Chiefs had already bumped the continental United States to DEFCON 3, so his next response could move the needle closer to war. He had to be sure of the enemy.

"Lieutenant?" His aide was there like magic. "Get me every flight, every satellite, every ground station with eyes in the sky above the central United States during the past twelve hours. If a plane deviated for ten seconds, I want to know. If a satellite glitched for a micro-second, get me its transponder code. If there was a kid videoing his dog humping a scarecrow when the light went by, I want to friggin' see it."

"Sir." The man stifled a grin and hustled off.

"You know what I mean," he called after him.

Nowhere in the brief did it categorically deny the one thing that probably wouldn't show up in any of their sensors. He wasn't a believer, but he had to keep his mind open until the door was shut on every possibility. That was why he included ground-based observations in his data gathering.

Someone please tell me this wasn't a UFO. Damn Giorgio making everyone think there are aliens.

Queens, New York

The rush of people leaving the airport continued to grow as Garth and Sam got on the bus. The driver waved everyone aboard that could possibly fit, and the boys were the last ones on. They had to squeeze behind the white line, and stood body to body with the other riders, which made him instantly glad they'd taken the time to wipe off most of the cologne.

"These people are missing out," Sam whispered. "We could have nuked the whole bus if we still wore the good stuff."

"Shh!" Garth shot back in an even quieter voice. "You can't say nuked on a crowded bus."

He caught the stink-eyes of a few of the riders standing behind Sam. "We're cool. We used to smell terrible."

The driver shut the door before he could gauge their reaction.

A computer voice droned from hidden speakers. "M60 bus service to Manhattan. Next stop, Ditmars Boulevard and Grand Central Parkway."

Everyone shifted as the driver hit the gas.

There was an unnatural calm for a few seconds as the bus crossed the airport property, but as soon as it turned onto a side street, everyone seemed to speak at the same time. At first, many people complained about the spotty phone service, but that talk died down after people realized it affected everyone. People then talked about their other problems.

Garth heard tiny pieces of many conversations but chose to focus on an elderly couple sitting in the second seat. The woman seemed confident the airport wouldn't be re-opening. That was his problem.

Garth leaned over toward the woman. "Excuse me. They're keeping it shut down?"

The woman gave him a harsh look in return. "That's very rude. I was talking."

He'd been brought up to respect his elders. Plus, he did interrupt her. "Sorry."

"As I was saying, Aloysius and I were standing right there when the plane blew up. It was driving across the runway and poof. It exploded into a bajillion bits."

"That's not right, ma'am," Garth replied politely. "It fell from the sky and got destroyed. It wasn't already on the ground."

The old woman shook her head. "No, I tell you, it was on the ground. I know what I saw." She elbowed her companion. "Back me up, Al."

The gray-haired man smiled. "I cannot tell a lie; I was in the can. My bladder wasn't happy with me for having two Bloody Marys on the flight in. She had a few as well."

The woman scoffed. "Just agree with your wife, you old coot!"

The guy looked to a young woman in a business suit standing a few slots behind Sam. "I'm available to start a new life. This one's about *spent*."

"You wouldn't know what to do with a young thing like her." The lady looked right at Garth. "But maybe he and I could show you how it's done."

Sam cracked up laughing until the old woman looked over to him.

"You too, blondie."

Garth backed up a few steps out of sheer panic.

"Behind the line, please." The driver was courteous but insistent.

"Sorry," he mumbled.

He purposefully looked away from the old couple. Two young men in suits sat in the front seat behind the driver. They appeared to be headed to the financial district. One of them guarded a dark leather briefcase on his lap.

"You're sure your guy knew what he was talking about?" someone from the aisle asked one of the men.

"Yes. I deal with them all the time. Intermountain Systems is the computer supplier for numerous science and tech companies. If anyone would know, it's them."

"Know what?" Garth asked.

The guy looked up at him. "Oh, hey. I don't know if you heard me, but I know people who know people. They told me that blue light was caused by a failure at a nuclear power plant. Full on Chernobyl-type stuff."

"Bullshit," someone voiced from a couple of rows back. "There was no meltdown. We would have heard about it."

"Maybe," the guy in the front seat allowed. "But the people in charge always try to get their friends out first. That rush can lead to safety protocols being ignored. Such haste might cause planes to drop out of the sky, or it might mean transit buses are loaded well beyond capacity. Take your pick."

"These are your people," Sam whispered. "Nutters."

Garth shushed him. While they rode the M60 to the subway stop, he tried to pick up clues for what caused the plane crash as well as how that blue light shot across the sky. There had to be a simple explanation.

The computer voice announced their arrival at the subway station. The old woman hopped up before the bus came to a complete stop.

"Excuse me," she said in a demanding voice.

Garth didn't let her into the aisle until he and Sam cleared out.

I can see why your husband wants a change.

She came off the bus not far behind them but was soon lost in the crowd. Most of the passengers went right for the stairs up to the subway platform, which was thirty yards down the sidewalk.

"Standard seating?" Sam asked.

"Agreed," he answered. The boys preferred to ride in the last car.

For a short time, they walked with their usual slow pace, but people began to pass them, including the old woman and her husband. There was really no reason for him to feel panicked, but there was an urgency in people's strides that tapped into a primitive area of his brain. When they'd been passed by perhaps half of the passengers, he suddenly felt the urge to run and get ahead of them.

He pulled Sam by the elbow because he wasn't moving nearly fast enough toward the steps. They had to be first to the stairs and get up to the top fast as possible.

Garth's heart took on the cadence of speed metal as they moved toward the front part of the group of walkers.

"Go faster," he said under his breath.

Sam kept moving but wasn't as adamant about the goal. "Dude, we got it made in the shade. We'll get the last car. We're already ahead of most everyone."

"Not good enough," Garth insisted.

Garth wasn't afraid of missing the last car.

He was afraid of missing the last train.

CHAPTER 10

Search for Nuclear, Astrophysics, and Kronometric Extremes (SNAKE). Red Mesa, Colorado

Faith had the conference room all to herself again. It was her chance to use her car key to finish scratching out the lame words etched into the wood. The mindless activity sent her imagination on tangents, but all at once, she figured out something critical.

Bob did this.

It came down on her like a ten-ton hammer. Her ex-fiancé not only tried to undermine her in the meeting, but he was the one who scratched her name into the expensive wooden table. Probably to the applause of some of his computer buddies.

Yep, it was him.

"May I come in?" a gentleman's voice inquired from behind.

She flung her key away from the scratch-work and slid a folder over the repair effort. "Sure. Come in."

"Donald," she said with relief when she realized it wasn't Bob.

Donald Perkins was a PhD from a time before time, as he often said. The octogenarian had been a mainstay at the SNAKE lab since the day they turned on the lights. During those difficult early times, she grew to think of the man as a mentor, and friend.

"Rough day, huh? May I sit down?"

"Always."

She rose from her chair, but he waved her not to bother. "Please, Faith. I can handle this part. It's the getting up where I might need a hand."

His ability to laugh at himself was a lesson she tried to take to heart.

"I can't seem to do anything right, at least according to *some* people." She twisted a knife into the word 'some,' and Donald was smart enough to pick up on it.

"Bob being Bob again? Did he write that, too?" He motioned toward her folder and what it covered.

"You know about that?" she said with shock.

He nodded sadly.

"Does everyone?"

"It's been there for the past couple meetings. My old eyes couldn't read it until today, and I didn't want to call attention to it during your speech. I presume everyone who is not an asshole thinks it is childish and immature. It doesn't even make sense."

"That's what I've been thinking!" she said with surprising engagement. "They got the charge all wrong."

Donald laughed with her. "It's just like you to see past the ill intent and cut to the core of the problem. The writer of that statement is an idiot. He was also an idiot for trying to sabotage the meeting."

Faith was already high-strung from her talk with Bob, not to mention shutting down a billion-dollar machine earlier, but her mentor's words hit her in the feels.

"Thank you. I really needed some fucking sympathy today."

"No problem. Glad to help. But, Faith, we do still have a very serious issue—"

"Can't it wait? If I have one more failure today, Bob the Asshat says I'm going to lose my job. He's ready to swoop in and save this whole facility. In the name of science, and all."

Donald's distinguished eyes remained fixed on hers. "I'm afraid it can't. None of the teams can tell us exactly what caused the shutdown of our experiment. Maybe there is a more complicated answer, but we should look first at why the power failover didn't kick in."

"Shit," she said by way of agreement. "Can it be that simple?"

The SNAKE complex drew a little over 500 megawatts of power from the main electrical grid running through Denver, so if Denver went down for any reason, they'd go dark, too. However, the system was designed so any failure in Denver would result in power grabs from Pueblo, Colorado, and Cheyenne, Wyoming. That relief valve didn't work today.

"Is it too late to build our own private reactor?" she said in jest.

"Far too late," he replied. "You'd have to go back to 1975 to get a permit."

"Then I guess we are at the mercy of municipal power for the time being. Whatever happened out there today really jacked us up inside here. I only wish someone had the answer for what caused it, so we could work up a plan for how to prevent it from shutting us down again. That's what Bob would do."

By E.E. Isherwood & Craig Martelle

Donald gently put his hand on her wrist. "Don't base your response around assholes, Faith. You do what Faith would do, okay? You've gotten us this far down the road. This is one of the most sophisticated pieces of scientific equipment in the world. Who knows what kind of care we need to give it?"

The SNAKE facility was less than a year old. It was built as a cooperative venture between the University of Colorado and several emergent technology companies, including Mr. Shinano's Azurasia. The initial meet-and-greet between the science team and the wealthy industrialists had been one of the most nerve-wracking two hours of her life. Each of those powerful corporate leaders was probably now asking their boards of directors what the hell happened at SNAKE.

If the shutdown was due to a grid rollover error, those leaders will crucify me.

"I overlooked something. If I want to save my job, I have to find out why some mysterious blue light overrode our failsafes and shut us down. I'll need an answer for how we can keep it from wrecking the next experiment. I'd like to do it without Bob's interference, if at all possible. It can be anyone else on the team, just not him."

She glanced at Donald, hoping he would slap her on the back and congratulate her for toughing it out. But that wasn't his style.

"Mind if I help you scratch?" He nodded toward the folder. "It will give this fancy table some much-needed character."

She pulled back the manila envelope and revealed her handiwork. There was no doubt she'd made it messier by scratching over the words.

"Thanks." She sniffled. "This is exactly what I needed."

Faith happily keyed at the graffiti but considered her next moves.

I must solve this.

Wollemi National Park, New South Wales, Australia

Destiny held the club over the stumbling Tasmanian tiger. She'd caught it in the eye with a pointy knob on her weapon and put a major hurt on the animal.

"Stop this," she demanded. "I don't want to kill you."

She coughed from the smoke.

"Let's both call it a day and get the hell out of here, yeah?"

The tiger shook its head as if to clear the stars out of its good eye. Then it took another run at her.

Fuck.

The tiger didn't move nearly as fast as it had before, and her adrenaline-fortified awareness ached to end the fight. For a long moment, she felt cocky enough to strike it in the side as a way of safely encouraging it to move along, but her sister's voice reminded her not to be heroic for no damned good reason.

Destiny struck the tiger near the injured eye socket with all the power she had left. The pointy knob bashed its skull and made a satisfying crack.

The animal rolled over like it had been turned off.

Her chest heaved as she tried to get enough good air into her lungs.

She'd shattered the tiger's orbital bone and blood poured out of its ruined eye socket. It should have been a victory, but the prone body made her regret her choice. "What have I done?"

You did what you had to survive, her sister would say.

I'm supposed to help animals.

The little voice provided no comeback for that. In all her years in the field, she'd never voluntarily killed anything bigger than a mosquito.

I'm supposed to help...

A short time later, she realized she'd been staring at the dead animal.

"I've got to get out of here," she said to herself. The fire raged down in the valley and came most of the way up the escarpment. Safety was over the ridge and down the hill toward camp.

"Camp!" she shouted to herself.

Destiny pulled the radio off her belt and tried calling them again.

"Camp. I'm good. I'm on the ridge. Are you there?" They would never leave her, but each second the line remained silent, more doubt entered her mind.

She changed tact. "You'll never guess what I've found. A Tasmanian tiger." She giggled. "It's illegal to trap them to get the bounty, but I didn't trap this one. I had to fight him off. I should get something for that, right?"

The line came back with only static.

"Come on, guys. I'm bushed. I need help."

Nothing like playing on the male egos to come to my rescue.

"I'm coming down," she croaked. Her throat was as dry as Ayers Rock at noon in the summertime. Thinking about that longneck beer didn't help with her thirst.

She'd gotten about fifty feet across the ridgeline when she stopped.

"Shit," she declared. "Why not?"

By E.E. Isherwood & Craig Martelle

Destiny trudged back to the body of the tiger and whipped out her phone.

"No one is going to believe this," she said.

The flames were everywhere around her, but she took her time to get several well-focused snapshots. They were a lot better than the dark blurs she snapped of it earlier. These new pictures were now irrefutable proof of the continuing existence of this species.

It upset her to be the one responsible for killing it, so the least she could do was properly catalogue it. She geo-tagged the location, threw the phone back in her pocket, and calmly walked away from the fiery ledge.

Her eyes became watery pools as soon as she descended the backside of the ridge. Her campmates were somewhere down in the valley. There was no fire within view, and she could finally breathe in fresh air. It was her moment.

She pulled out her radio again but spoke slowly because she was exhausted. "I'm coming down. Be there in fifteen. If you get the drone working, the tiger is up on top of the ridge in the open. You can't miss it. Oh, and just so you know, I'll kiss the first person who brings me a drink." She didn't care who it was.

Only silence answered her. The more she walked, the more she saw of the camping area below her. It hit her like an anvil. They had left her behind.

I-5 South of Sacramento

Buck had gone another mile while waiting for the other driver to come back on the CB. He passed marker 500 before he decided he'd waited long enough.

"Tenstepn, you got your ears on?" Buck waited a few seconds before adding, "What's going on up there?"

Traffic still ran at a good clip on the northbound lanes, but there were fewer cars heading south, though they still drove like fiends.

"That's where they're coming from," he said to Mac. A car crossed the center median on a gravel U-turn lane reserved for emergency vehicles. He jammed the gearbox as he considered whether he should do the same.

Come on, bubba. Get on your radio.

Buck passed the turnaround, but it was firmly in his brain that he might need to get off the highway.

"Bucky, come back. I'm entering this storm. No choice. It moved too fast." The other driver's words were drawn out, like it had been recorded and then played back at a slightly slower speed.

"Tenstepn, where are the other fast movers? There's almost no one coming south."

"Don't know. Can only see taillights in front of me. At least my truck is getting clean." His voice sounded mechanical and slow.

"Jesus," he said to himself. He keyed the mic. "What marker are you at?"

"509. Last known." That time, his voice echoed like it was inside a coffee can.

"Shit, I'm getting close," he said to himself. A decision had to be made. It wasn't that he normally went out of his way to avoid rainstorms, but there was something unnatural about the one ahead of him. It was larger than anything he'd ever seen before and the lightning strikes seemed to have a life of their own.

A few drops of water splashed on his windshield. Big Mac whined when he clicked on the wipers for a second to clear them.

"It's okay, bud. It's just a little rain." He wondered if his own tense posture gave the dog the wrong impression.

Buck took a deep breath. "Everything is cool."

Mac sat up and cocked his head as if to interpret his words.

"That's right. We're all right." Buck laughed to ease the tension. It didn't work.

Multiple strikes of lightning pulsed across the darkened sky right as he said it. He visualized ten growing cracks in a giant pane of glass, and each one split into more and more offshoots, like an infinite fractal of electricity.

The thunder lasted for ten seconds and rose to an intense crescendo that rocked his cab.

"Good god!" he screamed somewhere in the middle of it.

The radio hissed like hot grease in a frying pan for a few seconds, but then someone called his name.

"Bucky. This is bad. It's—"

"We're fine," he replied to himself, and to Mac.

When he looked over to his pal, the dog wasn't there. He had to look back over his shoulder to see where he'd gone. For the first time in history, Mac voluntarily went into his crate.

"Oh, shit," he said dryly.

He   knows   what's   coming.

CHAPTER 11

Queens, NY

Garth and Sam made it to the top step of the subway platform before most of the other riders. His fear of being left behind was for nothing, because the train cars were almost empty. However, he still held his friend back.

"I know you want the end car, but let's get any one she's not on." The group of bus riders from the airport trudged up the steps to the elevated station, but once on top, they were free to pick from any of the ten subway carriages. Garth pointed to the old woman who'd propositioned him.

"Aw, come on. She's not so bad. I bet even you could get a date with her." Sam pointed to the woman as she and her husband walked for one of the front cars.

"Nice burn," Garth deadpanned.

The boys went for the rearmost door on the last car.

He tried to get a dig back at him. "I think I can see why Tammy didn't want to go out with you."

"Harsh, dude. I assure you, it had nothing to do with my great sense of humor."

"Uh huh," he agreed.

The door shut once they stepped inside. A woman's voice came over the intercom: "This is a Manhattan-bound W local train. The next stop is Broadway."

A male voice added: "Stand clear of the closing doors, please."

Garth watched stragglers run to make it before the doors sealed shut. The pair of guys who looked like investment bankers were the last ones into their car. They sat at the front with a few others.

"It's nice to have a little room," Sam said from across the railcar. They each owned one of the wide seats facing each other.

The train smoothly accelerated out of the station. For a few moments, he watched the endless brick apartment buildings from the elevated railway, but he quickly grew bored. He pulled out his phone to see if his dad had called or texted while he was on the crowded bus. He had to think of something to say if Dad asked about the plane crash.

Sam had his phone out, too.

"Anything from your parents?" Garth carefully asked.

"Nah. I'm sure they'll call when they can. I'm just playing this dumb-assed brick breaker game."

He didn't have any messages, either, and the network symbol at the top of the screen had a line through it, which told him he probably wouldn't get anything anytime soon.

Garth sat and stared at his phone for a long time as the subway stopped at a couple stations. A part of him wanted to get in touch with his dad and let him know he was fine, but another part didn't want to be the little kid who cried to daddy. Sam hardly seemed to care that his parents missed landing today, so why should he care about his own father who was clear across the country and not scheduled to come home for another week?

Serves him right for what he did.

He tried to muster the energy to be mad, but he'd burned through most of his anger the week before. Garth's dad rode him hard about personal responsibility. Once his mom had passed away, things were tough for both of them. With only one income, his dad took the best-paying job he could find, which also meant he was gone for weeks at a time. By the time he got back, he probably wouldn't remember what they argued about. Garth wasn't sure it was worth staying angry.

He turned inward some more until he heard a familiar station on the intercom.

"This is Queensboro Plaza. Transfers are available to the 7 train."

Garth turned to Sam. "Say good-bye to the sky. We're going into the tunnel."

His friend leaned forward to get as close as possible so the few other passengers near the front wouldn't hear him. "I say we go to Union Station and mess with the tourists. We can play the part of cranky New Yawkers." Sam added some local twang to his speech.

He shook his head, seeing Sam in a new light now that his parents weren't coming. "It sounds like fun any other time, but with that crash, don't you think we should stay on this line and go to the ferry? Get back home? Maybe it would be better to load up on pizza, Mountain Dew, and binge-watch some Netflix?"

"Nah. We can do that all night. I think we should make ourselves available to the foreign ladies."

"Aha! So that's what this is about." Garth felt like he'd caught him in a huge lie, but quickly settled into the fact that that was how Sam thought about things most of the time. He had unusual names for girl-watching.

Sam was never caught flat-footed. "Dude. Would you rather sit alone in my house, just you and I, or would you rather polish your lady-killer skills out in the field?"

His first instinct was to say he preferred to go home, but he realized that was what Dad would prefer, too. The anger from their last argument had ebbed but wasn't yet extinguished. He put his phone away and resolved to stop pretending to be the responsible one.

"I'd rather be out and about."

I-5 South of Sacramento, CA

Buck slowed the Peterbilt to about twenty miles per hour. The southbound lanes were now empty of traffic, but cars, what truckers called four-wheelers, passed by on his driver's side like they were in a hurry to get to the mammoth storm. He took little comfort that this was no different than any other change in the weather. People went too fast in rain, sleet, and snow because many drivers operated without their brain. He would willingly join them if his scout told him all was well up ahead.

"Come in, Tenstepn. What is the situation? I'm at 504 and running out of blacktop." He held the mic with his right hand and kept his left on the wheel. His knuckles started to turn white from gripping as if his life depended on it.

The storm was bigger than anything he'd ever seen. The churning clouds on the front face were like a horde of zombies standing behind a chain-link fence. When they broke through, they would spill out on Buck and the other drivers.

"Break 4. Anyone north of mile 504, come in." There were other wagon-pullers on the highway ahead, but no one replied. He figured they weren't on the citizens band, or on channel 4. He broke into channel 19 but got no reply there, either.

"Mile 505," he said to Mac as another of the markers went by. "I don't think this is going to end well."

A voice echoed distantly on the CB. Buck leaned in to listen. For a few seconds, there was only static again, before he heard a man's shouts.

"...nuclear bomb went off. Horri..."

Static swallowed the voice.

What the—

"Tenstepn? That you? Come back." He was on 19, so he didn't think it was.

Nothing but static came out of the little radio. The voice was gone. He jumped off 19 and poked around on some of the other channels, but they had all gone silent.

He wiped sweat from his brow as he considered those words.

Nuclear bomb.

He had never seen one except in the movies. The clouds rose high in the sky like a nuke, but they couldn't have been formed by a detonation. There would have been a flash...

The blue light. That was a kind of flash. What if it was the leading edge of a blast coming from some other city? San Francisco was just over the Diablo Range from Sacramento. San Jose and Oakland were over there, too.

It made sense until he recalled that the blue wave came out of the east. Maybe Denver or Salt Lake City blew up?

The smooth lay of the land made it easy to see the squall line ahead. Maybe modern bombs would take on the appearance of a giant storm over a city, especially if there was already a storm in progress. The wall of storm looked more ominous the closer it got.

Someone honked as they flew by.

"Yeah, fuck you, too!" he shouted at his windshield.

It wasn't safe to go slow on the highway, but he didn't think it was safe to go into that rain, either. In all his miles of driving, no storm had enough power to shut down all radio broadcasts. Even the FM band was static. He wasn't convinced it was anything as deadly as a nuclear mushroom cloud, but he was positive that leaving the highway was the best course of action.

"There. That's our stage right." Buck pointed to a bridge over the highway up ahead and the paved ramp going up to it. The timing was perfect because the storm's leading edge was a few hundred yards on the far side of it. "Exit 506.

"Tenstepn, I don't know if you can hear me. I hope so. I'm getting off the highway at 506. You should turn around, too. Anyone hearing this on the northbound slope should shuffle back to the south. This storm looks like it packs a punch."

Nothing came back on channel 19. It was as if the world had abandoned him.

Buck accelerated as he hit the off ramp, but his truck's weight and the incline kept him from getting much speed on the climb. He shared the ramp with a few vehicles also trying to abandon the highway, but he noted that one motorcycle and several cars stayed on the main highway and parked under the overpass.

When he got to the top of the ramp, he had a clear view of the storm and what remained of the road. The lanes appeared to end at the bank of clouds, mist, and rain. The whole mass moved to the south.

He was faced with a choice. He could turn right and go into the suburbs of Sacramento and maybe find somewhere to hole up. Or he could turn left and get back on the highway heading south.

Lightning snapped through the air and wrapped around a tall light pole at his intersection. The dim bulb was already on because of the surrounding darkness, but it doubled in brightness as the electromagnetic energy surged through it.

Buck watched with awe as the seconds took an eternity to roll by. The lightning clung to the light pole like it was tied to it. A second finger of energy zapped out of the cloud wall and attached to the same pole. The bulb got even brighter before it exploded, yet the lightning continued sparking near the top.

He was fully aware when the effects of the strange EM burst reached his cabin.

There was no rearview mirror to confirm what he experienced, but he put his hand on top of his head.

His wild hair now stood straight up.

Manhattan, New York

Garth looked toward the other people in the front of the well-lit train car.

"Are we under the water, Mommy?" A boy of about five looked out his window at the dark walls of the subway tunnel. Tired rectangular lights passed by at regular intervals as the train rolled on.

"I don't know, baby." For a reason Garth couldn't figure out, the mother looked back to him. She sat toward the front, but he wasn't far from her son.

"Yeah," he said when prompted. "You are under the East River right now."

"Are there boats on the river?" the child asked. "I like the boats."

The mother smiled at him, almost like she was embarrassed. "We take the ferry to Staten Island. He's telling the truth; he loves all the interesting boats."

"So do we!" Garth agreed. Sam's family also lived on the island, so he was familiar with the ferry boats, barges of trash, and all the pleasure craft jetting about within view of the Statue of Liberty.

The computer woman making the announcements came on to indicate they were approaching the next station, but he ignored that so he could talk to the mother and her kid some more.

"Look alive, G-man. This is our stop."

"Right," he said in a distracted way.

The subway train slowed gently for a few seconds like it always did as it came into a station.

"So, where are you two—" he tried to say.

The car jerked to a hard stop. The boy and his mother were turned around on their seat, so they fell off and tumbled to the front of the carriage. Garth and Sam were veteran riders and held on to the safety bars. They'd taken the same tumble several times over the years, because people sometimes fell off the platforms at the stations, and the driver had to hit the brakes.

He jumped out of his seat once the train stopped.

"Are you all right, ma'am?" he asked the mother. Others ended up in heaps on the floor, too, but no one appeared to be seriously hurt.

The boy laughed like it was a game. "Can we do that again, Mommy?"

Garth helped the woman to her feet as the announcer came on the speakers.

"This is Lexington Avenue 59th Street. Transfers available for 4, 5, and 6 lines."

"We stopped short, I guess." It happened every so often, so he tried to stay calm for the sake of the kid.

Sam came to the front. "I think we hit a cow."

The little boy looked at him like he was Superman. "Really?"

Sam snickered. "I don't know. Maybe!"

"No," Garth said in a reasonable voice that reminded him of his father's. "There are no cows in New York City."

"What about at the circus?" Sam challenged.

"Have you been to a circus lately? There are no cows there."

"Mommy, I want to see the cow!"

Sam seemed proud of the confusion he'd caused.

Garth shook his head but inwardly laughed at how easily his buddy came up with that nonsense. "We'll have to go to the front," he suggested in a relaxed voice.

The two guys in suits heard his advice and were the first ones to go through the passageway to the next car. Garth gave the mom some room, so she could get out next.

"Thank you," she said. The boy followed his mom but peered around her legs as if searching for the cow.

Garth laughed as he waved Sam toward the inter-car doorway. "After you."

When his friend got close to the door, Garth nodded graciously like he was going to let him go first, but then he jumped into the gap next to him. As planned, neither of them could fit through the narrow frame.

Both cracked up, even though they'd each pulled that gag a hundred times.

"After you," they said in unison while fruitlessly trying to wave each other through.

Garth laughed as he watched the boy and his mother get to a small crowd of people standing at the far end of the next car. However, his mood shifted when he caught sight of Lexington Station. Overhead lights illuminated the platform, but they cut off in a sharp line, leaving most of the station in the dark. He was familiar with the large size of the popular subway stop. He estimated ninety percent of the platform was lost to an impenetrable blackness.

Sam pushed ahead because Garth lost his focus on their competition. "Eat it, sucker!"

He ignored his friend and started walking after the boy.

"Come on, man," Sam replied. "You can't let me win that easy."

"Sam, look," he said dryly.

He tried to square what he saw as he moved forward. The lighting was all messed up outside, but the car ahead was dark as well. Garth ignored the handful of people hovering around and pushed through to the next one.

There were only a few people standing inside the darkened third-to-last car, including the boy and his mom.

"Mommy, what happened? Where are the people?"

One of the finance guys touched a solid block of rock in front of them. "It looks like something fell and cut the train and Lex Station in half."

Garth experienced insta-guilt because his selfishness might have saved his life. He'd been happy to let riders go to the front cars, so he and Sam had the rear one mostly to themselves. How many cars did the collapsed wall of bedrock smash?

Garth whistled the equivalent of "wow."

"What the hell happened?" Sam asked, ignorant of the small ears nearby.

Garth didn't know, but something caught his eye where the train's outer body met the fallen rock face. In the odd light of the dim carriage, it was hard to see unless you looked right at it.

Garth felt the bile rise in his stomach. Sam was a terrible cook, and his pancakes were awful. He was aware they would taste almost as bad coming back up.

He tried to speak, but the combination of fluttering stomach and disbelief made it impossible to open his mouth. All he could do was slap Sam on the back and point to the object.

"What is it, Garth?"

Garth pointed emphatically at the dark shape.

A man's hand held one of the metal supports as if the rider was still sitting on a chair waiting for the train to stop. It gripped the pole, but everything above the elbow was somewhere inside the rock. Garth couldn't figure out how the block could have fallen fast enough to sever the arm like that without moving it an inch. The longer he looked at the connection, the harder it was to understand. It was like looking at a funhouse mirror that refused to yield the truth.

Garth only wanted his friend to confirm it was real, so he pointed over and over.

The young boy saw it first.

"Whose hand is that, Mommy?"

CHAPTER 12

I-5 at City Limits of Sacramento, CA

"Just drive, Buck," he ordered himself.

He turned his rig to the left, painfully crushing the clutch over and over as he hammered on the gear box. His intention was to cross the 4-lane bridge to the far side of I-5. From there, he'd merge right onto the cloverleaf ramp, which would take him back down to the southbound lanes of the interstate.

The wall cloud loomed close as if daring him to try to make it.

"Just drive," he gulped.

As soon as his truck touched the bridge, the cabin became charged with energy. He only needed to look out his windows to see why. Blueish lightning bounced between several light poles at the interchange as if trying to drive life into Frankenstein's monster. The nonstop claps of deafening thunder suggested the beast was close to re-animation.

"Sit tight back there," he said to Big Mac in a voice that betrayed his fear. There was something sinister about the endless razor cuts of lightning, and he desperately wanted to sneak around the curved ramp before they tagged him. "We have to get through this cloverleaf and we'll be in the clear."

When he missed a gear, the pucker factor went to twelve.

Steady, Buck, he thought. *Git 'er done.*

He was most of the way across the bridge when a nudge in his steering caught him by surprise. Endless days on the road helped him identify the strong wind pushing against his truck, and he was prepared to hold the wheel steady, but the direction was unexpected.

"Shit," he exclaimed. "How is it blowing *toward* the storm?"

The gusts came in from the left, and the rear tandem tires swerved from side to side like a shadow boxer trying to avoid an opponent, but the boxy trailer absorbed every blow square on the face. A tip-over knockout was a real possibility.

Mac whimpered in his crate.

"It's going to be—" He couldn't hear himself finish the sentence because a clap of thunder shook the entire vehicle.

"Fuck! It's going to be close!"

Buck guided the fast-moving truck off the bridge despite the high winds, and he entered the cloverleaf loop at a speed that would have made his commercial driver's license instructor loose his lunch. At the beginning of the curve, he drove straight at the storm, which did help with wind shear from behind him, but as soon as he rounded the turn a bit more, the agitated gusts jabbed at the trailer from the right.

Leaves and debris flew sideways toward the storm as surely as if it were trying to vacuum that stretch of California. His giant truck offered little safety. Brown dust came out of the interior vents, but he didn't have time to adjust them. He leaned into the turn, hung onto the wheel, and sucked in the dirt. There was nothing to do except drive the eighteen-wheeler like he stole it.

Years of trash tossed in the highway median now flew sideways at him.

"This is it!" he shouted.

He was scared beyond words, but he had a job to do. If it wasn't to save himself, it was to save Mac. The little pup counted on him to get out of the maw of the storm.

And I have to get home to Garth.

The rear van took the full brunt of the wind as he neared the exit of the cloverleaf circle. The dust and debris made it difficult to see it happen, but the right tires of the van seemed to come off the pavement. When it slammed back down, it shook the kingpin inside the fifth wheel, and thus it shook the cab.

"Whoa, Nellie!"

The turbulence diminished as he returned to I-5 and put the nose into the wind. Little particles of junk struck the front windshield as he went under the overpass he'd just crossed. The dust streaking toward him evoked memories of the big haboob sandstorms in the Iraqi desert, but he forgot all that when he came up to another car parked under the bridge.

"Idiot! Drive!" He encouraged the motorist with a blast on his air horn.

He was tempted to stop and see if the person needed any help, but the dust-covered sedan had all the windows up and it was impossible to see if anyone was inside. Risking his life for someone in need was one thing but doing it for a potentially empty vehicle had the makings of suicide.

Electricity arced between his Peterbilt and the parked car as he accelerated past it.

"This is insane!"

On the northbound side of the highway, the cars and motorcycle were still parked beneath the overpass where he'd last seen them. Several more cars joined them, cramming under cover as best they could. He caught glimpses of clothing up where the bridge met the embankment. Was that a safe spot to hide from the storm? He was already out from under the span and speeding away before he had time to wonder if he should have hid under the strong bridge, too.

A few stragglers still drove up the 506 exit ramp, but he wasn't sure where they'd go to get safe. The tide of clouds now lapped over the road across the bridge. The vehicles' only real option was to turn around and drive the wrong way on the highway. He didn't want to see what happened to them.

"Come on, baby," he said to his truck, "just a little more."

He drove out of the leading edge of the storm. A final swirl of plastic bottles and Styrofoam cups bounced off his windshield and front grille, and then the wind seemed to turn off. It didn't make him feel much safer.

He checked the side mirror a dozen times to make sure the storm wasn't speeding up to get him. It was a huge weight off his shoulders to see it fall behind. He couldn't help but think of those under the bridge. Fight or flight? Shelter or run? He grew more comfortable with his decision to turn around. The other drivers had their chance.

He wondered if this was it. Every man for himself. He needed to get to Garth. Buck gave that his singular focus, and it helped him shove the guilt from his mind.

He exhaled every ounce of air in his lungs and felt a little of his tension release. "What the hell was that?" he pondered quietly.

The Peterbilt gave him 85 miles per hour.

There was less traffic in the northbound lanes than a few minutes earlier. The storm had grown so large that many drivers turned around well before it was too late. Dozens of vehicles crossed the flat, rocky median and put the hammer down in the southbound lanes.

"They're the smart ones," he said to Mac.

For a couple minutes, his brain picked through every detail of his windy escape; it was angry it allowed Buck to get so close to major bodily harm. He almost reveled in the introspection until he glanced to the far lanes and saw a few trucks and cars that weren't turning around. He could at least help the truckers.

"Break, break, Channel 19. All northbound traffic on the 5 needs to turn around before Sacramento. There's a—" Buck didn't know what to call it. What was a cross between a haboob and a nuclear bomb? "There's an evil storm the size of Montana heading south down the Central Valley along Interstate 5. I say again—"

Helping others also helped Buck calm down and regain his composure. He filed away all the details of how close he'd come to losing his load, and potentially his life. They were lessons that might save his life the next time. The wisdom of experience.

"I told you we'd make it," he said matter-of-factly. "Piece of cake."

Mac didn't come out of his kennel.

Behind him, in the side mirror, the storm continued its relentless march.

Manhattan, New York

Garth ran out of the smashed subway car to make a deposit of pancakes and orange juice in the gap next to the station platform. His stomach betrayed him after seeing that unnatural hand still gripping the support.

Sam came out a few moments later. "Did you SEE that?"

"What do you think? I'm throwing up for shits and gigs?"

"It had to be some kind of gag, right? Whoever was sitting there before must have slung that hand on the pipe because it looked funny. I mean, he got you pretty good."

A teen girl about their age came out of the car behind Sam. She was pretty, with golden-blonde hair down to the middle of her back, but her gaze was rigid like she'd seen something horrible. His heart skipped a beat as she neared, but he wasn't sure if it was her or his embarrassment at tossing his fear.

"Hey," Garth said to her. Belatedly, he used his sleeve to wipe his mouth.

"What is the number for 999?" she asked in a British accent with her phone in hand.

"You mean the emergency number?" Garth asked. "Shit. Of course, we should call for help."

"It's 9-1-1," Sam said. "Lots of people are calling." He pointed into the subway car. "If their phones work. Ours don't."

She breathed out in relief. "Oh, that's cracking."

Sam kept the conversation alive. "Don't mind us. We're trying to solve the riddle about what happened."

The girl looked back to the second-to-last car. "I was on that one. We slowed way down and almost reached the station when the wall fell and cut off everyone up front. All the other cars got smushed to bits." Her accent was mild, and the young men found it intriguing. "I've heard about these problems on the telly. Does this happen a lot in your country?"

A lot?

Sam ignored the slight because he was blinded by her beauty. Garth recognized the look immediately. "Hi. I'm Sam. This is Garth. We were on the last car, but we didn't see it happen. Do you want to talk about it?"

Garth was impressed how easily his buddy directed the conversation where he wanted it to go, but he was also a little ticked he was talking to the girl at all. He didn't just throw up for nothing. There was something weird going on.

He purposefully stood in a way that blocked her view of where he got sick, but he was certain her eyes avoided it, too.

"Sam, old chum, we don't need to bother her."

"It's okay," she droned. "I'm Pippi. Me and my family are here on holiday. We're from London."

Garth re-evaluated everything that had happened in the last two minutes. After the train stopped, he must have walked past Pippi and her family without even noticing them. He hated to think he'd overlook a blonde as attractive as her, but he was following the kid and his mom. The most important thing on his mind, he hated to admit, was whether she saw him puke.

"I'm sorry we missed you inside. We came out here to get a little air, and so others could see the weird collapsed wall."

She smiled for the first time. "I saw you dropping pavement pizza. I wanted to do the same thing. Are all those people dead? Or are there survivors on the other side of the wall?"

Sam chose that moment to jump in. He acted like they were about to embark on an adventure. "Garth and I are going up the exit stairs to find out. Want to come with?"

"No thanks," she said. "I have to stay with my parents. They're right here. Where is the stairwell?"

Sam visibly deflated as he pointed to the red exit sign at the end of what was once a very long loading platform.

"Right. When they get here, we'll follow you two to the top. We have similar exits on our tube, so we'll be fine, thanks."

Garth and Sam stood there for a few moments as if unsure what to say.

"Great. Thank you so much for your help." Pippi's tone was friendly, but Garth picked up she was done talking.

Sam pulled out his phone. As sure as the sun rises, Sam intended to get her digits, but Garth cut him off before he could make the departure even more awkward.

"Sam, could you help me with something?"

Sam appeared like he was going to refuse, but then he shrugged. They moved across the platform and stood next to the fallen block of concrete.

Garth got right to it. "Dude, this isn't the time to be hitting on girls. There was a hand in there. A freaking hand!" His stomach fluttered at the recall.

Sam stood close and spoke quietly. "I saw it, G, but there's no way it could have been real. What was that about? Where did this wall even come from? This station is fucked up beyond all regulations."

"Recognition," Garth corrected. "FUBAR is fucked up beyond all recognition. That's exactly what this is."

"Right." Sam shook himself all over like a wet dog. "Ignore me, dude. I'm coping."

Garth chucked him on the shoulder. "Me too."

They shared a brief smile, then he glanced at the people coming out of the shortened train. Between the two and a half cars, there were maybe twenty riders.

"Exit time?" Garth asked.

"Exit time," Sam agreed.

"Things will seem better once we get up to street level."

Sam gave him a thumbs up. "I'm sure it will."

Garth had to believe.

"This way to the top!" Garth yelled to the small crew, waving his arm for them to follow. For once, he was prepared to use his New York City transit knowledge for a good cause.

NORAD, Cheyenne Mountain, Colorado

"General. We've got some intel you have to see." Lieutenant Chris Darren placed a large blueprint on the general's desk.

"It better be good, Chris" he said in his gruff voice.

"It is, sir." Lt. Darren used his arm to smooth the sheet, then he pointed to all the dots. "We've found some discrepancies in these."

The general studied the large paper. It carried the markings of the 50th Space Wing USAF. "You've found problems with our GPS satellites?"

"No, sir. Well, not really. A minor problem, perhaps."

"You don't sound very sure of yourself. You want to re-think this meeting?" He didn't have time for guessing.

"No, sir, there is a problem," he said with more confidence. "Maybe one that doesn't matter, but I don't want to ignore this."

The general sighed. "Let's have it then, and soon."

"Right." Lt. Darren pointed to the blue line drawing. Numerous black dots blanketed an outline of the Earth. "These represent the global positioning satellites visible to the northern hemisphere. For the sake of this discussion, I'd like to focus on these, but the problem does affect all of them."

"Did we lose some of them?"

"No, sir. But they did lose something important. As you know, the world network of satellites relies on accurate timekeeping so the trilateration between any four stations in the sky will assign a location to a point on the surface. That is what gives the user accuracy to within thirty centimeters."

"Go on."

"Well, you told me to check satellites for any anomalous behavior in the last twelve hours. I sent the request to the 50th, and they shot this back almost right away. This data shows each of the satellites is slightly out of sync with the calibration equipment."

"Out of sync? By how much? Which ones?"

"That's the funny part, sir. Every single one shows the exact same error. I've checked this five times from five different ground stations. The satellites are all wrong."

"It's got to be a calibration error, right? The ground stations sent bad data."

"I asked the same question because it seems logical, but the commander over at Schriever assures me this error was not caused by the Earth-bound stations. They checked all six nodes in the ground tracking system. They confirm the entire constellation of thirty-one active satellites got recalibrated in space."

"Well? What happened? Did the blue wave knock them into next week?" The general laughed a little at his own joke because he didn't want to believe anything could mess up all the satellites. Rare solar events might affect the internals of a satellite here or there, but those were always localized. Not universal. If the satellites were tweaked just a little, it could be a probe by an enemy power to see US response time. Maybe it was a prelude to war.

"No. They aren't knocked out, thank god, or we'd have a real traffic crisis down here on the ground." Chris's laugh was hollow. "But every satellite in the GPS grid, without exception, has lost point-six-six-six seconds."

General Smith sat down in his leather office chair. "Six-six-six?"

Lieutenant Darren's face turned pale.

The general steepled his fingers in front of his face. "You a religious man?" he asked, taking a stab of logic.

A nod.

Obadias turned serious. "This isn't the devil's work, son. This is the first piece of evidence that shows the burst of energy did *something*. I want every byte of telemetric data for each of the satellites in the constellation. I want..."

He rattled off a laundry list of requests he had for the boys and girls at the 50th Space Wing.

And he did everything possible to avoid thinking   of   the   evil   number.

CHAPTER 13

Search for Nuclear, Astrophysics, and Kronometric Extremes (SNAKE). Red Mesa, Colorado

"I can leave you alone, if you'd like," Bob said as he approached at the window overlooking the experimental equipment.

Yes, I'd like that.

"No, it's still a free country." She couldn't tell her chief computer mathematician to pound sand, even if he was Dr. Bob Stafford, chief asshole in residence.

Bob was a head taller than her and built like a professional football player. His trim beard had a touch of gray to give him the distinguished look of a scientist. It was the contrast of brainy and brawny that first attracted her to him those many years ago, but like those bosons and neutrinos written into the table, even the stars couldn't hold them together forever. Now she saw him as nothing more than an ape in a lab-coat.

The ape started his statement with a sigh. "I won't undermine you like that again. Happy?"

She pursed her lips while studying his face to see which way she wanted their chat to go. His wire-frame glasses seemingly added ten points to his IQ, which was already considerable. He always made sure people knew it, too. For many years, she was drawn to his incredible intellect and they rose through the University of Colorado science department as an unstoppable team, but their relationship imploded soon after the SNAKE lab came online. She always assumed it was because he wanted the head job, instead of her, but they never talked about it. It was easier to let the implosion happen.

"I can fire you, you know," she deadpanned.

"Nah, you need me. This shutdown problem is too complicated for you to handle on your own."

Though technically true, she wasn't going to admit any such thing.

"Well? What is it? What caused the shutdown? I'm waiting."

She stared out the glass again. The experimental underground chamber was the size of a large aircraft hangar with people walking along railings eight floors up. It was built around a piece of equipment fifty feet-tall and a hundred long that looked like the world's largest automotive transmission, or a horn of plenty. It was mated with a similar-sized cylinder in the leftmost part of the room. When the two pieces mashed together...

It's like watching the universe make love.

The small trace of romance near Bob brought her out of her reverie. "Well? Nothing? What are you good for?"

He snickered. "I kept the reporter off your back. He was snooping around the conference room while you and pops were in there. I told him you would explain the shutdown as soon as you could."

Faith gritted her teeth. As part of the Colorado education system, the administrators above her didn't want the place locked down with high security. Anyone could get in by showing a driver's license at the front desk. "Why would you tell him that? I'm not going to talk to a reporter. I have no idea what shut us down."

He shrugged. Somehow, it had a belligerence to it. "As I said, I'm working on the answer for you. But if you want to take everything personally, I can bonk off for the afternoon and take a pleasant drive up Mt. Evans."

Her blood was already boiling. She pursed her lips and squinted her eyes because every word out of his mouth clawed at a chalkboard just behind her eyes. It was made worse because he knew she couldn't refuse his help.

She forced herself to speak with her normal, calm authority. "Correction: I'm not going to talk to anyone until I know the answer to every question they're going to ask. That's good public relations, right? And you apparently are hot to prove my incompetence by coming up with the answers I seek. Go find them already."

"And then you'll talk to the press?"

"When I'm good and ready," she snapped.

Inside, she was already planning to avoid the reporter for as long as she could. Bob was a genius, but his motives were often broadcast with the clumsiness of a child. It came from his self-assurance and absolute belief that the rest of humanity were a bunch of idiots. For a while, she found his braggadocio charming. Now, it repulsed her.

"Fair enough." He stretched his arms above his head, like he'd just gotten out of bed. It was another annoyingly childish trait that signaled he was about to ask something entirely different. "So. Have you given any thought to finishing the experiment, if it's possible? If we plug this bad boy back in now, we can be up and running in three hours."

She tapped on the window with her knuckles. "CERN is offline. There is talk of a meteor somewhere out there. Maybe UFOs are flying around." She didn't believe that last part for a second, but there was no need to be rational with an ape. "There is no way we can fire up the engine while we still have no clue why it was shut down."

"True," he agreed a little too fast. "It's good to know the answer. I hate to lose research time is all. Hell, maybe we caused all the world's problems. That would be the ultimate roundhouse kick to SNAKE's beanbags."

"That's bullshit!"

Her chest heaved up and down, and her hands were balls of pent-up anxiety. She glared at Bob because she'd let her anger get too close to the surface, and she knew it. His very presence made her think and say stupid things.

"Sorry," she said in her business voice. "But it is absolutely crazy and those words cannot escape anyone's lips here, not even in jest."

"Of course. I'm just saying it might be better to get in front of the worst possible outcome. Tell the reporter you're working on proving we didn't cause that blue light, or whatever it was. When the real source is discovered somewhere else, your shutdown will seem irrelevant by comparison." Bob's voice was cool and oily, like he'd planned to say those exact words.

He wants to blame me for the blue light. Fucking great!

She spoke in a mechanical tone. "I'll think about it."

The fuck I will, she thought.

"That's all I can ask." He was as agreeable as the devil after discussing a fire-singed contract.

Bob departed the observation deck. She caught a whiff of his cologne and cursed herself for drawing in even a molecule of it. In a moment of weakness, she remembered a time when she pined for his scent, but the memory soured when she thought of him as he was today. He woke up and made a choice to wear that same cologne just to piss her off. It was as transparent as everything else he did.

She stalked off in the opposite direction, determined to solve the mystery of what shut them down. She preferred to find the answers without his help.

I-5 South of Sacramento, CA

By E.E. Isherwood *&* Craig Martelle

Buck found his groove as he sped south on the I-5 freeway. He flashed his lights continuously and became the town crier on the CB. Whenever he made contact with a northbound trucker, he told them about the storm ahead and convinced them to turn around. Those drivers, in turn, began sending out warnings on channels other than 19.

It was easy to coordinate while driving the arrow-straight segments of flat interstate between Sacramento and Stockton. He was high on adrenaline when he noticed the wig-wags and flashing red and blues in his side mirror.

"Fuck, no. He must be crazy. Mac, we've got a bear nosing our back door." He enjoyed sharing trucker slang with his small friend.

There was no doubt he was speeding. His foot was a brick on the accelerator for every bit of the miles he'd already traveled away from the storm. The dial said he was doing 85 miles per hour, which was about as fast as he felt safe with such a heavy load. A fully-laden train might have better stopping distance than him.

He didn't let off the gas.

"Go around me!" He rolled down the window and waved the cop by. It was a long shot, but it could save both their lives, so he was willing to attempt the act.

The black and white Crown Vic sped up in the hammer lane, but matched his pace instead of moving ahead.

The officer leaned forward over his steering wheel, so Buck could see him from up above. The gesture was unmistakable: pull over.

The dark storm was still back there, but he'd gained a lot of distance on it, so it wasn't instant death to stop, as long as it was brief. There was a math problem if he wanted to solve it: after going almost ninety miles an hour for fifteen minutes, how much time does bubba have before a storm moving fifty miles an hour catches him?

I can explain to the officer what's behind us.

He let off the gas.

The second he had the Peterbilt off to the side of the road, he opened the door and jumped down.

Buck halted reflexively as a black panel van rode the white stripe along the shoulder and whizzed by within inches of his face.

"Holy shit!"

Without thinking, he hopped back onto his sidestep and hung to a handle as he re-evaluated another of today's dubious life choices. He patted over his heart and felt something hard in the pocket of his shirt.

Picking up that quarter started my bad luck.

Everyone he'd been advising to turn around was now burning rubber to head south, but no one slowed down or switched lanes out of courtesy when they passed his rig. Car after car roared by as if he wasn't there. It didn't seem that fast when he was in the flow of traffic, but now it seemed like a NASCAR race.

And I'm the one who got busted. More bad luck.

He waited for a break in traffic and then ran to the front of his black rig.

"Damn, girl. What have you been eating?" The once-shiny front grille was now caked over with dust, small branches, and drink lids. The stiff winds and fast escape hadn't allowed any of the junk to fall off.

He picked out a few of the larger pieces and was about to walk around the far side of the truck when an officer appeared by the front right tire, gun drawn.

"Hold it! Show me your hands!"

Buck dropped the last of the debris and held both palms up. "I'm unarmed."

"Why'd you get out of your vehicle?" The guy looked at the ground near the front bumper. "Were you dumping drugs?"

Buck's mind moved faster than the traffic on the highway. The storm. The wind. The lightning. It was all jumbled and messy in his field of vision at that instant. But there was nothing larger in his consciousness than the Smith and Wesson aimed at his chest.

"P-please, Officer," he stammered. "There's been a misunderstanding. I was coming around to see you, but I almost got cut in half when I jumped down to the slab."

The young male officer looked at him from under his tan wide-brimmed hat. "You're supposed to stay in your cab. It's the law."

Did the officer not know about the insane weather?

"I'm sorry, sir. I'm driving scared shitless after almost dying in the storm."

The other man seemed to think about it, then he relaxed his stance and lowered his sidearm. "I saw it driving up here. I turned around when I saw you flashing your headlights, distracting other drivers. That's also a regulation."

Buck's eyes wanted to pop out of his head. The greater Sacramento area was turning into a shit sandwich and this guy wanted to talk about what condiments to add.

"Officer, I assure you, my intentions were noble. I'm also on channel 19 turning other truckers away. You can't let people in cars go north into the storm. It isn't..."

He didn't know what word to use. The guy didn't seem like a free thinker, so it would do no good to try to scare him into action.

"It isn't a safe storm to drive through. There are high winds, literally zero visibility, and more lightning than I've ever seen in my life. Lots of wrecks. If you call up there, I'm sure someone will confirm. I'm trying to save some lives."

Including my own.

The trooper took a few steps back, then holstered his semi-automatic.

"I'll have to call it in. I'll be right back with your citations."

Buck absently nodded but looked beyond the young man. Suddenly, fifteen minutes at ninety miles an hour didn't seem like near enough distance from the hellish storm. His respect for the law would only go so far when his life was on the line, but he was willing to spare two minutes...

A breeze swirled into a miniature dust devil at the side of the road.

He was willing to spare one minute...

Three Mile Island Nuclear Generating Station, Pennsylvania

Carl stepped away from Pete's body. The blackened indicator on the radiation badge proved the other man had been doused with radiation. He mentioned a blue light...

He considered using the phone to call back over to the control room, but he didn't want to touch it. Even though his badge beeped a couple of times, it was currently silent. If he stayed where he was, maybe the radiation wouldn't get him.

That's not how it works.

A few more seconds went by while he deliberated. The containment room was behind the heavy door inset in the nearby wall. If he opened it and looked inside, it was possible he'd finally figure out what Pete discovered. On the other hand, opening the door might be the last thing he ever did. Like the other man.

He forced his legs to go backward.

"I'll figure this out, Pete. I promise."

When he was near the front door, he spun and sprinted through. The specter of radiation tagged along, and he imagined getting saturated with 20,000 roentgens per second like the boys at Chernobyl. 500 per hour was considered lethal, and Pete died in minutes.

He barely noticed the heat of the afternoon as he sprinted across the courtyard. Why was Pete's badge black, but with none of the dozens of alarms near that room going off? He thought again of the odds of multiple sensors going out at the same time. Did they somehow hit the 1-in-88 quadrillion jackpot?

More to the point, was his badge defective? Was he already a dead man walking?

Carl charged through the doors into the familiar control room.

"Sound the alarm. We have a leak. A big one!"

One of the control specialists gave him a sideways glance after checking his board. "But we don't have any radiation detectors showing a problem. Are you sure?"

"Pete's outside of containment. His badge is black, and he's dead on the floor. Would you like a picture?"

His team jumped into action.

The drone of sirens started up a few seconds later.

"Put containment on the main screen. Let's see how big of a disaster we've caused." A feeling deep in the recesses of his stomach told him the meltdown in 1979 was going to look like a dance party compared to the one today.

"Get me the governor," he added with gravity.

"Let's see what we've got."

CHAPTER 14

Manhattan, NY

Garth and Sam led the small group up the steps and out of the subway, but once they reached the sunshine up on the surface, he lost some of his motivation to go back down.

He briefly pointed to the stairs at the subway exit across the street. "Should we go over there and see if anyone needs help?" Garth's tone said the opposite. If the fallen wall was narrow, maybe only the one guy got hurt. But if the collapse was bigger, there could be lots of injuries.

"Think we should make sure emergency vehicles show up?" Sam suggested.

"Right," Garth said with relief. "That's smart. All those people dialed 911. I'm sure they'll be here soon enough."

They would not commit to anything more.

Pippi and her parents strode by while they debated the issue. Garth smiled, but the girl didn't seem as interested in him as she was in getting well away from the subway entrance. He felt the same way.

Garth studied the busy street. Cars and trucks crowded the narrow avenue like any other day. Pedestrians walked by like nothing had happened below their feet. "Shouldn't there be a cave-in or something from where the rock fell?"

Sam shrugged. "Doesn't look like it." He pointed to the E 60th Street sign on the corner. "Only sixty blocks to the battery."

Garth did a double-take. "You want to go home already?"

Sam got serious for a moment, then cracked up laughing. "Dude. I'm messing with you. I'm not walking sixty blocks. That's like twenty miles!"

He shook his head in a feel-sorry way. "It's barely five from the battery to Central Park. We are one block more. How could it be twenty miles?"

"What are you, Magellan, now? How am I supposed to know how far it is?"

"Is this what we've become? I'm the brains, and you're the..." He couldn't give him a compliment. "You're the plucky comic guy."

Sam whipped his arm around like he was going to playfully strike, but he held up at the last moment. "Yeah, I like that. I'm the comic relief to your lame-ass science talk. We can be like a team. Sam and the Garbage Man."

"Son of a bitch! You know how much I hate that nickname." Sam never used it in a derogatory way like some of the assholes at school, but he still didn't like hearing it from his best friend.

"Nothing rhymes with Garth, yo. What else can I call you?"

He kept his mouth shut. If he picked a better nickname for himself, it would mean he could never use it. Sam would never stand for Garth having a better one. It was part of their friendly competition.

"How about our duo is Garth and the AmperSam? Sounds better to me." He had to explain what an ampersand was the first time he used it, and he assumed he would hate it, but Sam rolled with the nickname like he did everything else.

Sam grabbed his arm and dragged him along Lexington Street. "How about we don't use nicknames and simply agree I'm the funny one? Once people see that old-school 'cake is a lie' shirt you wear, they'll come to the same conclusion on their own anyway, right?"

Garth's dad had gotten him the orange T-shirt a few years ago, but he kept wearing it because he liked it, even if the meme was long dead, and the threads were well-faded.

Sam laughed as he hopped over a ventilation grate on the wide sidewalk. It was one of the active ones that smelled like death. Garth got a face full of the mist but held his breath until he was clear.

"So, what should we do?" Garth inquired. "Take a cab?"

"We have all day. We'll just see what happens. Besides, do you have enough money for a cab?"

"No," Garth replied. His wallet had about five bucks and one 30-day Metrocard. The former would buy him a small bottle of soda at any of the high-dollar delis in the area. The latter allowed him to ride all over the city on the subway at no cost. Dad bought it for him before he left because he knew the boys would need to get to the airport to meet Sam's parents, but Garth might as well have tossed it in the trash because he wasn't going down in those tunnels again.

"Walk it is, then." Sam looked up at the clear skies. "Besides, I prefer to let the day take us where it will. No plans. No place to be. Just you, me, and the city."

"I'm sure your parents will be worried once they land. We should probably get home and wait for the call."

Sam pursed his lips in thought, but didn't reply.

They walked in silence along the block-long storefront for Bloomingdale's. The squat, ten-story building wasn't very inviting and barely had any display windows to show off what he couldn't afford. When free of parents, they'd hang out there and find good-natured trouble, like pretending to get eaten by the escalators or daring each other to go to the women's unmentionables section and ask the help what those tiny scraps of lingerie were for. However, after several adventures inside lately, it was now a fifty-fifty proposition they'd get kicked out on sight. Sam's inability to laugh at a reasonable volume also made him an easy target.

When they finally reached 59th Street, Sam tested a look over his shoulder and became uncharacteristically serious. "What do you think the hand was all about, back there? Why did the wall move?"

Recognizing the moment, Garth tried to be serious as well. "I don't know. I've never seen or heard of anything like it."

"I was kind of joking about it being fake. There's no way that could have been planned, you know? Who carries a hand in their jacket just to stick a one-in-a-million gag?"

He nodded, then looked back up the street toward the subway entrances. "There still aren't any emergency vehicles. Do you think we should go back?" He allowed Sam to talk him out of going back down, but Garth didn't like the idea of not helping.

Sam broke into his personal space and stood painfully close. "I've got to admit something, G. I can't go back. I can't see the hand again. I can't."

He pushed him back a step. "It's okay. I don't think I can, either. I almost got hit by flying crap at the airport, then we almost get decapitated in the subway. I think someone has it out for us."

"What do you mean? Some angel of fate is trying to *Final Destination* us to death?"

"Fuck, dude, don't say it like that. No, I mean we've been super lucky today. I say we make our way south toward the ferry but keep our heads on a swivel. If someone is out to get us, we have to be ready."

Sam was all over it. "So, to quote *Star Wars*, we want to have some fun, but not look like we're having fun."

"That's a loose quote, but yes. Let's stay away from the subway and we should be good to go. We'll hoof it the whole way if we have to. What can hurt us just walking around, minding our own business?"

"Nothing," Sam replied with a growing smile. He looked like he was going to step into the street to cross it, but he doubled back and cracked Garth on the upper arm the way he liked.

"Thanks, man," Sam said in his serious voice. "I was gonna lose my shit if you wanted to go back into Lexington Station to see smashed or sliced people. I don't want to be a wimp, but that was too messed up for me."

"Me too," he readily agreed. "That's why I tossed my breakfast. Have no fear. There's no way we'll see anything worse today."

In his head, Garth imagined the universe's response to the bold proclamation.

Challenge accepted!

I-5 near Stockton, CA

Buck didn't dwell on the police officer's gun a second longer than necessary because it would only piss him off. The trooper opened his car's passenger door and leaned inside, presumably to file his paperwork and issue the numerous citations Buck deserved for trying to do a good deed.

His mood changed when he saw his puppy in the window.

"Hey, Mac!"

Buck hopped up to the passenger door and opened it a crack, then he reached in and grabbed his golden friend by the collar. He carried him so he didn't have to jump from the elevated door.

"Go make!" he shouted to the dog once he was on the ground, even though he'd already done a number on his front seat.

Mac ran around looking for grass, but there was nothing but dirt along the highway. The nearby orchards were also devoid of grass or other ground cover, too.

"Just go here," he said calmly as he climbed back into the doorway.

He looked away to give Mac his privacy. He mopped up the towel on the front seat and tossed it into the back. He wanted to be ready to run with the storm coming, and that included a clean seat for his dog.

When he was done, he climbed down and stood impatiently. "Come on, Officer. What are you waiting for?"

The storm lost some of its cohesion as it moved south. It was still fairly linear where the clouds met the interstate, but the eastern part of the storm seemed to move faster to the south, giving it a hook.

She's flanking us.

He looked back to the officer, but he was still dinking around in his car. There was nothing Buck could do to express his feeling of helplessness except pace back and forth.

Mac made his deposit and came over to the step. Buck did their usual procedure and opened the door.

"Up, pup," he said.

Mac's toenails rattled on the metal step as he hopped from it to get into the cabin. Despite the difficulties getting down, he had no problems climbing back in. Buck shut the door and stood on the gravel, looking up. A second later, Mac got on his hind legs and pawed at the window, as if to sensibly suggest Buck get his butt in gear.

"I'm coming, buddy. We have to wait for this jag..."

He held his tongue and cancelled the word 'off' just as the officer sidled up next to him.

The trooper was not amused. "This jag-what?"

Buck feigned a laugh. "Judge Advocate General? Like from the TV show? Didn't I see you on there?"

The trooper gave him a stony stare.

"I'm sorry, sir. I was just joking with my dog." He pointed to Mac doing his own impression of a lovable TV star. He licked the window and let out a single bark to try to help Buck out.

The officer spoke slowly, as if unsure of Buck's intentions. "I'm going to need to see your logbook and registration papers."

Buck wanted to scream. The wind blew through his hair as if to remind him what was on its way.

"Officer, you can follow me ten miles thataway and I'll provide whatever you need, but the storm is coming right for us and I'm scared for our lives, I've got to tell you."

The officer didn't look back. "Yeah. I've seen it. We've got plenty of time before you get your hair wet."

"There's lightning and shit!" he said with excitement. He pointed behind the trailer to the approaching system. The top of the storm disappeared into the atmosphere, but the base was still a few miles away. Lightning strikes reached out from the front sheet of precipitation and dust, like the *Psycho* guy reaching through the shower curtain with a deadly knife.

"Look, bub, I don't appreciate the backtalk. I might have let you go with a warning if you hadn't just called me a jagoff. That's very disrespectful."

Buck saw what was going on. The young officer was one of those guys who needed to be top dog. Running a strip of highway as a trooper was one way to get it—no one with any sense would try to dis him. Except dumbasses like Buck.

"I've got nothing but love for you, sir. I have a son not much younger than you. I've always taught him to respect the law above all else, and I've failed to live up to my own lessons. I'll take five tickets if you let me drive ten miles toward safety."

A monstrous spiderweb of lightning traveled over the orchard next to them. An instant slap of thunder came with it.

"Fuck me!" the officer yelled.

Wind grabbed the trooper's hat and carried it into the southbound lanes of traffic where another big rig immediately crushed it.

The guy shook his head and seemed to consider his position. "I need to write you a citation. It'll be quick. Quotas, you know?" He hustled off without waiting for a response from Buck.

His ears began to buzz. The hairs on his forearm stood on end.

"Aw shit," he drawled.

Buck climbed the passenger side and held Mac out of his way. Lightning struck again with an instant crack of thunder behind it. He jumped in surprise, but the Golden Retriever lost his marbles during the endless rumble. The dog went out the door before Buck could shut it.

"No!"

Spurred by fear, the dog launched from the cabin and dropped the four feet to the dirt. Buck had been worried the jump would hurt him, which was why he always helped him down, but he stuck the landing like a well-trained Olympian.

"Mac!" he yelled from the open door. "Get back here! COME!"

Mac barked angrily like he was telling the storm who was in charge. If he heard Buck use the magic word for return, he didn't show any acknowledgement.

More lightning struck close. Mac heard it and made a quick right turn. That put the wind at his back, and he seemed to float away with all the debris in the air.

Buck had never felt so helpless.

CHAPTER 15

Wollemi National Park, New South Wales, Australia

Destiny stumbled out of the trees hoping to find her team waiting for her, but when she came into the clearing where all the tents were supposed to be, no one was there.

"What the piss?"

The sprawling campsite had been abandoned. The tents and no-see-um nets were gone. All the tables were cleared off, and the firepits were cold. The trucks weren't there, either.

She blinked to see if her eyes registered the scene correctly, but dehydration had followed her out of the smoky fire. Her eyelids scraped her eyeballs with the weird dryness of a cat's tongue.

Oh my god. I'm so thirsty.

She went into the middle of the open space and stood there like she'd gotten lost.

"Hello?"

She hoped against all odds this was all a big mistake, and the rovers would race back to pick her up.

Her voice box was as dry as the rest of her. "Please."

She had the mental fortitude to pull out her phone and tap around to the instant messaging. She picked the first name in her recents list.

"Susan," she mouthed. "Help me." Susan was in charge of the support team. If someone moved the camp, she would know where it went. And why.

She texted words to that effect, then tried to keep her eyes from gluing shut as she watched patiently for a reply.

A minute went by before she tried another name.

Darrien Bobbs was next. He was one of the grad students, from the UK, but he was in his late 20s and had a bit of sense to him.

"Come on, Darrien."

She sent the text, then waited.

A few minutes went by as nothing happened on her phone. The dull gray smoke of the fire drifted high above, but it wasn't as thick on her side of the hill. That allowed the morning sun to peek through and brighten things up.

She sent text messages to everyone in her phone when she realized those first few weren't going to answer. She cut and pasted the same message over and over.

'This is Dez. At Wollemi. Need help. Respond plz.'

With each entry, she became more despondent.

"Where is everyone?"

She was ready to fall over with exhaustion and thirst when she finally had the mental clarity to see there was no network service at her location.

"Well then, why the fuck did you let me send them?" She intended to scream at the world, but it came out as more of a dry hiss.

Her eyes fell on a small mousepad. Someone had tossed it in the tall grass in the middle of the field. She groaned when she bent over to pick it up.

"Oh no."

The white pad bore the Sydney Harbor Foundation logo, which was a kangaroo with a Mohawk hairdo resembling the distinctive Sydney Opera House.

"They left me." She was hardly able to speak.

Destiny threw the pad back down and noticed some of the nearby treetops were on fire. Debris drifted on the wind, some of it ash and sparks, so the threat of fire stayed with her. But she barely found the energy to care.

Water became her primary mission.

She didn't have far to go. The campsite was ideal because it backed up to a small creek that ran down the valley. One of the group's "fun" activities was sending a few lucky people down to collect water in blue Jerry cans and carry them back for everyday use. She didn't mind as much as some of the others because she wasn't a complainer.

A final challenge met her at the stream. Since she spent the bulk of her life researching animals in the bush and deserts of the deadliest continent on earth, she knew the risks to drinking water straight out of the ground. But she didn't have a filter, water purification tablets, or a pot to boil it.

"Burn to death or die from tainted water?" she wheezed.

With survival at stake, it was an easy choice.

She dove in.

I-5 South of Sacramento, CA

"Mac! No!" Buck called after his Golden Retriever puppy, instantly knowing he wouldn't come back. In those first few seconds of guilt, he beat himself up good and hard. On a normal day, Big Mac would never run away; he didn't even have a leash. But today was the king of all jacked-up days. The thunder made the pup go insane.

He released the tension he'd been holding in his gut because he knew what he had to do. It was his fault Mac got out, so he had to rescue him.

Buck landed on the gravel next to the truck but glanced to his right to judge how much time he had left. All that anxiety came right back.

The storm bore down on his tractor-trailer and the cop car parked behind it. The monster system sucked in the air just as it did at the cloverleaf, and the wind speed rose with each second.

"Mac!"

The dog was a flash of golden fur out on the flat ground next to the interstate, but he'd turned around again and now headed to the left. He went for the edge of a farm growing endless rows of grapevines.

Buck vaguely heard the police officer yell at him, but he ignored everything that wasn't his frightened friend. He got up to his best sprint, but his war-injured leg made him feel like he was skipping across the dusty field. He made better time running in a combat crouch.

"Stop!"

Each footfall of his work boots made the dirt leap into the air, so it could be sucked toward the all-consuming storm. The increasing wind speed echoed loudly in his ears and he resisted the urge to look back.

There he is.

Mac had gone fifty yards through the empty field to reach leafy cover. He cowered behind the first row of vines but turned and barked at the giant monster chasing them both.

Buck ran a bunch of scenarios through his mind on how he was going to get the dog to go back to the truck. If Mac was scared and ran deeper into the vineyard, he might never come back. He couldn't yell at him because the wind noise was now well beyond his ability to shout.

Thunder rumbled every few seconds, though he tried not to think about the constant lightning filling the air. He felt like the flash-bulb paparazzi was in hot pursuit. The crackle of static surrounded him.

He'd almost arrived at the vines when lightning struck somewhere close. Mac hopped sideways in what seemed like a reaction to it.

I'll never get him.

But his futility turned to surprise when the dog darted around one of the bushy vines and ran past Buck. He tried to grab his collar, but Mac deftly avoided his reach.

"Whoa, boy!"

Mac's bark was almost completely lost in the freight-train howl, but the dog took up a fighting stance a few feet behind Buck. His mouth opened and closed with cries, but all sound was immediately swallowed by the intense wind. The golden puppy barked at the storm like a junkyard dog protecting his favorite chewy.

Now Buck got a good look at what his delay had cost him.

"Oh. Fuck." Only he heard his words.

The storm was thousands of feet tall and miles long, and it seemed to chew at the ground where it met the interstate. It looked like someone painted a black streak where the storm met the surface. It was an open mouth searching for things to eat.

He leaned toward the storm because of the wind.

No time, he thought.

Buck was proud of Mac for defending him against the creeping horror, but he wasn't ready to let him die that way. There were no buildings or structures within sight to give them cover, and there were no overpasses where he could park his rig and hide. The only hope was getting back in the truck and outrunning the storm.

He didn't think further than that.

"Sorry, little buddy!" he yelled into the wind as he bent down and scooped Mac into his arms.

Mac flailed for a few seconds at the surprise grab, but Buck held him tight as he ran for the truck.

"It's me," he said in the most soothing yell he could manage.

His bad leg strained under the heavier load as he ran with Mac in his arms. For an instant, his brain registered a memory of him carrying Garth during a bathroom emergency at his first professional baseball game. He held his tearful four-year-old in his arms as he raced him through the stands to get him to the men's room. The heroic mission ended in a messy disaster, but it was a life event he and Marnie had laughed about for years.

Buck briefly imagined stepping outside his body and looking down on the running figure of himself. It made no logical sense to rescue the dog and risk his own life doing it. The wind was so strong, he felt it push him forward a bit each time both feet left the ground.

Leave no man behind.

It was a mantra he'd not thought about for years, but one he recognized in the running figure straining to reach the Peterbilt.

He came back into the moment as he pulled open the passenger door. It took a lot of effort because the wind wanted it shut. He felt a twinge of panic at the notion of the wind conspiring with the mouth of the storm to kill him. Buck pulled it open again and used his body to block it.

"Get in there. Stay!" He used his command voice. There was no need to worry, however, because Mac went between the two front seats and jumped into his crate without looking back.

The door slammed shut as soon as he cleared the entrance and the instant silence was jarring. Buck didn't hesitate. He hopped over the passenger seat and slid into the command chair, then fired up the diesel engine. He sat there for a micro-second appreciating the fact he and Mac were still alive.

"We're getting out of here," he said a little too loud.

The air brakes released, he crushed the clutch under his boot, and he threw the shifter into first gear. The storm filled his mirror.

So did the flashing lights of the trooper's car.

"Move! Go!" Buck yelled at the officer, wondering if his paperwork and regulations were really the reason he was still there. Surely the man knew he was in danger.

Buck cycled his running lights, hoping the officer would see them and get the message.

He didn't hesitate for a second. His responsibility was to Mac and himself.

The trooper's lights faded as the darkness arrived. For a few seconds, he saw the glint of the cruiser's front grille as lightning touched down all along the stormfront, but then it was swallowed by the dirt and arriving rain.

Buck flew through the gears like he was going for the quarter-mile sprint record, but 34,000 pounds of canned goods still took a lot of effort to pull. The Peterbilt complied like it knew the stakes, but the laws of physics would not bend.

The storm was in top gear, too. Buck shouted at the windshield and willed his truck to win the race.

Search for Nuclear, Astrophysics, and Kronometric Extremes (SNAKE). Red Mesa, Colorado

Faith pored over the printouts Mindy brought into her office. Some of them were private missives from the Feds, which she was forced to at least scan. There were so many regulatory agencies involved with her facility, it was almost impossible to keep up with all the advisories and factsheets. Reports also came from Azurasia Heavy and other corporate teams, plus the numerous university partners.

"From MIT. Dear Mrs. Sinclair," she read aloud before adding, "it's Ms., thank you. We appreciate your diligence in managing the shutdown of AH's experiment but would respectfully request you resume operations with MIT's block in the next twenty-four hours. Our experiment is critical..."

MIT banked some time in the research park, and they were scheduled to go right after the Azurasia team. Delay affected everyone.

Faith pretended to type. "I respectfully request you shove it up your arse."

She turned to a stack of papers that was more relevant to her immediate problem. Public notices from news reports and state and federal agencies such as NASA and NOAA. She had to cut through them and solve the riddle before Bob came in and explained it to her.

She grabbed the top one of the stack and scanned for the meat of the report. "The Weather Channel notes warnings have been issued for Summer Storm Audrey and Summer Storm Bella in the west. Audrey has formed along the coast of the Carolinas and is moving steadily toward the I-95 corridor of New England..."

She skimmed ahead, because an East Coast storm was of no concern to her Colorado home. The other was slightly more relevant.

"Summer Storm Audrey started over Northern California, but unusually strong jet stream currents have already sent it into the Central Valley region. Sacramento. Stockton. Modesto. Merced. Fresno. Be prepared. The weather service..."

Faith tossed the sheet. Weird weather couldn't have stopped her experiment.

She leafed through a few more. An incredible amount of news had transpired in the past few hours.

"Russian fleet limps out of Murmansk."

Pass.

"Subway collapse in New York City. Aging infrastructure blamed. Mayor concerned after plane fell from sky at La Guardia."

Pass.

"Power grid collapse in Denver." She read a few lines before picking it up. "Authorities working with Xcel Energy to restore power to customers in Littleton, Ken Caryl, and Columbine. Additional outages reported in Castle Rock, Larkspur, and Monument."

"Bingo!"

The pattern of power loss was in the southwest corner of metro Denver, which was very close to SNAKE's infrastructure. The university chose the location because it was close to the talent pool of research schools in the Denver and Boulder area, but it was also close to the Denver Tech Center, which was the Silicon Valley of the Rockies.

She read deeper into the brief article. "At approximately 12:08 pm today, residential and business customers lost power."

That gave her pause.

The time should line up perfectly with the moment the experiment went offline, which was a few seconds before noon. It was impossible to forget the exact time because she'd been waiting all week for the experiment to wrap up.

Damn, it would have explained it nicely.

She made a mental note to check with the facilities staff on that one, because they maintained the power and plumbing infrastructure. Belatedly, Faith admitted if the answer was that simple, Bob would have figured it out.

She leaned back in her chair and absently brushed her bangs out of her eyes. "At approximately noon today, *something* happened and took our experiment offline..." She recalled the fax she'd given to Mr. Shinano. At the time, it was self-evident from government reporting that a meteor sent electromagnetic interference all over the planet and ruined his multi-million-dollar experiment, but upon reflection, it seemed odd Denver didn't go out until almost eight minutes later than SNAKE. Was there a design flaw she'd missed that made Denver survive the blue light a little longer? It would give Bob one more arrow for his career-takedown quiver.

She continued thinking out loud. "That same event caused storms on the coasts, a subway and plane crash in New York, and ships put out to sea in Russia. What the holy hell am I missing?"

She prided herself in thinking outside the box. As a scientist, that was a requirement for breaking new ground in her field, but as a woman, it served her well on the climb up the ladder of advancement. If there was no correlation among the reports after the noon event, maybe there was something recorded in the morning before the power was lost.

Faith thumbed the faxes and printouts but was unable to find one piece of relevant news from before the power failure.

She picked up the phone and spoke at warp speed. "Mindy? I want you to give me the hourlies for this morning and the overnight hours. I breezed through them already, but I would feel more comfortable looking at them on my desk. Also, get me any important news events that took place this morning, before noon. There is a news article about ships leaving Russia in a hurry. Could we be going to war? Perhaps the Feds drained our power for military use."

Mindy took a second to reply, as if she'd been writing it down. "I'll have it for you in fifteen minutes. Would you like something to eat, as well?"

It was unusual for her friend to offer food, but she'd been going at it since before lunchtime. The day was supposed to include a celebratory pizza party after the conclusion of their first experiment, but of course it was canceled. She was famished.

"Thank you, yes. I'll eat while I work. I'll call facilities while I wait."

She was confident the answer was close.

CHAPTER 16

I-5 between Sacramento and Stockton, CA

Buck cheered for his heavy metal steed. "Come on, baby, you can do it!"

He thought of his trusty Peterbilt as a member of his family, but he was afraid to think up a nickname. He tended to drive his cars and trucks until they fell apart, so getting overly attached would make the final separation much harder. Whatever it was called, the wind had arrived, and he needed the semi to escape the same forces that swallowed the police cruiser like it was a toy.

The tornadic updraft pushed against his front grille.

"You got this, girl," he said as he simultaneously downshifted and gave it more gas. The storm's wind was powerful enough now that if they'd been driving sideways along its front, the trailer would have been flipped, taking the truck with it. Since they were driving directly into the wind, all he had to do was keep the truck moving in a straight line. It helped she was fully laden with cargo.

The highway had a slight bend to the left ahead, and he was worried that it would be enough for the wind to side-swipe him.

The only solution was to get there ahead of the storm, so he struggled to get more speed out of the engine. For a few tense seconds, he imagined a powerful gust grabbing the truck and sending it into the sky, like in the movie *Twister*, but all at once, the wind lost its grip and the truck lurched forward as it escaped the menacing embrace.

"Yes!"

When the needle hit seventy-five, he exhaled in relief.

"Thank you. You're the best." He rubbed the dashboard, then looked to Mac. "This time, we're really in the clear. Never a doubt in my mind we'd get away."

Fortunately, his dog couldn't call him out on his fib.

To his surprise, there were still cars and trucks arriving on the northbound lanes. However, he didn't need to use his radio to get them to turn around. The storm kept growing behind him, and there was an endless stream of vehicles making U-turns across the median and hightailing it back south.

He slowly shook his head thinking of the trooper. "You should have gotten the hell out of there. Didn't anyone teach you common sense?"

Buck held up his right hand, disappointed to see a slight tremor. He was coming down off the adrenaline rush from rescuing Mac. Buck's leg was also hurting; the pin in his shin felt like he'd bent it during his run.

"We're okay," he said in a calming voice.

Channel 19 came back from the static, but he didn't want to take either of his hands off the wheel, lest that shaking become serious.

He drove for many minutes, lost in thought. Should he have tried harder to save the trooper? He shouted something when Buck got out of his cab, but he didn't see him when he brought Mac back home. The mental replay made him realize he didn't think about the officer again until he returned to his truck. What if he needed help?

Some people were beyond help. The trooper refused to listen. His own decisions had been his undoing. The trooper had to live with the consequences.

By E.E. Isherwood & Craig Martelle

Buck checked his mirror. He prayed he'd see the lights coming up behind him again. Not that he was going to pull over. He'd drive until he ran out of gas before he stopped in front of the storm again. Jail be damned.

"I hope he made it," he murmured.

He needed to change the subject. "Big Mac, you little demon baby, I've got to make sure you never go walkabout again. You hear me?" He chuckled at how close he'd come to being swept away to Oz. He wasn't mad at Mac, but he felt he'd let them both down with his lack of preparation.

"We're going anyplace in that direction." Buck pointed south toward clear skies, but the simple act came with a pang of professional guilt.

As a commercial freight hauler, one of his greatest enemies was going backward during a delivery. The quickest way to New York state was Interstate 80, and he was hardwired to get there, no matter what. The fact Garth was at the destination added to his tunnel vision about the short route. It took a near-death experience to make him consider other ways to get there. Going backward would cut into his schedule, but there was no other choice. It was as if an earthquake had put the Grand Canyon where the interstate used to be. He could no more drive through that storm than he could drive across the canyon.

He jumped in his seat when Freddy the GPS unit on his dashboard suddenly came to life. "You are off route. You are off route."

"No shit!" he said with a laugh before clicking the unit's mute button. It should have complained about the route change a long time ago, but he imagined the cloud bank went far up into the atmosphere and probably blocked the GPS signal.

He needed to get far away from the bad weather before it grew any larger. Step one on that journey was going due south on I-5. He'd go all the way back to Modesto if necessary.

"Yeah," he thought out loud, "Modesto is ass backward on our route, but we can use it to our advantage. We know the place well."

All of Buck's adult life had been spent preparing for the worst. First, on the battlefield. Later, he became one of "those guys" who stocked up on survival gear and freeze-dried food. Now, far from home, and after almost accidentally killing himself, the trip across the country suddenly seemed very dangerous. There could be other storms along the way.

Maybe that blue light was the planet finally getting tired of global warming?

Something wet nudged his elbow.

"Oh, hey, boy." Mac had come out of his crate and sat on his hindquarters like the whole thing was forgotten. He nosed at him, tennis ball in his mouth, ready to play ball. Fetch was his favorite game when they stopped at rest areas.

Almost losing Mac made him realize how bad he needed a companion on his trip across the nation. He'd crossed the United States countless times over the years, but he'd never felt so far from his son. The friendly dog took some of the edge off.

They shared a knowing look. He assumed they were thinking the same thing.

"Yeah, I don't know what I'd do without you, either."

Manhattan, NY

Garth and Sam walked at a brisk pace as they put distance between them and the subway exit. A few subway station entrances lurked down some of the streets they passed, reminding him that other riders might be in danger of being smashed next.

Sam stopped in front of a small deli. "I'm hungry, aren't you?"

"I don't have any money, but yeah."

"I'll cover you, dude. Just pay me back." That was Sam's way. His parents were loaded, and he always had lots of cash. He didn't flaunt it the way some of the kids at school liked to do, and Garth hated to take advantage of his friend's generosity, but he really was hungry.

They walked in the door when a guy at the counter called out. "We're closed. No power!"

Sam stopped and looked around. "Can't we just sit at a table until the power comes back on?"

The sun was almost overhead, and the eatery had nothing but bright, open windows on the front wall, so it was hard to tell the power was even off. Only when Garth looked at the price board and food case was it apparent there was no electricity.

"No. City says no customers during emergency." The dark-skinned man was foreign, but so was everyone in the city. He had no idea where he was from but could tell at a glance he wasn't messing around.

Still, he tried to break out the logic. "Wouldn't the city want you to serve us so that you don't lose your food to spoilage?"

The man leaned over the high counter and spoke in a quiet voice. "What I want is of no matter. If city inspector walk by and see me feed you, I lose license."

"Harsh, dude," Sam said in an off-hand way as he went back outside.

"Okay. We'll leave you." Garth started for the door.

"Wait," the man ordered. He walked around his dark food service counter with something in his hands. "Take this. It will be the first thing to go bad. You didn't get it here."

Garth accepted the hand-sized cheese wedge. "Can I pay you for it? I have five dollars."

"No. Take. Screw inspector. I live on the edge, like you!"

Garth smiled and walked out with the food, though he wondered if he and Sam were really living life on the edge. Sure, they'd seen some weird stuff today, but for most of the last year, they'd been nothing more than two boring kids wearing too much cologne to get a rise out of people. However, slicing meat could hardly be called an adventure, so anything he and Sam did would be awesome by comparison.

He caught up with Sam.

"Hey, check out what that guy gave us for free."

"Cheese?" He crossed his fingers like the wedge was a vampire bat. "If I touch it, we spend the rest of the day chasing unicorn toilets in Manhattan, dude. Is that what you want?"

Unicorn toilets were what the boys called clean restrooms. They were as rare as unicorns in the city.

"No," Garth conceded. "I forgot about your issues with cheese. It seems like you always have problems, no matter what you eat, but how could I forget the Great Cheese Pizza Emergency of freshman year?"

"Let the record show that was caused by leftover tacos I ate for breakfast."

"Oh, come on, man. It's almost like you want bathroom fails."

Sam laughed. "It makes for a hilarious story. I couldn't have done it without the help of Old Shaky here." He caressed his stomach like it was a beloved pet.

"I don't know..." Garth started to say.

"Hey! You two!" A female voice called from a second-story window in the apartment building above them.

The boys looked up to a middle-aged black woman sitting on the windowsill. She was close enough for him to see the fancy white letters stenciled into the chest pocket of her fluffy pink robe.

"Did Dinkins pay you to go into the Korean deli?" she inquired.

Garth and Sam glanced at each other, then turned back to the woman. Sam spoke first. "Yeah, he said it would piss off some woman living above the shop. That's why we went in."

Garth laughed for a second, then caught himself. He didn't know nationalities, but the deli guy couldn't have been Korean. Maybe Middle-Eastern or Indian, but not Korean. "No. Wait. We..."

"Smartasses, huh? The mayor shops at Korean stores, too. He's going to ruin this city sure as shit."

"Well, we thought it was great, so we think the mayor is doing a good job. We're going to vote for him again." Sam spoke with confidence, like he enjoyed the confrontation. Garth knew he was unpredictable when in public, and most times, he could keep his friend from stirring up shit with people, but this caught him off guard.

Sam smirked when he caught Garth's attention. "She's nuts!" he whispered.

"Don't encourage her," he insisted.

"I can't help myself," he said slyly. Sam's grin broadcast his intentions, then he spoke to the woman. "We're going to visit every Korean joint from here to Battery Park. We're real hungry!"

Garth pulled his arm to get him to clear out, but he wouldn't move.

"I'll show you white bread punks. I'm comin' down!" Garth watched her abandon the sill with a flourish. Her long robe flowed behind her, like Batman.

They looked at each other again.

"You think she'd really come for us?" Sam asked with disbelief.

Garth couldn't make himself move. The double front door of the building was twenty feet away, but still closed. It wasn't far from the entrance to the deli, so the woman probably knew she could catch people who lingered.

Suddenly, the whole interaction seemed stupid.

"We should run," he told Sam.

"She won't come down. She's just shitting with us."

The doors opened with "Hey you!"

The big woman came out the front door with a hustle. The pink robe was tied neatly with its companion belt, and she wielded a bright yellow broom as her weapon. She strode forward like she owned the street.

"Run," they said at the same time.

CHAPTER 17

Modesto, CA

When he wasn't shifting, Buck rubbed Mac's neck as they drove south, away from the storm. An hour later, he pulled into the familiar Modesto Walmart's parking lot and shut down the motor before giving his dog one final pat.

"I think we're finally safe." To be sure, he let go of the wheel with his other hand and confirmed it was no longer shaking on its own.

He melted into his captain's chair while silently replaying the scariest moment during his brush with the storm. It wasn't the lightning. It wasn't the wind nearly tipping him over. It wasn't even the trooper's delay that put him in mortal danger.

The scene that played over and over in his mind was Mac springing out the door.

"Don't ever do that again," he whispered.

Mac's escape was what brought him to Walmart.

"I can't let you come in with me, but I think you could use some quiet time in your crate, anyway."

He took a deep breath and stood up. Buck tried to motion Mac into his crate, but he wouldn't go in. That was actually a relief, because it was the dog's normal behavior. It was easy to get him in at bedtime, when the lights were low and the day was winding down, but he resisted going into the cage any other time.

The golden looked up at him with his typical smile of innocence.

Buck slowly shook his head. "You really are something. Can I leave you out of your cage while I'm gone?" He didn't plan on being long. "I'm getting something for you, so a little professional courtesy is in order, don't you think?"

Mac kept looking up, but he let out several brief whines as if he knew Buck was planning on leaving.

"Oh, you're fine," he stressed.

The dog barked once with excitement.

"I know you did. I won't hold peeing on the seat against you, Mac Daddy."

Mac became more agitated, and Buck felt bad for winding him up.

By E.E. Isherwood & Craig Martelle

"It's cool, kid. I have to get new shorts, too, after all that. Happens to the best of us." He backed away, but that got the puppy even more excited.

When Buck left Garth for this latest haul, he'd had no idea he was going to get a dog like Big Mac. Since Buck had to be on the road almost three weeks of every month, it left lots of time for Garth to be lonely. He'd overheard his son saying the summer months were the worst. Even though Garth spent most of his time with his friend Sam, there was still a black hole where his mother should have been.

"Just stay back there and rest, all right? I'll be back in a jiffy."

He scurried out the door and shut it without looking back at his friend. A couple of moments later, he heard the clicks of nails on the window at his back.

Sorry, buddy.

He'd found the Golden Retriever at a shelter right on Staten Island. He'd been in his pickup for five minutes, intending to drive to the terminal to pick up his Peterbilt, when he turned into the animal rescue center on a whim. It was a miracle to find a pure breed pup in such a place, and he took it as providence. They'd been together for two weeks as they delivered freight in Florida and along the Gulf Coast, and they'd grown closer in the trip across Texas, New Mexico, and Arizona. By the time he reached Modesto last night, they'd become inseparable.

But he still couldn't take him inside Walmart.

He ignored the scraping and walked back along the trailer. He told himself it was to check to make sure there was no wind damage in the thin skin of the sidewalls, but it was also to get out of Big Mac's line of sight.

Once he made it to the rear doors, he pulled at the lock to make sure it was secure.

"Keep an eye on things, Mac," he said quietly.

He parked at the far edge of the lot, so it took him a couple of minutes to walk to the store. He looked over his shoulder as if the dark clouds on the northern horizon were watching him. The storm was probably still forty miles from the parking lot, but after wasting time with the trooper, he felt the pressure to keep things moving.

Cars whizzed in and out of spaces on the busy lot, but there wasn't a true sense of urgency. Average people going about their business, in a hurry with the trivialities of day-to-day life.

The cool air hit him as he went through two sets of automatic sliding doors.

"Good afternoon. Welcome to Walmart." The greeter was about a hundred and wore a blue navy ballcap with the name of a warship he didn't recognize. Ten or fifteen pins adorned the edges of the golden logo in the middle.

He'd intended to haul right by the guy, but decided to spare a moment. "Thank you for your service," Buck said. "World War II?"

"Yeah, Battle of Coral Sea. Ever hear of it?"

Buck nodded. "Had to study it in OCS."

That got the old guy's attention. "Afghanistan?"

"And Iraq." Normally, he didn't like talking about his service, but he didn't mind giving a little back to another veteran.

"Thanks for that."

He gave a curt nod.

A young woman stocked a shelf nearby, so he spoke more quietly to the oldster.

"Hey, there's a giant storm coming. Lightning. Killer winds. Dust everywhere. You might want to keep an eye on it."

The man tapped the side of his hat. "Thanks, son."

"Good luck."

Buck raced off into the giant store.

Search for Nuclear, Astrophysical, and Kronometric Extremes (SNAKE). Red Mesa, Colorado

It took Faith an hour to read through the reports on her desk because Mindy kept bringing more. The weather service added new bulletins every ten minutes. The big storms on the coasts were fascinating, but they didn't relate to her problem, so she asked Mindy to stop bringing anything related to weather. Things moved faster once she could focus on the important news, but at the end of her research, she was still no closer to figuring out what took her experiment offline.

"That's all I can find," Mindy said from the doorway.

"Thank you, Mindy. Will you see if Dr. Perkins might be available for a short conversation? I'd like to talk about what I've found."

Or what I didn't find is more like it. She'd been unable to discover anything newsworthy that happened before the 11:59:58 moment her experiment went offline.

"He left the complex to go into Castle Rock." Her friend pulled out a notepad. "Said that he would be quick, but he ran out of his heart meds last night and he wanted to be ready in case we worked late this evening."

Faith and Mindy laughed together.

"He's an old pro at this, isn't he?" Faith asked.

"I think you're an old pro, too. You both don't know when to go home. Do I have to remind you of that time you stayed all night to ensure the new computers got delivered?"

"I remember it well. I like to make sure my team gets what it needs. Surely you're not thinking I should go now?"

"No. Of course not. I'm just saying you both take your jobs more seriously than anyone I've ever met."

So does Bob. He loves to upstage me.

"Fair enough," Faith replied.

"So, if the dedicated Donald is finally out, would you like me to get Sun? I know she's free."

"That's a great idea. I should probably tell her what is going on before she thinks I've forgotten about her."

Dr. Sinclair would hardly forget the leader of the particle physics team, even though she was a diminutive woman who spoke at a volume that would make a church mouse seem loud. She was one of the most brilliant minds in the particle world and probably would have been the leader of the whole project if she had a killer instinct to match her bursting intellect.

"I'll have her right in. I believe she is in the library."

Her assistant disappeared into the hallway.

The SNAKE administration level was built with a dormitory wing, recreation room, research library, and cafeteria. It wasn't designed for long-term stays, like a normal college dorm, but they provided temporary quarters for any scientist running a lengthy trial. The admin sections flanked the central experimental chamber, which was the focal point of everything in their underground world. Because of this, it wasn't long before Dr. Sunetra Chandrasekhar came in.

The exotic woman favored light, breezy dresses draped over colorful long pants. The flowery crimson material of her shoulder-to-knee dress seemed to shimmer as the doctor flowed into the office.

"Please, sit down, Sun." They were familiar enough that Faith could use her nickname. She waved at one of the two plastic chairs in front of her desk, while jotting down the time on her calendar. It was important to keep track of every meeting, especially when someone was gunning for her job.

"Thank you," the quiet woman replied.

"How are you? Everything going all right with your family?" It was difficult getting any information out of the private woman, but she did once mention she was trying to get her extended family to come to America. Her husband and two older teen boys were already here.

"Just fine, thank you." Sun sat there with no emotion on her face. Faith wondered about playing poker against the other scientist.

So much for small talk.

"I've been searching for any external cause that may have taken Azurasia's experiment offline." She pointed to the two-inch thick stack of papers at the edge of her desk. "As you can see, I have a lot of data, but no conclusions—"

"It has only been a few hours. It could take years to parse through all the data and discover the true cause."

Faith politely laughed. "If only my bosses would allow that. In the meantime, I need to know if you've found anything. I know Dr. Stafford is checking the software, but I figured you might have already discovered something in the hardware."

"With preliminary data, I can tell you it was all working to specs until the instant it wasn't."

Sun leaned forward at the edge of her chair with hands on her knees as if ready to get up.

"Have you checked all the linacs?" The linear accelerators fed energy into the main experimental chamber.

"Of course," she mewed. "Everything is working nominally."

Faith came close to bending the plastic pen in her hand. She'd heard Sun talk at a hundred miles an hour for half a day when she gave a symposium on dark matter, but tracking down power malfunctions apparently didn't do it for her.

Faith sat in an uncomfortable silence for ten or fifteen seconds before making up her mind that this was a dead end.

"You'll tell me if you find anything?"

Sun finally smiled. "Of course."

They stood together and looked at each other across the messy desk. Sun turned to leave, then hesitated. "I do hope you retain your position."

Her face became a mask as she tried to stop the smile from flagging. "Thank you. Once we figure this out, I'm sure things will go back to normal."

Sun tipped her head as a sign of respect, then hurried out of the room.

Faith felt completely alone.

Wollemi National Park, New South Wales, Australia

Destiny floated in the hip-deep pool of water like she was at a day spa. It was freezing cold, but her belly was topped off, and being low to the ground made it so she wasn't breathing in the worst of the smoke from the nearby fire.

She fought the urge to doze off, knowing it could lead to her drowning. She also didn't want to chance a poisonous snake joining her. Every animal at the edge of the forest fire was desperate to stay alive, just like her. That drove them to do unusual things. A snake could bite her for no reason, just the same as a Tasmanian tiger could attack because it was scared.

She stood up and listened as the water splashed around her legs.

"Aw! Fuck me!" She realized the walkie talkie was still attached to her belt. She snapped it from its link and tested the handheld device. It had been underwater for at least fifteen minutes.

"Dead," she said as she chucked it on the shore.

She reached into the front pocket of her spacious cargo pants for her phone. Unlike the walkie, knowing it had been underwater didn't make her angry. Everyone on her research team had phones hardened with waterproof cases that were designed for the rugged backcountry. She pulled it out, turned it on, and tapped the keys.

The discouragement returned as she realized none of the text messages had gone through, and thus no one had replied to her plea for help, but an approaching truck engine made her forget it.

"Yes! They're they are."

She stepped out of the water and stumbled up the rocky bank to the edge of the road. Her mates were coming back.

Destiny looked down the dusty gravel road. A small red truck came up the tree-lined path at a speed suggesting they weren't in any hurry. She didn't know who it was as none of her team had red trucks.

She used a tall bush to keep herself hidden at the edge of the road. If it wasn't her team, it was probably one of the locals, or maybe a tourist visiting the park. But it could also be some rando that would love to get his meaty hooks into someone like her.

The truck drew close, giving her little time to plan.

Was her team coming back? Was the fire worse than it seemed? The campground was still clear but more of the nearby trees had dots of fire high in their branches. Perhaps the team had no choice but to leave.

None of it made sense. Even if they had to bug out in a hurry, they would have left a note. They wouldn't have abandoned her without good reason, but whatever the cause, she was now alone. The only thing she knew was that she needed to get out of there before the fire closed in.

She stayed hidden until the last possible moment. Two large men filled the cab of the small ute, and the cargo bed was filled to the brim with firewood. Her first impression of them was not favorable. She imagined they were serial killers collecting wood, so they could burn the bodies.

How bad do I want to live? she wondered.

CHAPTER 18

Modesto, CA Supercenter Walmart

Buck left the aged veteran with mixed emotions. Thinking of his time overseas reminded him of Marnie's passing, and the start of all his troubles with Garth. The sadness never left him. It was a void that continued to steal his joy. But this Walmart reminded him of the one near Staten Island, and of the times he'd been there with his son, so it felt like he was already home. That made him happy.

Let's do this.

He grabbed one of the small, blue handheld baskets and took off for the pet section.

"Ma'am," he said when he saw a retiree-employee pulling dresses off a rack. "Do you know the way to the pet section?"

Most Walmarts shared similar layouts, but this was a supercenter, making it feel vastly larger. It was better to know for sure where to go, so he didn't waste a second of his time.

"Si," the woman answered as she pointed the way.

"Gracias," he responded with a wide smile.

He walked up the main aisle, but stopped as he noticed how ordinary it all appeared. Haboobs, service in the sandbox, and the Battle of Coral Sea seemed like events from another reality. This one was full of dull-eyed shoppers, fluorescent lighting, and the smell of plastic. Few citizens had any idea what happened in those overseas deployments, just like no one seemed to know about the violent storm a few miles to the north. *With experience comes wisdom*, Buck thought. *So what the hell are you standing here for?*

He shivered as he imagined the weather front getting closer. That made him pick up the pace as he walked toward the pet department.

Keep it together, Buck.

He made for the back of the store. The two main walkways met at an intersection, and he needed to make a left turn, but running footsteps came up behind him and made him turn around.

A bald, middle-aged man in a red shirt trotted the same path as Buck. His heavy work boots made loud clops with each step, which gave him away from a distance. His muscles tensed up at the perceived threat, but the guy didn't even seem to notice him. He turned right and ran toward automotive.

He shook his head and wondered when his nerves were going to settle back down to normal. There was nothing to do but laugh it off, though he moved even faster once he saw the pet care section up ahead.

Buck trotted by a couple of rows of dog and cat food before he found the one with the leashes and chew toys.

One of his two near-death experiences could have been avoided if he'd had a leash for Mac. It took him about ten seconds to find a nice one with a little box for spooling up the extra length. That would be fine for those times when he could walk his dog, but he also grabbed a red-cased metal wire that was designed to go on a spike drilled into the soil. He intended to keep his golden attached to the lead while inside his truck, so if the door opened again, he could not jump out.

A strange sensation poured over him, like he was being overly protective of the pooch. He considered leaving the red cable, but it was only a few dollars, so he used price as a smart reason to hold onto it.

"Better to have and not need..." he reminded himself. He put both in his basket and absentmindedly tossed in a bag of all-natural jerky treats.

He figured he'd hit the soda aisle on his way out. With proper hydration, he could drive all afternoon and get well clear of the storm.

A young woman in a blue Walmart smock ran past the end of the aisle closest to the rear of the store. Her long ponytail bounced back and forth in the brief moment he'd watched. He noted she went in the same direction as the man in red. *Something is going on. Where's the best place to be when shit hits the fan? Someplace else.*

"Stay alive, get a prize," he mumbled.

A female computer voice spoke evenly on the intercom. "Code 99, Department G."

He laughed at the thought of what constituted an emergency at a place like Walmart. They had endless spills, dropped glass, and god knew what else. There was no amount of money suitable for the janitors doing hard labor in those stores. Maybe the 99 code was for someone puking.

That caused him to chuckle, despite knowing it was immature.

Marnie always said I never mentally grew past seventeen. That memory stirred up his already mixed pot of emotions.

"Code 99. Department G. Code 99. Department B." The woman computer listed the codes and departments, then repeated herself one more time, as if the person pressing the button really wanted to make a statement.

When he got to the end of his aisle, several shoppers were stopped and faced toward where the running men had gone. He turned to see what it was all about, but the guys were out of sight already.

"What's going on?" he asked an older lady holding a hand basket filled with nothing but a white bag that might have been a prescription from the pharmacy.

"Probably a damned thief. Store is full of 'em."

She cradled her basket like Buck might take it, then turned and went toward the front of the store by cutting through the infant and toddler clothes section.

"Code 99. Depar—" The intercom cut off suddenly and an actual woman came on the line and spoke fast. "Code 99 in G, B, and F. Basically that whole corner of the store."

Buck thought about following the woman through the baby section and to the checkouts, but he thought of that noble veteran at the front of the store and was compelled to do right by him. If something was going down, perhaps he could lend a hand.

A thin, frail-looking young man came out of the cat food aisle, glanced at the people standing around, and asked Buck about the commotion exactly as he had done a few seconds earlier.

"I don't know," Buck replied. "I'm going to see if anyone needs help. Wanna go with me?" It wouldn't hurt to have an ally, even if the guy appeared harmless.

"No way, dude. Code 99 sounds dangerous. We should steer clear, if you ask me."

Buck paused for a few seconds, not sure if he was right about the dangerous part.

"Trust me," the thin man added.

"I do," he said as he walked away.

Shoppers had gone back to their tasks as he jogged the long aisle toward automotive. He was almost there when a man in a red shirt tumbled to the floor about fifty feet ahead. Boxes of oil filters slid around on the tiles like he'd knocked them off the shelves.

A male Walmart employee came after the guy and got a hold of him. Maybe the guy was a thief, as the woman had guessed, and now he was caught. However, he didn't roll over and accept his fate. The pair of men traded punches as they ran up against the windshield wiper section.

Buck instinctively moved closer to help the employee but halted when a second worker ran out of the aisle, apparently to support his friend. The new man threw his body against the guy in the red shirt. The thief grunted and cursed while trying to keep his footing, but the pair overwhelmed him, and they all fell sideways toward Buck.

"Shit," he said to himself.

Another man came out of the aisle with something silver in his hand. He was dressed like a normal person, not a worker. Buck recognized the weapon as a long socket wrench and for an instant saw him as a fellow good Samaritan who was going to help the two employees.

However, the new man held the wrench over his head behind the second Walmart employee.

Buck took a few steps forward, but he was too far away to help.

"Look out!" Buck shouted, knowing no one would know what he meant.

"Fuck you!" the wrench man shouted as he slammed the metal tool on the young man's skull. "I'm not a thief!"

The woman on the intercom began her next statement with a girly shriek. "Code 99. Code White. Code 300. All security to automotive. We are watching on the cameras."

He looked up at the black dome almost above his head, then at a few of the shoppers who, like him, were just curious enough to watch the action from a distance. Buck recognized the look of confusion and fear at what they saw.

"All patrons are advised to calmly make their way to the registers." The intercom woman sounded pleasant and restrained. Anyone not directly watching the fight wouldn't know of the life-or-death struggle taking place in the same store.

The injured man had fallen to the side with blood pouring out of his wound, and now the two male shoppers worked over the remaining employee, but more Walmart guys appeared in the tire center. Once they saw the fight, most of them headed right for it.

He made a command decision not to get involved. The men from the tire area looked like they could handle themselves, and first impressions were critical in emergencies like this. They all wore blue smocks; he did not. It would be easy to get confused as an enemy if he went over there.

Buck left the automotive area and shifted lanes to get out of sight of the tire guys. By the time he'd gone thirty feet, the mood in the store was back to normal. A group of five or six men stood at the sporting goods counter. They had to hear the punches and grunts from a few aisles over but made no effort to help.

"Can't you hear it? There's a fight..." Buck said in a loud voice.

A lone woman worked the counter. She stood in front of a glass case filled with ammo and had a black notebook in front of her that might have been a price chart. She leafed through it like she was in no hurry at all.

One of the guys in line turned to Buck. "Some guy came in and said the store had to be evacuated because a huge storm was just outside."

Uh oh.

Manhattan, NY

Sam laughed maniacally as the boys ran from the woman with the broom.

"She'll never catch us," Sam assured him.

They turned and ran west on the next street, but the woman came around the corner not far behind them. She ran surprisingly fast for someone wearing slippers.

"Stop!" she called out.

A handful of tourists avoided the two boys as they ran along the sidewalk, but a larger group of people stood outside the library up ahead.

"Should we go in?" Garth asked. Even if the woman followed, she wasn't going to start trouble in a public place.

"No, run through those people," Sam advised.

"Stop them!" the woman screamed again. "Help!"

Garth knew right away that the group of tourists were going to react to the woman's urgent cry. Several tall men in red and white tracksuits spread out to block the sidewalk.

"Now go into the library?" Garth asked again.

"No, we can cross—"

The tourist group seemed to be a basketball team, and they appeared anxious to help a woman in need. A few of the young men went into the narrow street as if anticipating their next move. Others fanned out toward the metal-framed front doors of the library.

Garth held up his hands and stopped because there was no way to outrun them all, even if they turned around. If his dad saw him acting like a jackass and running away from people, he would not have any kind words to say about it. He thought it was a better idea to act calm and explain the situation.

Sam went a few paces more, but also came to a stop.

"We didn't do anything," Garth professed. "This woman is crazy!"

"A total nutter," Sam added.

The basketball team regrouped as the broom-wielding woman got closer. Garth turned to her, intending to apologize, but she tried to poke him with the broom handle, so he had to dive to the side.

"Whoa!" Garth exclaimed. "We didn't do anything."

A college-aged woman in jeans and a red top jumped in front of Garth to prevent anyone from getting hurt. She appeared tiny next to the giant men flanking her, but she spoke like she was their leader. "What in a New York fucking minute is going on here? Did these two boys hurt you, ma'am?"

Garth was distressed that the woman would ask the crazy lady instead of him, but he was glad someone in authority was involved.

"Those two gave me lip about eating at that deli run by them Koreans. I told them not to do it, but they gone and did it."

The tourist woman seemed surprised. "You mean they ate there?"

"Yuh huh." The old woman pointed to Garth's cheese. "They got that."

He held up the block like it was a dead mouse. "She told us not to go in after we'd already come out."

"Mayor Dinkins went in, too. I'm doing my part to raise awareness and get him kicked out of office."

The young woman put her hands on her hips. "Ma'am, I go to school at Cornell and I've spent a lot of time in Belarus doing work-study with their national basketball team—" She pointed at the tall guys now crowding around them. "—but even I know the Mayor of New York is not named Dinkins. It's Del Rosario. Are you sure you're feeling all right?"

The woman swung the broom in a sweeping motion, but she was too far from the group to be a serious threat. "I see what's happening here. One piece of white bread gets with the next, and before you know it, I'm facing the whole loaf!"

She stepped back a few paces but kept the broom between her and the young woman. Once she was about twenty feet away, she paused. "I'm calling the police!"

She took off running.

The young woman from Cornell stood there for a few moments, as if savoring her victory, but then she spun around on her heels to face Garth and Sam. He assumed she was going to lecture them in some way, but all she did was smile and walk by.

"Wait!" Sam called after her. "Can I get your number, you know, in case we need to follow up about this incident?"

Garth stood there, unsure what to say.

The college girl flashed her star-white teeth. "Nice try. You boys are cute, but as you can see, I have my hands full with twenty-five men already, and we're late. Enjoy your stay in New York City."

"We live here," Sam blurted.

"Da pabachenya, boys," she said as she waved over her shoulder. "That means goodbye in Belarusian." The young woman led the team into the front doors of the city library without looking back.

Sam leaned over as the crowd of people went in the doors. "This is some seriously fucked up shit, yo."

"I know," Garth agreed, "This city is coming apart. First the airplane. Then the subway. Now we have women chasing us with brooms. Something is wrong with reality itself, don't you think?"

"No. Not all that." Sam pointed to the library. "Why the hell would foreign basketball players be going into an American library?"

Yep, the world's gone mad.

NORAD, Cheyenne Mountain, Colorado

"Come in." General Smith rubbed the bridge of his nose as if to pinch away the headache.

Lieutenant Chris Darren came into his office with his laptop already opened.

"Got something?"

"Yes, sir. You're going to want to watch this."

Lt. Darren placed the laptop on the immaculate desk and hit play without preamble. The computer display showed small dots around a digitized globe; it was the constellation of GPS satellites.

"As we discussed earlier, each satellite was .666 seconds out of sync with the rest of the planet, but the 50th Space Wing was all over this, sir. They discovered the sync glitch, as they call it, took place in each satellite at different times."

"So, it isn't a ground station calibration error," the general reasoned.

"No, sir, it's not, but we know exactly what it is."

The general glanced up. "I'm all ears."

Lt. Darren pressed some keys, and the screen changed slightly. The dots representing satellites were color coded.

"The red ones went out of sync first. Then the blue. Finally, the yellow."

The data representation was clear. The satellites closest to North America and the bordering oceans were red.

The junior officer continued with his presentation. "I'm sorry for the quality, but I kept things simple, so I could get this in front of you as soon as possible. Using the time-shift data, we drew this concentric ring as a stand-in for the blue light that went around the planet."

He pressed a button and a white oval showed up over North America like a big halo.

"If you use the track pad, you can expand it, sir. Like this." He moved the ring, so it got larger and spread in all directions over the part of the globe facing them. "We can go all the way to the other side and see where the ring ended up."

It was someplace in the Indian Ocean.

"I don't care about that. Show me where it came from!"

Lt. Darren reversed the path of the light until it was back over North America, but it stopped when it was about as big as the state of Colorado and Kansas put together. "I'm sorry, sir, but the ring represents fixed satellites in the constellation, not ground data."

The general growled deep in his chest.

"But I see what you want, sir. I'll have the programmer detach this ring and close it down to a point. That should be the source."

"Hmm. That's a start. Get your team to go over the data and get me the precise location of the earliest effects. Then we'll know who loaded up this bag of dicks."

"On it, sir."

CHAPTER 19

Search for Nuclear, Astrophysical, and Kronometric Extremes (SNAKE). Red Mesa, Colorado

Faith felt like she was a teenager again, sitting at the table and waiting for her parents to come home. She'd gone to the front patio of the big underground complex to get some air and, she admitted, to wait for Dr. Perkins to come back from his run to town. It had been several hours since her world was turned upside-down, and Donald seemed to be the only scientist who had genuine feelings for what she was going through.

"Hi, Dr. Sinclair."

"Heya," she replied to the young technician before he sat down with a group of his peers at another table.

Before she went back to reading emails on her phone, she took a moment to enjoy the view. The Red Mesa location overlooked the Dakota Hogback, which was a long, thin ridgeline that ran the entire length of western Denver. It was only about a hundred feet tall, but it was steep and pointed. Almost like a giant had taken a sharp knife and cut the rock from below. The upturned rocks made it a great place to find dinosaur bones, go hiking, or, as it turned out, use as the starting point to build hundreds of miles of tunnels for a scientific endeavor called SNAKE.

"Dammit, Donald, where are you?" She'd waited for over forty-five minutes and began to think he'd stopped somewhere for dinner.

She almost went back to reading her phone when his maroon sedan drove into the shady parking lot. None of the landscaping trees had grown much beyond saplings, yet, but the sun was already behind the Front Range Mountains and adjoining foothills, because it was late afternoon. He pulled into the nearest handicap parking space.

"Ahoy!" the man said as he got out of his car.

"Ahoy," she repeated with a touch of regret. She didn't want to come across as too eager, but there she was sitting at the bench ready to pounce on him.

"Did something happen?" he asked as he came up the walkway. He glanced down at his pager to see if it had gone off.

All the other staff had smart phones if she needed to get in touch, but Donald refused to carry a phone. As a compromise, he accepted a pager. If she needed him in an emergency, she could dial him up and he would find a payphone to call her back. She'd never needed to call the number, but she often wondered if he would bother to find a payphone if she had.

"I didn't page you. Mindy said you'd gone to town for your meds. Look, I'm sorry for catching you like this, Donald, but I'm running out of ideas for how we were shut down." She let him come over and sit next to her, but she never stopped talking. "I've asked Bob if he was willing to share anything, and you already know what he said to that. Then I asked Sun for her opinion, but I get the feeling she is content to let me deal with this political quagmire. I even had Mindy give me printouts of every piece of news she could find that might have affected us, but that has done nothing but made me aware of all the problems in the rest of the world."

She turned to look at him. "I need the answers to the problems in *my* world."

He nodded grimly, but she didn't think he looked right.

"Are you okay, Donald? You look like you've eaten a sock."

By E.E. Isherwood & Craig Martelle

He belched politely. "I got my medicine, just as Mindy said, but a wave of nausea struck me on the drive back and I had to pull over for a short while. It went away until I sat down here with you."

Faith held off recommending he go lie down, which was what she thought he needed.

"Do you have any ideas, Donald? I could really use an assist, here."

He sat up as if he was going to answer her, but then he squirmed like something was wrong with his stomach.

"Oh, Donald, I'm sorry. I'm not being a good friend. You really need to lie down. My problems can wait."

Donald tried to stand up, but he flopped back on his butt before he got all the way up.

"Here, let me help you." She held out her hand and he immediately grabbed on.

"I'm fine," he whispered. "Been a busy day, right?"

Both of them stood about five-foot-nine, but he was mostly skin and bones, so she pulled him up almost effortlessly.

Dr. Perkins was impressed. "Whoa! You've been lifting weights, Faith."

"No, I don't know how my arms got this strong," she lied. "I mostly ride bikes."

She walked him across the patio toward the front door, but he stopped her a few yards short.

"Faith. I've been thinking about the wave of blue light. Where did it come from? Where did it go? Was it affected by clouds, or by mountains? Did any air traffic travel through it and gather any data for us? If we can figure out how the light affected other locations, we can extrapolate how it affected us."

That was what she wanted to hear. "Jackpot!"

She reached for the glass front door to help get Donald inside, but as she leaned forward, she happened to notice one of the men sitting at a nearby table. He kept his back to her and wore a nondescript lab-coat, but she recognized the dirty blond hair and first hint of a bald spot.

Bob heard me.

Supercenter Walmart, Modesto, CA

Buck stepped away from the ammo counter like he'd seen a ghost. Someone had come in and spooked the people of Walmart. Alarms rang throughout his brain.

It couldn't have been me, could it?

The fight in automotive was the first sign of panic caused by the exaggerated rumor. He was certain the storm itself was miles away. No one was in danger.

There was nothing to be gained by hanging around. A bloody fight was in progress in modern-day Walmart. That shouldn't ever happen.

Let's skip the soda.

He went toward the center of the store, directly away from the violence. The sounds of the fight faded after he made a few turns down different aisles. He passed the vacuum cleaners, pots and pans, and came out in a section devoted to picture frames. A young mother stood by a cart with an infant in a car carrier strapped into the seat. He noticed the woman's smile and how her face lit up as she looked at an empty picture frame, oblivious to the danger around her.

"Ma'am, there's a fight in the back of the store. Get your baby out of here, okay?"

She seemed startled at first when Buck touched her cart, but she turned and listened for danger like a prairie dog on the high plains.

Buck waited to see what she'd do.

The woman tossed the frame onto the bottom shelf. "Thank you. We're leaving."

He resumed his swift trip to the checkout.

"We now have a code 99 at the ammo counter," the intercom lady blurted out.

His survivalist instinct asked him to consider dropping the basket and getting clear of the store immediately, but everything was calm at the front, and he still wanted the leash. He figured if things got worse, he would be the first person to run out the door. Helping others while on the run.

He made his way to the ten-items-or-less lanes. He chose the line with the least people, but that still put him third behind an elderly woman and a young woman with a little boy standing next to her.

The old lady had her stuff in bags, but she whipped out a checkbook to pay.

Oh for fuck's sake.

The older woman looked back as if she heard him thinking. "I'm sorry. It's all I have."

He smiled politely, intent to mask his ill-tempered inner monologue.

"Code 99. Sporting goods. Code 99. Automotive. Code 99. Paints."

It's spreading.

The little boy stood on the bottom shelf of the display stand next to the conveyor belt. Buck waited for the woman to tend to her charge, but she was staring daggers at the old woman.

The elderly lady fumbled for twenty seconds as she gathered the two small bags she needed, which made his inner voice scream endless obscenities. But when she looked back one last time, he retained his outward smile.

"I'm sorry again. I usually have cash dollars, but it is so dangerous to carry these days." She smiled at Buck, but her demeanor went right to fear when she looked at the young mother. Buck couldn't see the woman's expression from behind, but it must have been bad for the kindly old lady to change so dramatically.

The mother tossed her blue basket on the conveyor and made no effort to unload her stuff for the clerk.

Buck tried not to formulate an opinion about her. If she was fast, she could look at people any way she wanted.

"Momma, look what I did!" The toddler pulled at the hem of his mother's shirt.

"No," she deadpanned.

"Momma!" the kid screamed.

"No," she repeated.

He tried not to judge, but the clerk pulled several bottles of hooch from her basket and not much else, leading him to wonder if she watched her kid when drunk. Was she already drunk? She sure didn't seem to care about her young one. However, Buck forgave her right away, because she paid for the liquor with a wad of cash.

"Code 99. Breakaway protocol 11. Code Black." The woman on the intercom sounded nervous, almost like the code names she said were close to death sentences for someone she cared about.

"Momma, dammit, look at my fuggin' picture."

The mother finally looked. "Shit, kid. Curtis is going to give you a proper spankin' when we get home. You are cruising for—" She froze when she saw what he'd done.

Buck looked at it, too, because despite the chaos in the rear of the store, the woman and child were the biggest spectacle on lane 5.

The kid had taken the liberty of opening a pack of scissors, grabbing a sharp one, and then using the edge to scratch the blue paint right off the side of the checkout lane. He'd done it without anyone noticing until he was ready.

The five-year-old didn't seem bothered by the threats of his mother. He jumped back and pointed to his masterpiece.

"Elmo!"

The kid had drawn the character's furry smiling face with uncanny precision. Buck thought the boy was a natural artist and was going to compliment him on it, but before he could open his mouth, a gunshot exploded in the back of the store.

"Oh, fuck," the mother said.

By E.E. Isherwood & Craig Martelle

The cashier pointed to the woman's stuff. "Take it. Breakaway means we're supposed to get out of the store!"

Buck held up his basket to ask if he could still check out, but the cashier took off before he could catch her eye.

The mother threw her stuff into a bag and dragged her son toward the exit.

Screams came at him like a wave from the back of the store. Shoppers poured out of the clothing racks and housewares aisles as if the shooter was directly behind them.

He intended to pay cash, so he threw a pair of twenties onto the counter and held up the basket with two leashes and jerky treats to the black orb on the ceiling nearby. If anyone looked at the tape of what happened in the store, at least they'd know he paid for his goods.

Buck joined the crazy mob heading for the exit. The pop-pop sound of a small caliber gun continued as he neared the front doors, and daylight.

"I'm coming, Mac!" he said to bolster his spirit. *I should have left when I saw the first person running. I'm sorry, Mac. Sorry, Garth. What's wrong with me?* He'd been in the store for less than ten minutes, but his feet pounded the ground like sledgehammers as he tried to make up for lost time.

CHAPTER 20

Search for Nuclear, Astrophysical, and Kronometric Extremes (SNAKE). Red Mesa, Colorado

"Ladies and gentlemen, thank you for gathering. Yet again." Faith looked at her team stuffed into the large conference room. She thought it ironic that the builders of this scientific facility didn't include a conference room big enough to hold all the top-level people who would be required to run the program.

"It looks like everyone is here but Dr. Perkins. He's feeling a bit ill, so we'll carry on without him, for now." She expected him to come in at any second; he never missed a staff meeting, no matter how bad he felt.

Dr. Stafford raised his hand. She pointed at him to indicate he could speak. Deep inside, she wished she had the power keep him silent.

"It has been five hours since Mr. Shinano's Izanagi Project was shut down. Can you give the team an ETA on when we can expect to turn the power back on, so we can complete what we need to complete?"

Dickhead, exhibit fifty.

"Thank you, Dr. Stafford," she said through gritted teeth, "for bringing that up."

"You're welcome, Dr. Sinclair." Bob smiled, but his eyes remained fixed on her. They carried no happiness.

"Well, we're still not sure what ended the experiment. I've been working with the facilities people and both science departments to try to pin the exact cause of our shutdown, but so far, we haven't come up with anything solid. If we go live again without knowing why we were shut down, we could be right back where we started."

"But isn't it worth the risk? Maybe we get shut down. But that's where we are now. If we don't, we get some more experimental time in the books. It's a win-win, right?"

She couldn't refute his logic, so she held her response while she thought it over. Maybe she was holding back, just to stick it to him. She tried to search her feelings to eliminate that possibility, but she was unable to do so. Faith couldn't decide if that was morally right or wrong.

"The shutdown protocols were written by you guys." She pointed to the room, not just at Bob. "Those protocols dictate that each shutdown must be catalogued so that if a similar problem occurs in the future, we'll have a template from which to work. If we restart now, we may lose the opportunity to learn the cause of the shutdown or if something is wrong with the machine. We could create a catastrophic failure, destroy billions of dollars' worth of equipment. That would be a crime."

"Are you saying it was a criminal act?" a woman from the computer team asked.

"No, not at all. I'm sorry for taking the conversation there. The point I'm making is that I think we're close to figuring out the cause. We've certainly got enough data on what didn't shut it down. It wasn't a meteor or North Korean nukes, like I thought during our last meeting. Once I have a firm answer about what it was and am confident the machine isn't going to fail, we can get back to doing what we came here to do."

She looked around the room and tried to make a connection with each person. One on one, she could talk to anyone on the face of the earth, but in groups, she lost the ability to read their body language. She didn't know if she was getting through to them.

"Are you going to talk to Benny?" Dr. Stafford asked in his most charming voice. "Our young friend from the *Denver Post* is still waiting outside the facility on the patio."

She had a panicky thought wondering if Bob had already talked to the reporter. He'd been on the patio earlier, and the reporter was there now. He seemed adamant she go to the press and bare her soul, but he didn't threaten to do it himself. She hoped he would give her that small courtesy.

Bob went on. "Well, if we don't tell Benny what happened today, he may get the idea that we're hiding something in here, you know? He might decide to write a story that paints us as the bad guy, instead of as the victim. We don't want that, do we?"

Faith swished her tongue around her closed mouth as if deciding where to park it. Whatever Bob was angling for, she wasn't going to fall for it. Earlier, he brought up the idea that she was responsible for the blue light and all those problems stemming from it. The pile of documents Mindy gave her showed the results of that blue light, so its effects were considerable. She was now convinced that was the angle he hoped to use to drive her from the lead position.

And here he was in another meeting, ganking her, just like he said he wouldn't do.

Don't give him an inch.

"I'm in charge of public relations, Doctor, and I'll decide when any member of my team speaks to the press. Is that understood?"

"Crystal clear, ma'am," Bob said dryly.

They both knew he'd succeeded in forcing her hand.

Benny had been at the facility all day, because he was going to report on the ending of SNAKE's first experiment. She asked him to wait outside as a precaution. Her intention was to talk to him after the experiment wrapped up and she had something to tell him, but when it ended early, she had different priorities than dealing with a reporter.

She hoped he'd get bored and leave, but that turned out to be wishful thinking.

Faith would have to make a public statement soon, but she'd do it on her schedule, not Bob's.

Supercenter Walmart, Modesto, CA

Buck thought the Walmart Supercenter looked like someone had kicked the roach motel. Shoppers poured out of all the exits and ran for their cars in the huge parking lot. Even as the gunshots faded behind him, he looked to his right to see if the storm was getting close.

Finally, a piece of luck.

The storm appeared in the sky to the north, but it was still far away. He stopped kicking himself for taking too long inside the store.

He jogged down the long center aisle of the parking lot while carrying his basket of treasure. Cars and trucks pulled from the spaces and sped away. He'd parked at the edge of the lot, so he had a long way to run through the chaos, but no traffic to drive through.

Some of the shoppers managed to get their carts outside, and he wondered if they'd paid for their contents. It gave him a feeling of pride he didn't steal the leashes or jerky, but after passing more carts of fresh fruit, canned foods, and cereal, he realized what a missed opportunity he'd just had.

Every piece of survival gear he'd ever need was less than a hundred yards away, and he couldn't go back and buy any of it. There was no way he'd tangle with people shooting guns. Lots of supplies were worth fighting for, but nothing was worth dying for. There were other Walmarts. Modesto probably had six.

"Mac, I'm home!" he yelled when he was a few parking spaces away from his black Peterbilt.

As he said it, a silver SUV crossed from another aisle and sped right for Buck.

"Shit!" he screamed as he jumped aside.

The truck squealed its tires as it came to a stop. The driver jumped out and walked around the back with long strides. Grungy tennis shoes. Dirty blue jeans. A black t-shirt of a heavy metal band. He carried a small wood axe in one hand.

"Give me your fucking stuff," the guy said as he crossed behind his ride.

Buck had no time to think of a response, so he defaulted to his Marine persona.

He set down his basket and reached behind him, like he was going for something in his belt. Then he spoke in his military voice. "Stop! I'm authorized to carry a concealed pistol. I don't want to pull it out and kill you, but I will!"

The axe-guy skidded to a standstill about ten feet away.

Buck tipped his head toward his belongings in the see-through basket. "My treasure here is a couple of leashes for my dog and some meat sticks. Is that worth dying for?"

The man was about the same age as Buck, but that was where their similarities ended. The other guy's face was ravaged by pockmarks and blemishes that Buck recognized as caused by chronic drug use. He stood a little hunched over and his eyes were bloodshot pools of hatred.

The man lunged forward a couple of steps, but Buck reacted by stiffening his arm behind his back like he had the gun in his hand.

Both looked at each other across one 8-foot-wide parking space. The man's forehead and neck were waterfalls of perspiration. The afternoon was warm, but his problem seemed unrelated with the weather.

"Guy on the TV says rioters are at the Walmart." He half-turned to the store behind him. "But they must have meant the other store. I came to get in on the action."

The man's smile was almost black, like he had done too much chewing tobacco. He cackled and swung the axe back and forth in a threatening manner, but his sense of space wasn't good. He bashed his own taillight on one of the backswings.

The guy screamed in apparent agony. "Fuck!"

Instead of acting like a normal person who made a mistake, he used the axe to take several more chops at his light to make it worse. It cracked the remaining plastic, but his blows missed the light a few times and also bent the thin metal of the rear quarter panel.

The guy had issues.

Buck changed positions and held both hands in front of him. He heard and felt his heartbeat in both ears, and his hands wanted to shake with that same anxiety, but he forced himself not to quake in front of the other man. He had to project confidence.

"Look, man, I don't want to shoot anyone today. It doesn't look like it from the outside, but this Walmart is crapping the bed right this instant. People are shooting guns in there, and all the workers have left. You can go in there and take whatever you want. Just leave me and my leashes, okay?" He purposefully didn't mention the storm. With a little luck, the man would get caught inside the store when it arrived.

The druggy tapped his axe in the broken plastic where the taillight used to be. "Yeah, I could get a new light in there. Hell, I could get a new flat-screen TV. Then I could watch the riots in high def."

The guy looked at Buck. Perhaps he was figuring out if he was worth the hassle.

Buck played the part of a non-threatening but still dangerous man. Like a coiled snake that wanted to be left alone.

The man stepped back a few paces, then side-armed the axe toward Buck. It clanged off the rear bumper of the SUV because his throw was terrible. The axe only made it about halfway across the parking space.

Buck held his ground.

The unarmed fool ran to his driver's seat, put it in gear, and peeled out.

"Go crazy, buddy," Buck said with relief. People tended to lose their minds when big winter storms were expected back on the East Coast, but he'd never heard of people rioting over a rainstorm. Sure, it was dangerous and windy, but it wasn't worth going on a shooting spree or fist-fighting in the motor oil aisle.

He picked up the leashes and figured he'd better grab the axe, too, but soon realized the SUV's engine noise got louder, even as he drove away.

"Oh, shit," he said.

The silver SUV went up the aisle next to the middle one. The guy had no regard for people in his way; they jumped aside. He smashed into a few carts.

Drug man laid on the horn as one car tried to back out, but that didn't even slow him down. The SUV was doing at least fifty when it smashed into the blue safety pillars in front of the store. The vehicle also tagged a stone column next to the entryway, causing it to collapse.

Screams came from all over the front of the parking lot, but there was so much smoke and debris, it was hard to see what happened.

"I'm out of here," Buck said aloud.

He climbed into his cab, making certain Mac couldn't get out, locked his doors, then went into the sleeper area.

"I hope you appreciate these," he said as he tossed the leashes onto the bed. He set the axe on the floor. "I had to go through some trouble to get them." He removed one of the jerky treats and kept the rest of the bag to hide in a compartment above the windshield.

He laughed as he scratched behind Mac's ear.

"But there is one thing I need to do." He sat up on the bed and reached to the rearmost corner. He carefully pulled off the plastic sheeting of the cabin's wall. It was designed to be removed in case he needed to service any of the wires back there, but he used the secret space as a place to store some extra cash and a few other valuables.

He reached into the hole, brought out an item, and set it on the bed. When the axe-man threatened him, he reached behind his back like he carried a pistol in his waistband, but that was all a ruse. Buck didn't like to carry his sidearm because he crossed so many state lines. Some states frowned on concealed carry; some made it illegal. It was safer to keep it hidden and only pull it out when it was necessary.

Like now.

"Next time someone pulls an axe on me, I'll actually be able to defend myself."

The dog sniffed the gun, not sure what to make of it.

Manhattan, NY

Garth watched the last of the basketball players go into the library. "You know what? I say screw this shit. Let's go to the park and get away from people for a while."

Sam nodded agreement. "I've got nothing going on."

They both laughed, but Garth didn't wait for Sam to change his mind. His buddy was too unpredictable to expect him not to get distracted. He had to get them to Central Park in a hurry.

"This way," he said as he fast-walked west along the sidewalk. "The park is close."

"I know," Sam replied.

They caught the light at Park Avenue and crossed with other pedestrians. Park was one of the wider streets in Manhattan. It had four lanes going in each direction, and the north-south roadway was split by a flower-filled median.

"Come on. Keep up!" Garth jogged across the street and back into the narrow canyon of the side street. They walked against traffic, because the road was one-way toward the east.

They'd gone another block before Sam began to catch on.

"I need a break. Let's see what's around us."

Garth tried to keep walking. "Not yet. Almost there."

Sam kept pace for a short time, and they crossed another wide street, but that was it. "What's your problem, dude? Got to use the john?" He pointed to the next building on their walk. "Go in there."

They stood next to a twenty-story building that looked like a jail cell. Tall steel girders alternated with jet-black windows from top to bottom. The odd-looking structure was almost as long as the entire block.

Garth didn't think he could get him to the park without more of an explanation.

"Look, man, I love you like a brother, but sometimes I need to get you away from everyone, so I can relax."

"What the hell?" Sam chirped.

"It's not a bad thing, dude," he said to stave off any hard feelings. "I'm down with all the trouble we get into, but it's all this other stuff that has me worried. The plane. The subway. You know?"

"Maybe," Sam allowed.

"If we can get to the park and sit under a tree for ten minutes, I think I'll recover, and we can go look for something else to do after that."

Sam brightened. "We'll be closer to Times Square. We can go mess with tourists." One of their favorite things to do was pick up tossed maps and stand around like they were lost. Then they'd go up to pretty girls and ask for directions.

"Yeah, sure," Garth replied. "Give me ten minutes of peace, and you've got me all afternoon."

The park was only one corner away. Garth was confident they could make it there without incident, but the day had a weird energy to it. Trouble seemed to find them everywhere. He wasn't so sure the park was going to be any better.

"To the park!" Sam shouted as he took the lead.

Three Mile Island Nuclear Generating Station, Pennsylvania

Carl looked at his control room and felt impending doom, even when surrounded by twelve top-notch professionals and a thousand blinking lights calmly assuring his safety.

"Is it just me, or did we have a system-wide failure on our monitoring equipment?" The others in the control office gave him troubling looks. "Does anyone have a sensor that is working inside or near containment?"

He looked over to the containment department. Two men hunched over keyboards as if magically willing something to work. One of them looked up and shook his bald head. "As best we can tell, all the sensors have been shut off in there. Even the cameras." That was Ken.

The news raised his hackles. "Was this a terror attack?" Taking out a nuclear reactor would be a formidable achievement for a terrorist group. Doing it at Three Mile Island would have some significance, given its famous history.

"We're trying to find out."

Carl fell back into his chair. He briefly thought of issuing orders to put everyone into the spacesuits to protect them from radiation, but his badge hadn't made a peep since he'd seen Pete up close. Even if a terrorist took out all the other sensors, they couldn't have tampered with every badge worn by the employees, nor could they get inside the concrete bunker that served as containment for the nuclear fuel.

They were still safe.

"Get me the tortoise," he said with finality.

Ken looked up again. "Sir, we'll get a camera working before we need that. I can see the power feeds are online. That means the cameras should be sending something back. We have to be close."

"This ain't horseshoes, people. I need an answer right now. We're sending in the tortoise."

CHAPTER 21

Wollemi National Park, New South Wales, Australia

Destiny had just survived a forest fire, climbed a dangerous ridge, and fought off a Tasmanian tiger. She was committed to staying alive and tried to project the image of Wonder Woman. The strong naturalist stepped out of the brush to bravely face the oncoming truck and its two occupants.

She waved and got their attention right away.

When she got a better look at the two bearded men, her superhero mentality took a big hit. They could have been twins. Their heavy-set frames seemed to fill the entire volume inside the cab of the truck. She suddenly felt like a ninety-pound weakling, soaking wet. Since she'd just climbed out of the creek, that was exactly how she would have appeared to them.

"Where ya' headed, sweet-cheeks?" the burly driver said as he pulled up next to her. His black beard was at least a foot long and dotted with dry grass, like he dragged it through the weeds. He was probably roughly in his thirties. "Getting away from the fire, are ya?" His accent was total Ocker, which made him sound like he'd never seen pavement in his life.

"I'm here with my mates," she said, feeling distracted.

The man looked around. "Where are they?"

She hardly looked at him. "I don't know."

Her uncertainty came with seeing the men and their ride. The old Holden utility truck looked like something out of the nineties, with dinged-up hubcaps and tires that seemed too thin. The body of the truck was tiny and narrow, which gave the impression of the large men filling the entire cab. Their load of firewood was stacked high and in a jumble. If there was any other vehicle on the dirt track, she would pass on this one immediately.

Destiny met the man's eyes, but not before she saw him looking at her soaking wet clothes. "I think they left me. I almost died in the fire and came over the hill to find my team has gone and pissed off. I'm mad as a cut snake."

"You look it. Well, there probably won't be many cars behind us. Nothing but fire up there. We're heading down to the bottle-o to get a slab of four-X Gold. We can give you a lift if you don't mind two blokes with a little extra beef."

She leaned down to look at the second man. He was equally as large as his mate and sported the same messy beard and disheveled appearance. They might have woken up in a ditch not ten minutes before they pulled up.

Her mind was torn with indecision. If she didn't get a lift, it was a long way to blacktop, and fire was unpredictable. She tried to work through the logic of the situation, too. If the men were up to no good, they could jump out right now and attack her. If they just looked like a couple of bogans but were actually good guys, she would have turned them away for no good reason.

Don't judge them by the cover, she told herself.

"I guess it is a long way to the police station. I need to report this fire and find my lost friends. They could still be out there."

"We didn't see anyone up the valley. No cars, for sure. I think your mates might have gone down that way." He pointed down the valley, to her right.

"Okay. Can I ride in the bed?" She pointed to the pile of split logs.

"Oh, I wouldn't," the driver said with a laugh. "You might tip right out. We've already lost several pieces where it got bumpy. You'd be a lot safer inside, with us."

"Yeah, we'll protect you," the passenger added.

She clicked her tongue in rapid succession as she thought about it. If she took too long to decide, the men might get the idea she was asking herself whether they were rapists and murderers, rather than two guys who looked like they lived a bit too long in the bush.

She spoke in an even tone so as to not betray her misgivings. "Thank you for the ride."

The passenger opened his door and stepped out. The little red truck rose a few inches off the ground as the shock absorbers took a break. She walked around the front of the truck in order to get in on the far side.

"My name is Christian," the big guy said as he cleared some beer bottles from the floorboard and threw them to the side of the road.

Every ounce of her being wanted to complain about littering.

Don't do it, Dez.

"My name is Destiny." She wasn't going to give them an ounce of information about herself, besides her first name. After she said it, she realized she should have used a fake one.

She slid in on the bench seat but paused when her hand felt sogginess in the cloth. Since her clothes were already soaking wet, they seemed to absorb whatever was in the fabric where the big man had been sitting.

Oh, god, this is disgusting.

She slid more to the right and got as close to the driver as she dared. While dutifully ignoring the warmth on her back and bottom, she noticed the stick shift was going to be between her legs.

"My name is Stephen Irwin," the driver drawled in his exaggerated backwoods accent.

She brightened up. "Like the Crocodile Hunter! I love that show." As an animal lover, it truly was one of her favorites, though she admitted it was hard to watch the episodes after he passed away.

"Don't know about that." He tugged at his beard like it helped him think. "I don't fight the crocs, though. I steer clear."

"Or we fill 'em with lead." Christian slid next to Destiny and physically pushed her more toward the middle. It wasn't done in a rude way, but he was so large, it was necessary for him to fit on his seat. Once inside, he pulled the door closed with a grunt.

"That's what this is for," Christian continued as he pointed to the rifle behind her.

"Do you have a license for that?" It fell out before she could stop herself. It wasn't like she was going to check.

The driver giggled. "It's back with my other guns."

Christian laughed like it was the funniest thing he'd heard.

The two big men smelled like a rugby locker room gone bad, but there was also an acrid odor lingering, too, like someone had recently chundered in the cab. It was likely the only time she was grateful for the smoke inhalation. If someone had puked in there recently, she could only barely smell it.

"Hang on, little lady," the driver said cheerfully. "We're going to rescue you."

Destiny had nothing to worry about. She was packed in so tight between the men there was no room to move on either side.

She didn't even need a seatbelt.

Modesto, CA

Buck sat in his captain's chair looking out over the Walmart shopping center. After the crash of the SUV, most of the customers had gotten to their cars and escaped, but the lot wasn't empty. Every row had ten or fifteen vehicles remaining, like the owners decided to fight it out inside or took off on foot.

The storm loomed larger. The high-altitude, white-topped clouds were almost above him, and the business end of the dark storm was now coming into view in the north. He figured maybe fifteen minutes until it arrived.

But still he waited.

For the first time all day, he didn't know what to do next. Going north on I-5 was out of the question, as was taking alternate routes around Sacramento. The storm was broad enough that it looked as if it butted up against the Sierra mountains. He might find alternate routes paralleling Interstate 5, but he refused to bet his life on it.

He'd also grown less thrilled with his alternate plan, which was to go south to Bakersfield and then head east along Interstate 40. The GPS said the other route was a few hours longer to White Plains, but he had no idea if there were other storms in that direction. Any delay would make his trip back to Garth even more of a disaster than it already was.

Buck felt compelled to get over the Sierras as fast as possible. In his experience, storms spent all they had on the front side of mountain ranges. If he got over the pass and into Nevada, he'd be safe from this or any other California storm.

"What do you think, Mac? Should we go over the mountain?"

Big Mac barked once when he heard his name. His friend sat next to him, looking forward at the dashboard like it was the most interesting thing in the world.

"I hear you. It could be dangerous, though. We'd be on our own." Any good freight hauler knew to stick to the major highways when carrying a full load. The DOT also frowned on heavy trucks plowing over rickety bridges or slamming into low overpasses. The farther one got from the main shipping lanes, the more chances of getting into trouble. Heavyweight wreckers were endangered species high in the mountains, too. If trouble did find him, it could be days before he was rescued.

"We can wait for the storm to pass," he offered, "though I think we both agree that isn't smart, so let's toss that."

He patted Mac on the head, then got the lucky quarter out of his pocket.

"Heads, we go over the mountain to get to Garth on the shortest route possible. Tails, we don't go the longer route through Bakersfield."

The dog wouldn't understand odds.

Buck believed in making his own luck.

Search for Nuclear, Astrophysical, and Kronometric Extremes (SNAKE). Red Mesa, Colorado

Faith left the meeting angry and upset, which was becoming a regular thing. Bob had forced her hand about the *Denver Post* reporter, and now she had to go talk to him before anyone else did.

She poked her head into Mindy's office. "Did Dr. Perkins check in?"

"No, Faith, I'm sorry. I've left messages for him, but I guess he is sleeping hard."

She gritted her teeth. The duties of leading the SNAKE lab were supposed to be nothing but rewarding for her. A career capstone, they had called it. But today, she'd had her first experiment shut down and had to explain what happened to a reporter from a major metropolitan newspaper.

I'm not telling him shit.

She went out onto the patio. The shadows of the late afternoon were now deep as the sun fell behind the foothills of Denver. It was warmer outside than it was in the air-conditioned facility, but not by much.

A few administration people still hung out on the patio, but the reporter sat alone.

She went right over to him. "Hello, Benny."

He stood up. "Hello, Dr. Sinclair. Thanks for your time. I was beginning to think you guys were avoiding me."

She laughed it off. "Please. Dr. Sinclair was my mother's name. You can call me Faith, out here."

They'd talked before, so she found it odd he used her formal name.

"I'll try," he assured her.

"It has been a busy day. We've just wrapped up a long experiment and we're running diagnostics out the Yin-Yang." None of it was a lie.

They both sat down at the table, facing each other.

"I've heard that there was some kind of problem with your experiment. Is there any way I could get more information on that?"

Bob strikes again.

She'd talked to Benny a few times while the SNAKE lab was under construction and during a few of the test runs, but it was all formal and there were other people around. As such, she wasn't sure how to read him.

Faith took a chance she could keep him off the scent for a little while longer. "I'm afraid this all has to be off the record, if you agree?"

Benny looked disappointed. She knew enough that he was fresh out of his journalism apprenticeship at the paper and was keen to tackle bigger stories. For a time, nothing was bigger than SNAKE in the Denver region, but a year after the ribbon cutting, it was already a routine beat. It was an educated guess, but she figured he'd agree.

He put down his pen. "Are there other reporters inside? I've seen civilians going in and out that I don't recognize as workers. I only ask because I want to get this scoop, you know? I'll do this off the record, but I want to be there when you go back on."

Faith reached over the table to shake his hand. "Deal."

Benny smiled. "So, what can you tell me?"

Those were the magic words. She could control the message again.

"It is mostly as I said. We are poring through data today to figure out if the initial experiment was successful or not. Since this is our first live project, we really didn't know how long it would take to see meaningful results."

"And you still don't know?"

"That is correct."

He seemed to chew on that before going on. "Do you know about all the weird anomalies that happened after the blue light zapped the world?"

She feigned not knowing.

Benny pulled open his notebook. "It has been an unusually busy news day, and most of it happened after we reported the blue light. Several planes went down around the world, but the most noteworthy was the one in New York City. A subway collapsed near that crash site, too. Pieces of Skylab fell in Illinois. The Governor of Pennsylvania has reported an evacuation around Three Mile Island because of fears of a meltdown. Civil authorities reported mass chaos and destruction inside the city of Sacramento because of a freak storm."

"And don't forget the fleet out of Russia," she said without thinking.

"I know, right! How did you know about that? The international news is even more disturbing. The fleet scrambling. A Nazi-era dirigible spotted over the Paris-Charles De Gaulle Airport. Rumor has it there are old Russian tanks appearing inside Kabul. It's like things are coming out of the past."

She saw her opportunity.

"Do you mind if I get a list like that? While I'm working on our project report, I'd really be interested in learning more about what's going on around the world. That blue light didn't affect us, I'm sure, but you know us scientists and our data collection. Maybe we can help to understand what made those odd things happen..."

Benny tore the page from his notebook and handed it to her. "The paper is reporting on all these, so I don't need to keep track of them. I mainly used it to keep busy while I was waiting for you to tell me about your problems in there. I'm hoping you'll give me something. Anything?"

She detected a special emphasis on the word 'problems.'

Faith stood up with the sheet in hand. "I'm sorry I can't stay any longer. My comment at this time is, I'm afraid, no comment. I assure you, nothing is wrong beyond a little accounting mismatch. As a scientist, I can't report on something if I don't have complete accuracy, and that is why I'm not talking on the record."

Please be enough.

The young reporter seemed to study her. Though she was old enough to be his mother, she found him handsome and rugged, as if he spent his time cycling during the summer and skiing in the winter, like her. There was a touch of guilt at not telling him everything.

She glanced at the paper in her hand to defuse the situation.

"We should know more in the morning," she offered as an olive branch to their back and forth.

He shrugged. "I've got to tell you, I have a source who says the answer should be coming much sooner than that. I'll hang out here for a while longer and see what happens."

Fucking Bob!

She kept on the mask of leadership. "Suit yourself. Feel free to come into the lobby when it gets dark."

"Will do."

She turned and went back inside. In moments, she was in the dorm wing at Dr. Perkins' door. Her intention was to wake him up and then dump out all her anger, but she didn't think that was fair, or professional. Even if Donald was her friend, she couldn't reveal how events were getting under her skin.

The burden of leadership felt heavy.

I am going to do one thing.

She slid the list of worldwide events under his door. If anyone could make sense of them, it was the crafty old professor.

CHAPTER 22

Manhattan, New York

Garth and Sam sat on the stone steps of a large fountain on the edge of Central Park. Garth had meant to go deeper into the trees where it was grassy and shady, but Sam wouldn't go a step beyond the water feature.

He went to work checking on his phone, while Garth did the same.

Come on, Dad, where are you?

There were no text messages from Dad, which was starting to make him nervous. The last one Garth sent was hours ago when he and Sam were almost at the airport. His dad never replied to that one, which wouldn't have bothered him on any other day, but today it did.

I have so much to tell you.

He would never reveal it to Sam because he acted like he was glad his parents left him alone, but Garth hated when his dad was gone for so long. Sure, the first few days were fun living with Sam's family, and it was like being on vacation without real supervision, but that wore off fast. Eventually, all he wished for was to see his dad's pickup truck in their driveway.

"Anything from your pappy?" Sam asked in an offhand way.

"Nope. Anything from your parents?"

"Nope," Sam mimicked.

They both went back to working in silence.

Around him, the city felt like it finally knew about the subway collapse. Emergency sirens wailed. It was impossible to tell where they came from or where they were going because of the endless echoes between buildings. He guessed they were for the crash site. He wondered if leaving had been a mistake, like leaving the scene of an accident was a crime.

A few other people sat on the steps or benches near the fountain, but everyone kept to themselves. They had no idea about the strange things he'd seen today.

His mind's eye went back to the hand on the subway. That reminded him of the plane crash. He thought of the fireball on the tarmac and the shards of glass scattered through the ticketing terminal. If his dad knew how close Garth had come to getting sliced and diced like a cheap steak, he'd probably whip out his belt and spank him for real.

It was their running joke. Whenever Garth made the slightest error, Dad would claim he deserved to get a spanking for it.

Spill a soda—get the belt.

Get a B on a test instead of an A—the belt.

Leave his belt on the floor—that called for the belt.

Telling Garth he deserved the belt was his father's quirky brand of humor.

The funny part was Dad had never laid a hand on him in anger. He sometimes bonked him on the back of the head with a firm slap, but Garth admitted those only came out when he acted like a jackass in front of his father.

He wanted to hear Dad's cheesy humor again.

Garth dialed his dad's number, and it rang a bunch of times but didn't connect. Not even his voicemail would come up.

"Damn," Garth huffed.

"Still nothing?" Sam said without looking up. "I think the network is down, or overloaded, or worse. We should have had something by now."

A man wearing a Jewish yarmulke spoke up from a nearby bench. "I can't get a signal, either. I hope it's not Summer Storm Audrey causing all this disruption. My son told me this phone was the best. Paid the lowest price in town for it, too. But it has been nothing but disappointment to me today. I should have stayed with my other one. Just don't tell my son, okay?"

A couple of other people overheard him and agreed with the man. Some said their service went up and down. Others that it had been out for hours. They all seemed to have reliability problems with their phones, which was what they'd heard on the subway and bus back at the airport.

Garth gave the man a thumbs-up sign, then turned to Sam.

"Yeah. I hate to admit this, but I'm starting to get worried."

Sam looked at him sideways. "About a rainstorm?"

"No, not some lame-ass storm," Garth answered.

"Then don't say it," Sam chided.

Garth paused for a few seconds, wondering if his buddy knew him that well.

"How could you possibly know what I'm going to say?"

Sam laughed. "I've known you since third grade. I've got your mind dialed in. I can anticipate your every move."

"All right, Mr. Genius, what is it I'm going to say?"

"Easy," Sam deadpanned. "You want to call Mona."

Garth's brain couldn't wrap itself around the statement.

"Who the hell is Mona?" The instant he said it, the morning ride on the bus came back to him. "Oh, shit, dude. For real? I'm not calling some girl whose name was on a city bus."

"Well, I still have it in my phone, and you should do something fun like that, because it looks like you are going to ugly-cry. You want to go home, don't you?"

"How did you know that, dude?" Garth said with surprise.

"Like I said, I've known you since the third grade."

Garth listened to the water splash in the fountain, not sure how to respond. Was his friend being sympathetic for a change or poking fun at him? It was always hard to say with Sam.

"This blows," Sam said after a few moments of uncomfortable silence. He slipped his phone into his black jeans and looked over to Garth. "No signal. No voicemail. No email. What's the point of being out in the fresh air if your phone is busted?"

Sam's parents loved to make him go outside and "play" with Garth, but they seldom went outside to check on what the boys did, so their outdoor rec time was a lot like their indoor activity.

"I do want to head home, I guess," Garth said cautiously. "If your parents are arriving tomorrow, we can go back out on the town early, but I think I've had enough adventure today. I want to get home and see if my dad left a message on our machine."

That was part of it.

His dad had contingency plans for everything, and they once agreed to use the hallway answering machine at their house if their cell phones stopped working. However, in the two years since they got the machine, neither of them ever needed to call the landline.

The other part was he saw himself through his dad's eyes today. Dad would have said Garth needed to go home the second the plane crashed. His motto in any emergency was to get somewhere you knew was safe as fast as humanly possible. The bigger disasters, he said, often happened when your guard was down after surviving the smaller crisis.

Sam faked sounding pissed. "Fine, dude, I'll pay for a cab and we'll get you home, so your daddy can change your diaper."

Garth didn't take offense to his friend's needling. A passerby would think they hated each other, sometimes, but it was the way they talked, especially on topics of emotion. The undertone of Sam's statement indicated he knew what Garth was going through, and it was cool to head back home.

Garth chucked his friend on the arm with one hard punch.

"Thanks, asshole."

Modesto, CA

Buck was glad to be back on the move. He rolled out of the Walmart parking lot as the storm approached, though he judged he still had plenty of time to continue his escape. He'd made a mistake by lingering inside the store, but he wouldn't make a second one by dallying in the town.

"Take me out of here," he said to the GPS unit.

Freddy Krueger the GPS stayed true to its name and tried to get him killed. The first route it picked went north out of Modesto before it turned east to go over the mountains. It was the shortest route, but it went directly into the storm.

He clicked over to the secondary route, which started with a leg to the south, through the downtown of Modesto, before it went east to the mountains. It was a little longer, but a lot safer because it got him away from the dangerous clouds.

He'd learned his lesson about pushing his luck near bad weather.

The 9mm Beretta PX4 Storm sat snug in a waistband holster on his right hip. His hand touched the semi-automatic pistol one last time to ensure that it was there, ready to save his life. Laws be damned, he was going to carry the gun every second until he made it back to Garth.

"Mac, you buckled in?"

The Golden Retriever barked because he heard his name. Mac was outside his crate but connected to the secured red leash, so he was as buckled as could be. There was no way the pup could escape out the doors and therefore, Buck had one less thing to worry over.

"I hope I've thought of everything. Could use a nice meal again, though." His lunchtime hamburger and fries had all but worn off over the last few hours of driving and running around. If things would have worked out differently, he could have re-stocked his food supplies while at Walmart. As it was, he had a few bottles of water in the mini-fridge, but nothing beyond ketchup packets for food.

He could have stopped at any of the fast food joints along the southbound route through the bustling town, but it would have been a pain to find street parking and walk his sorry butt inside to order. Plus, he wasn't going to be an idiot and let the storm catch up to him.

Big Mac hopped into the passenger seat and sat tall, like he was a full member of the crew. Buck reached over and stroked him on the neck.

"Don't worry. Storm is gone, see? We're safe."

The weather system filled his side mirrors, but it was only because the clouds swallowed the entire horizon. It was huge, but still north of the city.

The wide four-lane roadway took him along miles of small retail shops, fast food eateries, and payday loan stores. It looked a lot like any street in a similar-sized town elsewhere in America. However, as he neared the central part of the city, the buildings got a little wider and taller.

The people also started to act strange.

The first sign was when a silver flash sped by at death-defying speed in the center turn lane. Initially he thought it was the drugged-out guy in the wrecked SUV, but it was instead some other crazy person in an urban assault vehicle, which was his name for minivans. He last saw it skidding with smoke pouring from its tires as it made a hard left turn at an intersection.

He stopped at the same light, impressed at the driving skill of whoever was behind the wheel. The minivan was gone, but as he looked to the left, he watched several people throw suitcases and other supplies into their cars.

"Hey, this is just like the movies," he said to his friend. "They are getting out of Dodge before the storm hits."

Buck drove on, winding his way through town along the route given to him by Freddy. He veered away from the downtown, which was fine with him because it would have the most congestion. A few minutes later, he came to a street name he recognized.

"Yosemite! This will probably take us right to the park, don't you think?" He'd set the destination for his route at Mono Lake, which was on the other side of the Sierras, near the Nevada border. Once there, he'd be able to travel north and get back onto Interstate 80. The most prominent landmark on the route was Yosemite National Park, so the street name hinted he was getting close, though the park was eighty miles away and in the mountains.

While waiting for the light to turn left on Yosemite and head east, Buck noticed a man on the street corner. He looked like any homeless bum holding a cardboard sign, but this one caught his eye.

"The Earth is an appel in the mouth of the Devil."

Buck couldn't resist saying something, but not to point out his bad grammar. He rolled down his window and shouted to the man. "Hey, buddy, what does that even mean?"

The homeless guy could have come from central casting. California was famous for panhandlers, especially the times he'd been up through San Francisco, and this guy was typical. Long, dirty hair. Unshaven. Filthy canvas pants that looked like a car had driven back and forth over them a million times.

"Look around you, friend. Evil has found us."

He assumed the guy was talking about the approaching clouds, which now blotted out the sun. "It's just a storm. I've been in it. Bad. But survivable." Buck figured a stout home would protect these residents much better than his tip over-prone land-sail ever could.

The light changed to green.

"Not the storm. I'm talking about the black light now bathing our planet. You saw it this morning. I know you did!" The bum held the sign over his head. "It's the light of evil!"

Buck maneuvered through the intersection. "The light was blue, you dumbass," he mumbled to himself.

"Ending!" the guy yelled as Buck drove away. He rolled up his window, feeling a little silly for how compelled he felt to get away from the preacher of doom and gloom.

"We're fine," he said to Mac. The dog sat where he was, oblivious to the words he'd spoken. His tongue lolled out the side of his mouth and he wore the look of his usual happy self.

He instantly felt better.

"Yeah, you're right," he said to Mac, "the guy was nuts. Honestly, it seems like that's the only type of people in California today. We need to get over the mountain range and get the hell out of this state."

Buck got the big rig up to speed as the houses, shops, and restaurants finally turned into more orchards and fields.

In thirty minutes, he checked his side mirrors to confirm if the storm had devoured Modesto. He cracked up thinking of that homeless preacher getting soaked and scared to death by the lightning and wind, but he also thought of the woman with her infant he met inside Walmart. Were they okay?

By E.E. Isherwood & Craig Martelle

The immense storm was everywhere behind him, and still built up in the north, but he'd made the right call by driving east. The mountains were ahead, and he'd slipped around the leading edge of the storm before it arrived at the western approaches to the rugged range.

"All I have to do is drive, and we'll be over the hump in no time."

Mac let out a loud sigh and did a few laps on his seat before laying down.

Yeah, I don't think it will be that easy, either.

CHAPTER 23

Wollemi National Park, New South Wales, Australia

Destiny made herself as small as possible while riding between the giant men, Christian and Stephen. It was unnatural for her to shrink when faced with adversity, but in this case, it was completely justified. The smaller she made herself, the less the big, sweaty hulks would brush up against her.

They'd driven for an hour along the bank of the creek. The dirt track was recently constructed into the national park, so tourists and researchers would have better access to the interior, but they paid little heed to drivability. When she and her team arrived with their 4x4 trucks, they had to use four-low several times to clear rocky sections. Now, going back down, the overloaded Holden seemed ill-equipped for the task.

"How did you guys make it up this road?" she asked.

Stephen, the driver, laughed. "We were empty coming up. Christian said this looked like a great place to get some firewood, so we drove up to have a gander. He was right. We struck paydirt."

"I hope you didn't cut down a Wollemi pine," she mused. "They thought they went extinct thirty million years ago, but then someone found them here in the park." A lot like her finding the Tasmanian tiger.

"Does it look like a Christmas tree?" Stephen asked sheepishly.

As a naturalist invested in preserving nature, she hated the notion of them cutting down any of the trees inside the park, but she couldn't hold it over them while at their mercy.

"No. In fact, the Wollemi pine isn't a pine at all. It's—"

Christian interrupted. "We cut what we cut from deadfall, so it was dry and ready for burning. No one will know the difference."

"Phew," she breathed in relief. "I would hate for you to take something important."

"What if we need it to stay alive?" Christian replied. "Could we take it then?"

She rose to the challenge. "And what would you need inside the wilderness that would keep you alive? I'm curious."

The driver swerved around a rock in the middle of the road before he answered. "Could we cut down one of them fancy pines if it would keep us alive in a cold winter? Like if we were going to Antarctica, or something."

It already was winter in Australia, and it wasn't very cold, so his example only worked if he went somewhere colder.

She thought about it as they continued down the rocky road. "Okay. If it was between saving my life or cutting down the last Wollemi pine—killing an entire species, forever—I'd think about it pretty seriously."

"Rubbish, if you ask me. Your life, for a tree? Hmf. Would you cut off some branches, if it saved your life?"

"I see what you're doing. This is an ethics test." It took her back a few years, but she'd studied similar questions at university.

"Not sure what you mean. Out here, you depend on the land to feed you, warm you, and bathe you."

Doesn't look like nature bathes you too often, she thought with some amusement.

Christian went on. "We take what we want because that's how we live."

His tone had a trace of condescension she didn't understand. Was it because she came across as a city dweller to the backwoods men?

"I grew up on a farm," she replied. "I know what it's like to live off the land." It was an exaggeration, because while her parents did own a farm, it wasn't where she and her sister had lived.

Christian shifted in his seat, which bumped her. "So, what's a pretty Sheila like you doing way out in the woods by yourself?"

"I told you. I was with my mates, then they left me."

The big man glanced over to her. "We thought you were a prostitute."

She folded her arms over her still-soaked chest. The breath caught in her throat as she considered if she'd walked right into a nightmare after all. "I-I'm not. I'm a naturalist with the Sydney Harbor Foundation. We were doing research." Her voice was uncertain. "I'll be expected back."

Stephen laughed. "Relax. We may look like we've got a few kangaroos loose in the top paddock, but we're all right. We'd give Jack the Ripper a ride out of that fire, but we'd rough him up when we got back to town, ya know?"

Destiny spoke cautiously. "So, you don't want to sleep with me?"

The driver roared. "No way. We're both happily married!"

Christian laughed, too, and for a minute, she thought there was a joke she was missing. Two guys, driving in the forest together. A load of firewood to keep warm.

"Are you married to each other?" she probed tentatively.

Stephen's head whipped in her direction, then he exploded with more laughter. "Can you imagine!"

The truck slammed down on a rock that felt like it was right under her feet, but they barely noticed.

The men laughed for several minutes.

She was compelled to find another topic of conversation when the laughing died down. "So, I guess it's a good thing you have this old beater truck, huh? These rocks are brutal on your undercarriage."

"Mine, too," Christian added as he shifted in his seat. His long legs barely fit into the space below the dashboard.

"Hold up," Stephen replied. "I only just bought this Holden Commodore this year. It doesn't look that rough, does it?"

She didn't know if the man was serious. It smelled like death inside, they used the floorboards to hold their empty beer cans, and the shocks were probably crushed by the overburdened cargo bed. She was pretty sure they'd left some parts on the road back where they'd scraped rocks. She didn't know what model year it was, but it looked like something rode hard every day since the eighties or nineties.

"No, not at all," she answered.

"Good," the man said in a way that suggested he took it personally.

Stephen seemed to focus hard on driving for a short time, and everyone sat in silence. Destiny tried to think of something to say to counteract the bad mood she'd given the driver, but she was soon distracted with something else.

The acrid smell of the forest fire came in through the air vents.

The driver stopped the Commodore and slammed his hands on the wheel. "Don't that beat fuck-all? The tree is on fire."

Hardly any trees were aflame up ahead, save the tall one closest to the road. It was almost a roadway signpost. An advisory as to what was ahead.

"We found the fire again," she declared. "My team said it was spreading like mad."

"It's cool. We're almost down to pavement. We can push through." Stephen put it in gear by hitting the shifter against her leg, then gave it some gas.

"Wait! No!"

The daredevil driver headed straight for the burn zone.

Coulterville, CA

Buck sat at the intersection of the little town as he decided whether he could trust Freddy the GPS. The monster storm was mostly behind him, but the tops of the high clouds made it seem much closer. The GPS wanted him to drive north for ten miles in order to catch highway 120, which would take him to Tioga Pass and over the mountains. But there was a shortcut to 120 if he took a turn in Coulterville.

"Should we flip for this one, or just do it, eh, Mac?"

He looked over at the dog, sound asleep on the comfy front seat.

His instinct told him to take the shortcut, so that was what he did.

The drive through town was brief. It wasn't even big enough to be a one-stoplight affair. It took him two minutes to pass the last home, and then it went back to the natural landscape of golden grasses and short, stubby trees. The road no longer sported a shoulder. It was barely wide enough for his tires to ride the lines on both sides of his lane.

Time to call, he thought.

He'd put his phone into the cradle attached to his dashboard, which let him touch the screen without having to hold it in his hand. He wasn't one to text and drive, but it did make it easier to call his son while keeping most of his focus on the two-lane blacktop out his front window. The road had no guardrails as it flowed through steep ravines, so he needed all his attention out there.

To his surprise, the call went through, but Garth's number rang for almost a minute. Right when he was going to hang up, the system clicked like someone picked up on the other end, then his son's answering machine message played.

Finally, a beep.

"Hey, Garth." He didn't know where to start. It was almost an afterthought to call his son. He hadn't planned anything. "I, uh, was delayed. I just left Modesto, California. I'm about an hour to the east and I'm going over the mountains into Nevada to get home sooner."

He felt nervous for some reason. There was so much he needed to say.

"Look. Just call me back the instant you get this, okay? I'm sorry I haven't called earlier, make sure you and I are good. No bullshitting around. I need you to call me. If you don't, I'm going to come at you with the belt." He laughed to iron out some of the anxiety from his voice. "So please call."

Buck stared at the phone for a long time while considering whether to add more to his message, but then he reached out and quickly hung up.

Call me, son. Then we can talk.

Search for Nuclear, Astrophysical, and Kronometric Extremes (SNAKE). Red Mesa, Colorado

Faith ran to Donald's door the second he called.

"Come in," the man said from inside.

She pushed through and was shocked at how old her friend suddenly appeared. He'd put on ten years since they'd been together an hour earlier.

"You look terrible," she blurted.

Dr. Perkins waved like it was a minor inconvenience. "Don't worry about me. I've made a discovery."

They sat together on a two-person sofa and looked over a number of papers he'd spread on the tiny coffee table.

"Thank you for leaving that list of events, Faith. It really helped me put this in perspective." He pointed to a piece of white printer paper with hand-drawn lines and data, like he'd tried to re-create a computer spreadsheet.

"It looks detailed," she said to be helpful.

"Indeed. I entered each news item as a datapoint. Here is the column for the name, here is for the location, and this third column is for the time."

He had all of the things from Benny's list, plus some others.

"What are these? I've never seen them." She pointed to the bottom half of his list. It mentioned a minor quake in San Francisco, a major forest fire in New South Wales, Australia, and the disappearance of several of the statues on Easter Island.

"I was lying here watching television, Faith. Each time the news would pan to a news item today, I entered it into my fancy guide. Now we have thirty datapoints to do our analysis."

Sure enough, the list was neatly numbered down the left side from one to thirty. He probably stopped it there because he'd run out of space on the front of the sheet.

"As I said, I've already made a discovery." He put his hand on his chest like he had heartburn.

She leaned to help, but he waved her off. "I'm all right. I need to show this to you, but then I have to lie down again. Fair?"

"You can lie down right now, Donald. I can come back." She wanted nothing more than to solve the mystery of what shut down the Izanagi experiment, but she wasn't willing to risk her friend's health.

"No." He stomped. "Listen." He pointed forcefully to his spreadsheet.

"I'm sorry," she replied softly.

"Please. I need to show this to you." He pointed to the first item. "This is a story about the Denver power grid failing. It happened almost the same time we went down. The next one is an odd story out of metro Chicago."

He moved his thin finger to point 24 down his list.

"A troop of Boy Scouts arrived at their forest campground in the early afternoon today and found the flaming wreckage of Skylab. Pieces of it must have stayed in orbit until today."

Dr. Perkins slid up to number 12 and 13.

"These two have been all over the news. The New York City plane crash and the subway collapse."

"Haven't there been lots of planes that fell out of the sky?" she asked.

"Yes, but this was unique because it fell in the middle of a city and, to make this more confusing, it was so torn up, we still don't know what airline it came from. Every plane in America has been accounted for."

She nodded. "How is that possible? How many flights crashed, yet all are accounted for?" she asked, but the look on his face suggested he didn't want to speculate. "So, what is your big discovery?"

He sat back on the sofa. His wiry frame was almost absorbed by the cushions. "If you drew a line through all four, you'd see they almost align perfectly from west to east. I meant to sketch a globe and enter all these points to see if there is an overall pattern, but I didn't have time."

She studied his coloring and body language. "Donald, I'm up to my hips in this nightmare. Bob has been asking me to make a statement to the press, but I've been putting it off. I want to keep putting it off for as long as I can, honestly. You could help me do that if you were feeling better."

Donald chuckled while holding his head back with eyes closed. "Oh, Faith, how I would love to get in there and get my hands dirty, like the old days, but the trip into Castle Rock took everything out of me. It's almost like—"

"What?" she asked with concern.

"No, that's impossible. I'm winded is all. What time are you talking to the press?"

She had told Benny to expect something tomorrow morning for an official press statement, but the reporter seemed convinced she would have something to say in the evening.

"I think Bob is going to force me to talk tonight."

Donald opened his eyes. "How can he make you talk, Faith? You give that man entirely too much credit. You schedule the press conferences, after all."

She stood up to go. "Yeah, but he could still talk to them on the sly. Oh, hell, I should get it over with and say something to Benny and get him out of here. But, Donald, I think you have something here. Do you mind if I take your papers while you get some rest? I'll plot a few more points on your map."

"Have it all," he said with a dismissive wave. "It will do me no good while my eyelids are closed."

She picked up all his research. "Thanks for this."

"I'd do the same for a friend," he said with his old charm.

"Har, har. Get some rest. I'll see you soon," she   said.

CHAPTER 24

Manhattan, New York

Garth and Sam hurried to Park Avenue, thinking it would be easier to catch a cab there rather than on the narrow side street. As they walked up to the intersection, a man in a black suit turned the corner and almost ran into them.

"Sorry," Garth said instinctively. He stepped aside, but the man was followed closely by a mechanical animal that bumped into him. It was bigger than a dog, but smaller than a horse.

The black and yellow machine stopped when it made contact with Garth's arm and let out three small chirps.

The noise made the man turn around. "Stand aside, boy."

"Sure," he said apologetically.

The man in the suit spun on his heels and walked away. The angular dog-horse continued its locomotion behind its master. A metal arm was folded and tucked in on the top of the long body. The robot's four-legged gait was hypnotic as it walked away.

"What the hell was that?" Garth asked Sam.

Sam looked back but was unimpressed. "This city has a million companies. There must be one that makes robots. Hey, we got one!" He waved the cab all the way up to the curb.

The driver was about his dad's age, with gray in his short beard. He wore glasses and a blue newsboy's hat. Only after they climbed in and shut the door did they notice the guy's cigar wedged into a dashboard ashtray.

The driver didn't wait for them to state their destination, he put on the gas and rejoined traffic on the busy street.

"We're going to Staten Island," Sam said without urgency.

"You'll never make it," the driver replied immediately. "None of us will."

Sam replied. "Just take Lincoln over to 95 and head south. Simple."

The driver accelerated south on Park like he was driving the heist's getaway car.

"Hey now!" Garth said through the partition.

"We want to get there alive, friend," Sam added.

"My name is Jeff, but today, I'm going by Dawson. Today, of all days, I want to be someone else."

Park Avenue was unusual in New York City because it cut through the bottom of a skyscraper. The three lanes of southbound traffic condensed to one lane and entered the tunnel cut through the building. The cabbie bullied other drivers and merged in front of them.

"I picked up you boys because you look like fighters." He turned around and peered intently at them. "You are fighters, aren't you?"

Sam nodded. "We are, sir."

"Good," Dawson said as he drove them through the tunnel.

They came out of the darkness next to Grand Central Station on a raised viaduct. They followed it for a short while and then turned left to the front of the historic structure. The narrow roadway went down a ramp in front of the building and then Park Avenue resumed to the south.

Garth absently noted it was where they shot battle scenes in *The Avengers* movie.

Sam leaned forward. "Sir, you need to turn right up here so we can get to the Lincoln Tunnel, okay?"

The driver bounced up and down like the road was ten times bumpier than it was. Garth had a sinking feeling in his stomach, like there was something wrong with the man's brain.

Dawson turned around to speak to them. He kept his left hand on the wheel, but fully faced them in the back seat. "That tunnel is dangerous. I saw the end of all things. The end. Boom. Poof. You know?"

Garth braced himself as the car sped along the parkway and toward a red light. Traffic around them was light at the moment, but vehicles crossed ahead on the intersecting street.

Oh, shit, Garth thought.

"Turn around and drive!" he yelled.

The cab barreled through the intersection and somehow avoided smacking into the sides of the other cars. Horns went crazy as they sped away.

Much too late, the cab driver turned back around and put both hands on the wheel.

Garth leaned over to Sam. "You can really pick 'em. He's nuts."

Sam took it in stride. "Every cabbie in New York has something wrong with them. We'll be fine. Trust me." Sam spoke to the driver like they were old friends. "Hey, Dawson, where you from?"

Unlike many cabbies, Dawson was obviously born and raised in America. He had no accent that would have pegged him as being from anywhere besides the city.

The driver picked up his stogie and took a hard pull, holding it in his lungs as they ran another red light. This time, a cab coming from the roadway to their right almost struck their side. Garth saw it happen like it was slo-mo. A young woman passenger was flung forward against the passenger's seat in the other cab.

"Dude!" Sam shouted. "You have to at least do check-stops at each light. This is crazy."

"We have to get out of the city," Dawson said by way of a reply.

"No kidding," Sam answered. "That's what the Lincoln Tunnel is for."

"No, no tunnels. Those are the places where the monsters can hide. We have to stay above the water."

Sam leaned over to him. "You may have a point on this guy. He's crazier than the usual cab driver."

It wasn't possible to pick your own cabbie when flagging them down, but Garth understood his joke.

"Bigfoot. UFOs. Loch Ness Monster. They're all real. All of them. I've seen them all today."

"Hey, where was Nessy?" Sam said to provoke the guy.

Garth poked him in the side. "Don't do that. Not him. We have to get out."

Dawson blew his smoke through the open plexiglass partition window, which made both of them cough. "You boys sit tight and hang on. When I tell you to get out and fight, you get out, okay?"

They both nodded. Garth was already planning to get out and run for his life the second they stopped. He was positive Sam had the same idea.

"And don't worry about Nessie. I saw her in Central Park. That's why we're going this way." He pointed down the slot canyon formed by the tall buildings on each side of Park Avenue.

"Hey, Garth," Sam said in a loud, sarcastic voice. "Don't worry about Nessie. She's back that way." He pointed out the rear window.

Dawson turned halfway around and used one hand to point to Sam. "He knows."

Garth slowly shook his head in disbelief.

Of all the cabs in New York City.

Near Yosemite National Park, California

At first, Buck found the drive into the Sierras a nice change of pace from the crowded highways and wild weather back in the Central Valley, but it became unsettling once he caught on that no cars were coming down the road from the other direction.

"Must be a lonely hundred miles," he said to his sleeping companion. As the miles ticked by, and he went deeper into the foothills, he began to think of rousing Big Mac.

Let him sleep a little longer.

Freddy the GPS said it was an even hundred miles from the start of his trip through the mountains until he came out at Mono Lake on the other side. He'd gone about fifteen when a sign caught his attention.

"Now entering Buck Meadows." He sat up in his seat, excited to see the town that shared his name.

He passed a sleepy campground and a rustic motel nestled into the pines. A few cars and pickups were parked at each place, which he found reassuring, but a minute later, he was back in empty forest. Buck Meadows was even smaller than Coulterville.

"Damn. I guess these are what passes for towns up this way."

Fortunately, the road was well-maintained and rated for 55 miles per hour, so it was easy driving. He used the opportunity to listen to the news.

The AM station from Fresno came in loud and clear.

"It has been a wild day in aviation, and no one seems willing to guess on the cause. We are joined by Dwight Allie of the Civil Air Patrol of Fresno Composite Squadron 112."

"Thank you for having me, Dean."

"You're welcome. I'll be blunt, Mr. Allie. What the heck is going on out there?"

"It would be fair to say no one really knows. All air traffic has been shut down over North America, pending investigation into the loss of twelve aircraft in various parts of the country. Was it a maintenance malfunction? A terrorist attack? We simply don't know."

The host spoke matter-of-factly. "It was caused by what people are calling the Blue Wave."

Mr. Allie seemed reluctant. "Maybe. No one really knows what it was, but thank god it wasn't a serious electromagnetic pulse, or we might have lost more planes, many more."

"And how many aircraft were lost overseas?" the host inquired.

"My intel is incomplete. At least another twelve are confirmed, but some nations aren't reporting anything at all. It leaves a few gaps. I can tell you I've spoken with aviation enthusiasts in Thailand and heard the lost Malaysian plane, MH370, landed in Bangkok at the Suvarnabhumi Airport. It is the one bright spot in a day of losses."

Buck stopped listening after the word *losses*. Something big was going on, and it was everywhere. That blue light started his own weird day, and the radio was talking about strange events all over the globe as a result.

Riots in Modesto. Storms in Sacramento. Plane crash in New York City.

"It's all part of the same thing," he said quietly. "And, Buck, you couldn't have seen the big picture right away, but you could have at least avoided the riot in Walmart."

He'd spent too much time in the store and got very little for his effort. Sure, the leash might save Mac's life, and keep him from having to chase the dog, but if this really was the start of the end of the world as they knew it, he could keep his pup safer by stuffing him in the crate for the next 3000 miles.

Buck glanced over at his friend and immediately knew he couldn't be quite that cruel, so he cut them both some slack.

"Okay, at least I got something useful at Walmart." He tapped the wheel. "And I couldn't have predicted the riot, either. It was perfectly calm when I walked in."

For the next few miles, he replayed the events. Could he have figured out the red-shirted running guy was up to no good? Was that the precise starting point of the riot? Could he objectively point to the exact moment when he should have run out of there? The lesson was clear.

Don't go into a Walmart. Ever.

It was advice that made some sense to him.

Garth.

He hit the keypad on the phone to try Garth again.

After many rings, it made the odd click and went to his voicemail like before.

"Hey, son. I don't want to worry you, but there are some unusual things going on here in California. I'm taking a detour over the mountains by Yosemite National Park because of a freak storm. Whatever you do, don't go around people." He paused, knowing how it would sound to a boy in a city of millions. "What I mean is, don't go into places like Walmart or Macy's or Bloomies. I just came out of a Walmart full of people fist-fighting and shooting guns."

He wondered if he should tell Garth anything more about his ideas for survival. Board the windows of the house. Get out the guns. Stock up on water. But he decided to leave it at that because he wanted his boy to focus on the most important item.

"Call me as soon as you get this," he said in a soothing voice. "Let's plan this right, okay?"

Buck's heart thumped against his ribcage because of what he'd admitted. The Walmart debacle was the final tipoff. Society teetered on the edge because of the strange flash of blue light in everyone's faces. Once the assholes of the world figured it out, the criminals and opportunists would take to the streets.

The drugged-out guy in the silver SUV was the tip of that spear. Despite the encounter, Buck was thankful he now had a small axe.

Ahead, the two-lane road pointed deep into endless forest. He was doing fifty on a curvy strip of mountain road when he needed to be doing eighty on a smooth ribbon of interstate.

It felt a lot like going backwards.

For the next ten miles, he drove aggressively and at the limits of safety because he wanted to get up and over Tioga Pass as soon as possible. However, when he came around a curve, he was forced to lay on the brakes. The sleeping Mac slid off his seat and went to the floor. The trailer tandem howled under the stresses and for a few oh-shit seconds, he thought he was going to crush the rear vehicle in the line ahead. By the time he stopped, the green car was almost hidden from view because it was below his hood.

"You gonna make it?" he asked his dog in his friendly voice, so he didn't show any anxiety.

The retriever came out from under the dash and lazily stood with his paws on the side windowsill. He wasn't hurt or shaken up; he only wanted to see what they'd hit.

He laughed. "Good pup."

A line of about ten cars waited at a roadblock up ahead.

Every driver's door hung ajar, like the occupants had opened them and jumped into the empty lane of traffic going in the opposite direction.

The screeching of tires didn't bring anyone running to see what happened.

It was a first.

Something ain't right here.

CHAPTER 25

Wollemi National Park, New South Wales, Australia

Destiny couldn't afford to be polite any longer, because her life was back on the line. Heat from the burning tree came through the open windows, adding to her urgency. "You really are from woop-woop. Everyone here knows you don't drive into a fire. Turn around, dammit."

"Don't spit the dummy, little lady. I drive through 'em all the time. It doesn't get hot as long as you keep moving." He glanced over to her. "I liked you better standing outside the car. First you insult my ute, then you have a go at me for driving it the wrong way."

She rolled her eyes.

"Look. I'm sorry, okay? I've had a pretty shit day and I thought you two were my saviors. I was going to get you a fucking medal, in fact. But listen, we're going to die if we drive any farther into this fire. It must be huge."

They made it beyond the burning tree without incident, but the woodlands on the far side of the creek burned wildly, supporting her claim that it was time to turn around.

Stephen looked out the back window and drew his own conclusions. "See, we made it just fine."

The truck hit another rock and the three of them bounced six inches off the seat like it was choreographed. When they came back down, the springs of the bench complained with squeaks and metallic groans. She felt like a tiny Pomeranian trapped between two Great Danes.

"We're close," the driver said in an agreeable tone.

They drove along the edge of the fire for another five minutes. Destiny prayed it would become clear they were driving into danger, but neither of the men seemed to get it. Christian coughed from a patch of smoke, which she assumed would wake him up to the threat.

"Now, do you see—" she started to say.

Christian reached in front of her and turned on the tape deck.

As soon as she heard the harmonica, she knew the song.

"Is this some kind of a joke?" she shouted.

"How do you mean?" Stephen replied with a chuckle. "I like this song."

"It's called Suicide Blonde. You really don't see it?" She reached for a lock of her hair, which was blonde. Playing the song by INXS couldn't be a coincidence. It was a message. They didn't want to listen to her anymore.

"It's not about you," the driver continued as he picked at his beard. "It's the first song on the album. Just enjoy it."

They motored down the rocky path while the song blasted from the speakers. She kept watch and hoped the men were correct, though she knew they weren't.

The forest was aflame on the far side of the creek. Many of the tallest trees reminded her of skyscrapers as they loomed high above, but the flaming bark and torch-top crowns made them nothing but majestic threats. Patches of the burning undergrowth met the waterway less than fifty feet away, and, as she expected, it wasn't long before more of the trees on her side showed evidence of burning branches.

The fast pace of the song made it seem an appropriate soundtrack to the ongoing disaster, but she refused to be labeled as a suicidal blonde.

Fuck this.

She clicked off the tape deck.

"Let me out. I'll run back if I have to. You two are the ones who are suicidal, not me and my blonde hair."

Stephen seemed surprised. "Hey, I'll turn on the air conditioner. We'll be fine. I promise." He rolled up his window and fiddled with buttons on the dash.

"Please, guys. I'm sorry I made a mistake about your Commodore, and I don't really think you two are losers from woop woop, but please don't drive me into this fire. I've seen it from up close already."

The driver brightened. "There, that's better. I may look the part of a footy player, but I'm more of a lover, you see? My wife would beat me black and blue if I ever did anything as dangerous as you say. We're almost through to the main road."

Destiny was convinced he didn't know what he was talking about. He probably made up the whole thing about driving through fires as a macho attempt to show off, but it fell flat with her. Rolling up the windows and using the cool air was something a five-year-old would do, not a grown man.

"Stop. The. Car." She used her most commanding voice.

I'll start punching if I have to.

Stephen applied the brakes, which halted them immediately because they were never going that fast. He spoke with great importance. "We have to stop."

She shifted in her seat as if Christian was going to let her out. "Thank you," she said with relief.

"No, look." The driver pointed ahead.

Several tall trees had already fallen across the creek, their flaming tops blocking the primitive road. The downed trees acted like drawbridges, and she could almost see the path the fire took onto her side. A small chunk of the forest on the hill to their left was already aflame, and it spread like a plague while she watched.

"Chuck a uwie," she demanded.

"Yeah, yeah," Stephen said with sudden acceptance. "That's smart."

"How close are we to the blacktop?" she asked while the driver did a twenty-point U-turn on the narrow road. The heat of the burning trees warmed the cab ten degrees before they drove away.

"I thought we'd be there already, to be honest with you. That's why I didn't think any of this was a big deal. I'm sure it's right ahead."

Destiny spoke rapidly. "And this road goes far into the forest, past where you found me, but it eventually dead ends, right?" She'd studied her maps before they went into the national park and had undoubtedly looked at the end of the road, but her present anxiety blotted out all memory of it.

"We drove away from the fire near the end," the driver replied. "We can't get out that way even if the road went through."

The fire was huge and had spread to various parts of the park, but she already had a plan. "So, we have to get away from the fire on this end. That's obvious. We'll go back up the road to where it's clear, then hike out in another direction. If we're as close as you say, we should be able to go around the fire and find help. Should be a piece of cake."

"Lady, no offense, but that's a shit plan. Me and me mate are staying with the Commie, okay?"

"I, uh..." She didn't know what to say to that mentality.

They drove a few minutes back the way they came, and for the first time that day, she wasn't surprised to see more fire. The blaze had spread to their side of the creek, even in the short time since they'd been by.

"Now will you let me out?"

Near Yosemite National Park, California

Buck sat and watched the empty line of cars for several minutes. A white National Park Service SUV blocked both lanes of the road at the front, its lights flashing.

Tall pines crowded in toward both sides of the road, revealing nothing that might have coaxed people from their vehicles. Ten cars with engines running and doors open. Not a driver in sight. Not a tourist with their phone taking pictures. *No one.*

Freddy the GPS said he still had seventy miles to go, and there was no turning back. Buck was less than amused. "If the riot in Walmart was anything to go by, this could be more of the same. Men with guns exerting their authority. Wouldn't that be something?" Buck tapped the nine-millimeter before moving it under his leg to make sure he could pull it in an instant if needed.

"All right, Mac-O, we're not going to sit here with our thumbs up our tailpipes, are we? It's time to do something." Buck put the truck in reverse and slowly backed the big rig down the narrow road.

Despite the Jake brakes to stop and the slow reverse, no one showed up to stop him. When he had the truck a couple hundred yards down the road, he parked.

"I'm going to get out, okay?" he told the dog. "But I'm not going anywhere. I need to get one more tool, so I can protect us from...whatever's out there."

He watched the pine forest, his mind running rampant with wild theories. Though the thought was completely irrational, his many dealings with ambushes while serving overseas made him consider whether the people in those cars had been jumped by the criminal element he'd been fearing. The police truck could be part of the setup.

The nine-millimeter pistol was fine for a close-in defensive situation, but he needed something that could reach much farther. Back home, he had ten rifles that would have been perfect to have over his shoulder while in the woods. They offered long-range protection against coyotes, feral dogs, and even bears.

And the worst animal of all...

"I'll do anything to protect my son," he intoned, as if a mantra. He detached another panel from the inside of his sleeper. He'd put the object at the bottom of the compartment, so he had to reach in up to his shoulder to grab it. He pulled out a rifle's lower receiver group.

Buck set it on his bed.

"Now for the other piece," he said to his friend. "I have to step outside for a sec. Be right back."

Mac crouched under the steering wheel column like he was going to go outside, but the red wire caught and held him fast as Buck shut the door. The Golden Retriever jumped into the driver's seat and looked down at Buck from the window like he'd been betrayed.

"It's all right. I promise." Buck signaled with a calming hand and a smile. For the past two weeks, the dog had been great about coming out with him and staying by his side, almost like he had been trained that way. "Soon, buddy. You and me, figuring this out."

Buck strode to the side of his tractor and flicked open the hood tie-down, then he trotted around and opened the one on the passenger side. With both released, he pulled on the wing-like hood ornament to pivot open the black fiberglass hood. The casing swung on hinges toward the front until the hood was almost vertical, exposing the Peterbilt's big diesel motor to the world.

"No one shoot at the dumbass checking his oil," he said aloud.

Many what-if scenarios competed for Buck's attention as he worked to retrieve the thing he'd hidden inside the hood. Buck pulled the long tube out of the secret panel he'd tack-welded to the underside of the stainless-steel grille.

"Got ya!"

It took thirty seconds to close the hood, secure the latches, and rejoin Mac inside the cabin. When back in his seat, he scanned the forest for any signs that something was about to happen.

But it was exactly the same as it had looked minutes earlier.

"Didn't see anything, huh, buddy?" He imagined Mac was still pouting about being kept inside, but he hopped up on the passenger seat like they were going to drive again. His drooling, smiling face suggested the supposed infraction was already forgotten.

Buck slid one of the jerky treats from his stash and handed it to Mac.

"You really are a great dog," he said while rubbing his heavy coat.

After both seemed satisfied to have their partner back, he made his way to the rear of his sleeper and plopped down on the bed. The dog followed him and hopped up, too.

It only took Buck a few seconds to finish his project.

He twisted the stainless barrel and mated it to the synthetic stock until it looked like a proper rifle. Because he traveled the lower 48 states, he had to contend with 48 different laws about whether he could carry a rifle in his truck. He hid the pieces separately as a hedge against those laws and because he didn't want it to get stolen. He wanted it available when he needed it, though he'd never seriously believed he would.

"Mac, my friend, we have ourselves a 10/22 Takedown."

He pulled the box of ammunition from the same compartment where he'd kept his pistol. It calmed his nerves while he slid cartridges into the 25-round banana mag.

"Now, let's go check out that roadblock."

Search for Nuclear, Astrophysical, and Kronometric Extremes (SNAKE). Red Mesa, Colorado

Faith found Bob talking to some of his team in an empty office.

"Dr. Stafford, come with me, please," she said to be polite.

She didn't wait for him to follow but strode down the hallway and waited at the door a few offices down. The rooms were reserved for additional staff, so no one would be along to interrupt her. She went inside when he saw her, then she went and stood by the large window overlooking the photogenic hogback.

Dr. Stafford stuck his head. "Did you change your mind about a news conference?"

"Come in, please. Shut the door."

Bob closed the door but stayed near it. She looked at him from across an empty desk. "I'm in charge here. If you want to talk to a reporter, you come through me. If you want to schedule research time, you come through me. If you want to push for restarting the device, you do what?"

He pursed his lips like he'd eaten something unsavory.

"Say it," she persisted. "Because if you don't, I'm inclined to remove you from my team and send you to the offsite lab in Boulder." It was one of the data nodes for the giant project, so technically, it was a lateral move, but being banished from the main campus of SNAKE was the equivalent of firing him; something even she couldn't do inside the endless bureaucracy of the University of Colorado.

"I'll go through you, but I don't like the way you run things," he said quietly.

"Then stop complaining. Help me, for god's sake. That's what we're supposed to do for other scientists."

The sour look didn't disappear from his face.

"I'm holding a press conference tonight at seven o'clock in the main auditorium. Come if you want to, but I'm holding this because it's necessary for our operation, not because you said I should. Let's get that clear right here and now. This is my show."

"But I suggested it—"

"Dammit, Bob. Of course we're going to have a press conference. I've been resisting the idea because you kept pushing it and it was annoying; that's on me. There's something big going on outside, and we're just a part of it. We need to have a presser, get them off our back, and then get back to the science."

"That's all I ever wanted." Bob sounded contrite, but she knew better. Still, it was better than being at loggerheads.

"And you've got your wish," she said in a steely voice, before softening an ounce. "I want the same thing, Bob. I want to explore the universe and make discoveries, like we always said when we were together. The power interruptions and press nonsense will pass. We've got to be able to work alongside each other or I really will send you to Boulder."

"Fine," he huffed.

She wasn't holding out for more. "I've got to go." She showed him the bundle of papers she'd taken from Donald's room. "My research includes some stuff Dr. Perkins dug up on the web. I think it may explain that blue light and how it shut us down."

She walked by him and opened the door but stopped before stepping through. If anyone was going to bury the hatchet, it would be her.

"I want your team ready with computer time when we go live. Plan for it in the next twenty-four hours. The second we have this shutdown licked, I'm going to get us going again. I promise you, I'm trying." It burned her to give him what he wanted, but she wasn't just his ex, she was his boss, and the leader of an exotic group of physics researchers. She accepted that he was part of her team and needed to know she had his back.

That took some of the cringe from his face.

"We'll be ready," he replied.

She ran out the door, anxious to look at Donald's   findings.

CHAPTER 26

Yosemite National Park, Big Oak Flat Entrance

Buck drove his truck back up the road at barely a walking pace. He drove into the oncoming traffic lane and eased past the parked cars. When he rolled to the front of the line and could see around the next bend in the road, a little more of the situation became clear.

"Looks like they're keeping people out of the park. I wonder why."

Three brown wooden booths stood in the road ahead. National Park Service attendants used them to take entrance fees and hand out maps to visitors who came into Yosemite from this direction. If the police wanted a roadblock, it made sense to do it on two lanes where he was, rather than the four lanes at the formal entrance.

As best he could tell, it was a simple roadblock by the police, as one might expect if an accident was up ahead. There were a few spent flares scattered around the pavement, too.

But where are the people?

A scene from *Close Encounters of the Third Kind* played in his head. It was the one where an alien light shines from total darkness above the guy in the pickup truck as he waits at a railroad crossing. A powerful energy shakes the crossing lights, and the audience thinks he's going to be abducted. If he'd been taken, his truck would sit there empty, a lot like the cars Buck was looking at.

Without realizing it, the hairs on his neck stood straight up.

"The people are somewhere," he said sincerely to Mac. "Right, pup?"

The door on the park police SUV hung open the same as all the others. The buzzing sense of danger wouldn't go away, but his choices were limited unless he wanted to ram his not-paid-for Peterbilt into the government vehicle.

Buck sucked in some air and exhaled slow and deliberately. Lose his commercial driver's license. Not be able to make payments on his truck. Still a country away from his son.

"Let's save that option for last, and then still do something different. I'll be right back." He was already tired of saying that to Mac. "No, you know what? You're coming with me."

He swapped the leashes so Big Mac wore the long, black one. Securing him during a huge wind storm was fine, but if there was something going on with the world, they would depend on each other for survival.

In this scenario, he wanted Mac's ears to tell him if someone was sneaking around on the pine needle-covered ground. Unlike regular leaves, the needles would muffle footfalls, so he needed the heightened senses of his four-footed friend.

"Come on," he said like they were going out to play. Buck considered lifting him down, like he'd done every time for the last two weeks, but decided they were past the coddling stage, especially since he'd seen the dog jump out and land without a scratch. He let Mac hop onto the sidestep, then onto the ground. "Good job, buddy."

Once on the pavement, Mac pulled at the leash and went directly to the nearest tree. Buck had to let out about ten feet of the cord, but it was enough for the dog to reach the lodgepole pine.

"Go make!"

In the need for speed, he'd forgotten to stop so his little buddy could relieve himself. It was a wonder the dog didn't let loose on the seat again. While providing overwatch of his teammate, Buck appreciated the clean, pine-scented air and listened as the wind blew through the branches. He watched for any movement using the heightened awareness of his peripheral vision.

Buck held the Ruger 10/22 at the low ready, as he had been trained. There had to be a simple explanation, but after so many weird things in the news and on his own adventure today, he wasn't going to walk around without a weapon close by.

Mac showed no signs of stopping. "Wow. You really had to go."

Buck flicked the safety off and then back on, as practice. There was already a round in the chamber. By keeping the rifle aimed at the ground, he could at least ensure it was convenient for him to wield it, but it wasn't so threatening that he would accidentally shoot a kid on vacation. He was convinced the tourists were somewhere close by, as were the park service employees. His desire to protect vacationers was balanced by constant vigilance and drills, but he'd go hot the second he saw trouble.

When Mac was finally done, they walked around the police truck to see if he could discover what had happened. The service vehicle had been parked facing the right side of the road, so the driver's door was on the opposite side from the cars.

No one was in the SUV's front seat, so he stepped closer to look inside. The key was still in the ignition because all the instruments were on, as was the laptop affixed to the center console. The door chime wasn't going off as it should have been.

"Let's get this over with."

Buck scanned the bases of the pine trees to make sure there wasn't an officer wringing his hands like a villain, waiting for him to break the law. When satisfied with his sweep, he peered inside the truck to check for cameras or an officer lying in wait. He had the greatest respect for law enforcement, so he didn't think they were out to get him, but nothing felt right.

He turned to Mac and dropped the leash to the pavement. "Stay."

The dog sat on his butt.

"Good pup." He wished he'd brought one of the jerky treats.

Buck slid into the driver's seat and kicked off the emergency brake. There was just enough downslope to the road grade that the SUV rolled ahead toward the dirt shoulder. When he judged he had enough clearance to get his Peterbilt through, he stopped and re-did the parking brake.

"If there's a camera in here, I'm sorry for getting in. I only wanted to get by."

Buck had high hopes things would clear up by the time he got into Nevada, and he would look pretty stupid by going full-on Rambo in this forest if the rest of the world was still at condition green. Although the police vehicle would have to contain valuable survival supplies, he wasn't ready to take them. The world hadn't crossed that line, not yet anyway, but it was getting close.

When he stood up, Mac still hadn't moved. "I knew you wouldn't let me down. You're such a good dog. How'd I get so lucky to find you?" He bent down and detached the leash, confident there wasn't a threat.

But Mac almost hopped when he saw something kick up dust next to the trunk of one of the nearest trees. Buck saw Mac's reaction and quickly grabbed the dog.

"Holy shit," he whispered. "What'd you see?" He spoke breathlessly but also at the lowest volume. "We're exposed!"

Buck pulled Mac by the scruff until they both crouched behind the open door of the SUV. The dog seemed anxious to go running, but Buck wouldn't allow it. His own heart rate accelerated to hummingbird-speed as he considered his options. The world might be green, but this encounter had gone right to emergency red.

Let's get a look at you, shall we?

Buck leaned down and looked under the SUV, but he couldn't see into the woods beyond. He slowly rose, with just his eyes looking through the open door. He smirked at what he saw. "If you're not afraid, I'm not afraid," Buck whispered at the foraging rabbit. The presence of wildlife was the best indicator that people weren't around.

Buck raised his 10/22 and set it on the sill of the open window so he had a stable shooting platform.

"Stay," he said to his furry partner.

Buck lined up the iron sights of the small rifle. He needed a high-caliber long gun to do any serious hunting of big game, including the bipedal kind, but this was dinner and called for a lighter touch.

The rabbit moved slowly as it foraged. Buck waited patiently, twenty, thirty seconds. There was an ambush, after all, but Buck was the one who delivered.

He exhaled, froze, and pulled the trigger. The 10/22 hardly made a noise. At best, it was a loud snap. For a Marine sharpshooter, it was more than enough.

Buck stood up, relieved.

"All right, Mac, go get that rabbit." Mac bolted for the woods, reaching the fallen prey and barking viciously as he pranced back and forth. "Bring the rabbit!" Mac continued to bark and prance, nipping at the dead rabbit as he lunged in and jumped away.

Buck searched the area to see if the shot drew any visitors of the human variety, but silence and calm had returned to the park entrance.

Manhattan Bridge, between Manhattan and Brooklyn, NY

Garth and Sam swished around the back seat of the cab as the driver made a screeching left onto the bridge.

"Sir, um, Mr. Dawson, we'll be getting out here if you don't mind," Garth said as if this was any other cab trip. Yelling and screaming hadn't worked, so he went for calm and cool.

After passing Grand Central, the driver seemed to come off his suicidal high, but red lights were still optional for him. He refused to do more than look for cross-traffic as he sped through intersections all the way through midtown. And he adamantly refused to let the boys out each time they asked.

"Where the fuck is he taking us?" Garth grumbled to himself.

Dawson kept saying he was driving them to a battle. Garth's imagination ran wild with fight scenes from innumerable movies, but it settled on the idea they were being driven to a warehouse down at the marine terminal. There, several gangs would converge in one large, bloody to-the-death.

The eccentric cabbie gave them no other clues.

"At least we're getting closer to Staten Island, and home," Sam said to Garth in his own calm voice.

"We're not going to Staten," the driver replied while hitting the Manhattan Bridge at 80 miles an hour. He dodged the occasional slow-moving car, which sent Garth's heart into his throat each time.

"Sir, could you at least do the speed limit?" Garth asked to be sensible.

Cabbies always drove fast, but Dawson's foot was either pressed to the floor in acceleration or stomped on the brake to slow them down. He had no middle.

"We made it off the island, fellas. Get yourselves together. We're almost to the dinosaur!" Dawson guffawed, then spoke like he was announcing a movie trailer. "They won't know what hit them. Three knights in a yellow cab, armed to the teeth, go to meet their fate. Who will win? Dinosaurs created by aliens, or friends created by disaster?"

Garth watched helplessly as they zoomed past the first metal archway holding the suspension cables of the iconic bridge. The towers of lower Manhattan, the Brooklyn Bridge, and, in the distance, the Statue of Liberty, but he wasn't in the mood for sightseeing.

He whispered to Sam, "Remember, the second this thing stops, we make a run for it."

"No shit. I'd rather walk all the way home than spend another second with this guy."

As if on command, Dawson locked up the tires and skidded behind a box truck that took up both lanes while barely doing the speed limit. He laid on the horn, got the truck to move to the right, then pounced on the gas. When they sped past the other driver, the man looked down at Garth with anger.

"Help," Garth mouthed to the man. The message wasn't received, however, because the man raised his hand and showed off his middle finger.

It only took a few more seconds to reach the Brooklyn side. The ramp took them several blocks into the city, and Dawson exited the main road the first chance he got. The boys tumbled to the left during one maneuver, then they both slammed to the right moments later.

"Coming up on the dinosaur," Dawson said as he picked up his cigar. "Be ready. I have weapons in the trunk." He took a long drag and exhaled a cloud of stench like it was pure luxury.

"Yeah, no problem," Sam replied.

Garth looked at him like he was crazy, but his buddy shrugged. "What am I supposed to say?"

It wasn't clear if the cab belonged to Dawson, or if he stole it. The man was jacked in the head, yet the guy drove like he knew every corner, pothole, and stop sign, and he avoided too many fender-benders for it all to be luck.

They careened down a narrow one-way street. There were people out his window, Garth was sure of that, but they went by far too fast to get a good look at them. He didn't want to peek at the speedometer, but the blur of parked cars suggested sixty or seventy miles per hour. And they kept accelerating because Dawson's foot wouldn't come off the floor.

"We're toast, dude," Garth said with finality after shutting his eyes.

The motor screamed as they went even faster, but Dawson finally spoke up. "One more turn."

Garth and Sam crumpled against the front seats as Dawson hit the brakes. The tires dragged like a cat's claws on the urban street, and the car shuddered as it fought to slow down.

"Hang on!" Dawson shouted, sounding a little frightened himself.

The car drifted and slid into a right turn like a race car, but it screeched as metal rubbed metal. The sound only lasted an instant, and the rear side window above Sam exploded at the same time. Safety glass rained on the boys.

"Jesus," Sam shrieked.

Dawson didn't seem to care about the wreck. "There's the dinosaur!" He pounded the gas pedal like it was a cockroach that needed to be smashed.

"We just hit a car," Garth advised. "Shouldn't we pull over?"

The boys climbed back onto their seats. The acceleration made them slide into place and stay there. Ahead, Garth got a troubling first look at where they might be going.

A lot of it was blue water.

Dad, I'm sorry I got into this mess.

He tried to think of what his dad would do. Garth had no weapons, but if he did, now might be the time to risk using one. At worst, he'd knock out Dawson and they'd get into a fiery crash. The alternative was drowning...

The street ended in a huge pier with some green-turfed soccer fields on it. A giant black crane and the blackness of water threatened him from beyond the last pair of teams.

"Get ready for war!" Dawson exclaimed.

The insane driver crushed through a pair of picnic tables and tore through black netting designed to keep the soccer balls inside the designated fun zone. Dawson drove the cab onto the playing surface where games were already in progress. A few of the nearest kids jumped aside before the yellow arrow could get them.

"He's going to kill us," Garth said like he'd just figured it out.

Dawson's foot got heavy again.

NORAD, Cheyenne Mountain, Colorado

General Smith was inundated with information but little real data and no sound conclusions. He stood at a large table in the center of the action, with all the reports he could handle. As the afternoon wore on, it became clear the blue light preceded the mayhem around the world. Was the blue light the cause or was it a visual indicator of the underlying cause? The intelligence reporting was wild speculation at worst and empty at best.

"Lieutenant, read this to me aloud. I can't be the only one who thinks this is a joke."

The general handed over a printout with a few lines highlighted.

"Yes, sir. JSOC reports the 75th Ranger regiment has captured a platoon of Soviet T-62s deep inside Afghanistan. Their markings indicate the Russians are part of a larger formation of the 5th Guards Motor Rifle Division."

"Impressions?" The general liked to probe his people relentlessly. Lieutenant Darren was sharp.

"5th Guards hasn't been around since the late 80s. We studied their missions inside Afghanistan during their war. Their unit history helped with some of our mission planning when we went in."

The general nodded, satisfied with the answer. "So, what do you make of this report? Is Special Operations Command smoking crack?" Technically, he didn't have responsibility for operations in Afghanistan. His mission was to keep watch on the North American airspace, but he'd concluded the blue light originated inside his area of operations before it circled the world, so everything was now on his professional radar.

Lt. Darren was ready with more. "Could be militants dressed as Soviets, perhaps to draw in Russian involvement. The Soviets did leave behind some of their tanks when they left. I don't know why militants would bother, though. A-10s could kill those tanks almost without leaving their dugouts."

The general tapped his chin. "Agreed. Using those tanks as a ruse seems possible but highly unlikely. What are we missing?"

That wasn't even the strangest report. Somehow, in the last several hours, the lost Malaysian MH370 flight came in for a landing in Thailand, an entire supertanker dropped off radar in the Straits of Hormuz and showed up minutes later in the Red Sea, and the Indian government sent notice that someone plowed over the Taj Mahal. All of it seemed impossible.

That was the reason he had his staff read some of it out loud.

His biggest fear was one he wouldn't dare express in front of his subordinates. As a four-star general, that meant everyone. He wasn't allowed to speculate except within the confines of his own mind.

This weird shit could be explained if it was done by aliens.

"Sir!" Lt. Darren caught his attention again.

He blinked a few times to get back into the moment.

"Go ahead."

"I got the intel you wanted back from the 50th." Lt. Darren swung his laptop on the table and clicked his secure email. A globe appeared on his screen with the same white halo over North America as the general had been shown before.

"Here, now it compresses down to its smallest point. They tell me this still may not be accurate down to more than a thousand meters, but it's what we have."

General Smith leaned in to finally see the root cause of his day's problems.

"This is the scene of the crime?" he asked the junior officer. "That's the SNAKE lab, isn't it?" It became clear he could cross UFO off his list.

"That's what it shows on the map, yes."

"What are the odds? It isn't even that far away."

The small circle represented an object powerful enough to send a ring of energy around the entire planet. To an untrained observer, the obscure patch of hills southwest of Denver metro was the last place anyone would look for such a source. There was one lonely road to that location, and a few buildings standing among the foothills.

The energy was underground.

Lt. Darren knew what came next. "We can have a security team dispatched from Peterson Air Force Base and be there inside of an hour."

"Do it!" the general snapped. "Tell NorthCom we're sending everything we can, just in case there is a terrorist component we're not seeing from here."

CHAPTER 27

Search for Nuclear, Astrophysical, and Kronometric Extremes (SNAKE). Red Mesa, Colorado

Faith spent an hour locked in her office, ignoring all calls. Dr. Perkins' papers spilled across her desk, and she'd been poking pins into a laminated world map on the wall corresponding to each news item. She had intended to use pushpins to mark the home cities of the scientists who stopped in, as an ice breaker, but she'd usurped its purpose based on her compelling need to get to the bottom of the outage.

There were pins all over North America, but fewer overseas. It made sense, since American networks had to cover news for their home audiences. She was certain there were overseas events that had not seen their way onto the American news.

She tapped her fingernails near the red pin over New York City. "This tells me nothing."

Donald linked three dots using a straight line, so she used a marker and ruler to trace a path along the same three points. Denver. Chicago. New York City.

She tried drawing similar lines through other points on the map, but the lines weren't straight. On a whim, she tried to link the pin in New York to one in Europe, but that didn't line up either.

Maybe it's the map projection?

If she had a globe, the lines would be easier to draw around the curvature of the planet, but she didn't have one. She would make do as scientists had done through the ages and compensate with her mind.

"Maybe it goes the other way?" she said as she traced the line from New York back through Denver and over to a blue pin on Yosemite Park, California. The line wasn't exact, but it was close enough, given the scale of the map.

"What happened in Yosemite?" She scanned Donald's spreadsheet and found a weird news item concerning an unexplained disappearance of several park visitors as well as staff. And beyond that...

"Oh, shit." She continued the line to San Francisco, where a green pin waited for her. "What happened there?"

She checked the list.

"The north half of the Golden Gate Bridge had all its paint stripped off down to bare metal. Hmm. Weird one, but why is that news?"

Faith stepped back from the map to see what she'd drawn. It was a line from the West Coast to the East Coast, linking five datapoints. The connection was right in front of her.

"Of course!"

Faith scrambled to her desktop computer and pulled up a website with national news. She went to the story on the Golden Gate.

"Blah blah blah, paint stripped. Blue light earlier in the day. Came from the east."

She clicked out of that and searched for the story of the fallen plane in New York.

"Authorities are at a loss for how it happened." She scanned several paragraphs looking for her clue. "Blue light came from the west."

"Am I really this dense? The source is somewhere between the two."

Faith looked over her shoulder to the world map.

No! Her shoulders slumped as she dug further.

She checked the news reports for the Chicago Skylab wreck and the Yosemite Park incident. Then she hunted for more clues in other locations on her list. A grain silo collapse in North Dakota. A fishing boat tossed on a beach in Belize.

Each time the blue light came from a different direction.

At that point, it was rudimentary geometry. She drew arrows from each news item denoting the direction where the blue light originated. Four of them pointed to a middle location. It was the one place in the world she wasn't searching for the cause of the blue beam of energy.

SNAKE.

"Holy shit," she lamented, rubbing at the throbbing pain that had appeared in her temples. "This is unbelievable."

Faith was shaken to the core. The Izanagi test wasn't shut down by the loss of power from Denver. She'd been looking at it from the wrong direction. The power was shut down by an energy surge from inside SNAKE.

She stood up to look at her pushpins.

Her voice wavered while gently touching pin after pin across the United States, the timestamps from each event emblazoned in her mind. "We caused this?"

Was it even possible? They dealt with energy, yes, but not in dangerous amounts that could spontaneously travel around the entire planet and do the kinds of things reported in the news.

Unless there was more to the Izanagi Project than she was led to believe.

Her breathing sped up as her excitement rose. "Who do I tell first?"

She picked up her desk phone.

Donald was number one on her list, but he wouldn't answer.

"I've got to tell the world." Faith sat for a second, then snapped her fingers at how it was all so obvious. "The press conference!"

It came together in her mind. First, she'd organize her data and provide a bulletproof digital presentation rather than her current scratchpad scribbles. Then, she'd go to the press conference and announce the big news to everyone else on the planet.

Her rationale was simple: if she told the world, it would help everyone stay calm and not get rattled by the unusual occurrences. The scientists of the world could work cooperatively to find a solution to fix it...

But people had died, and it was her fault, or had they died for some other reason? She pushed that thought away.

Faith was bursting to tell someone right that moment, so she decided to send a text to her sister. It couldn't hurt to warn her.

Sis, be on the lookout for weird events.

Yosemite National Park, CA

As a professional driver, Buck had little time to stop and sight-see during his deliveries, but over the years, he'd seen a lot of scenic destinations. His notebook was filled with hundreds of places he intended to visit later with Garth. The Grand Canyon. Badlands. Every beach in Florida.

Despite the roadblock and missing people, Yosemite was on his list for a future trip. Until then, he only had one mission. He wasn't going to stop until he made it home to his son.

"Maybe we'll come back as a family," he said to his dog.

Miles later, he almost went back on that resolution.

"Hey, pup. Check that out." He pointed to get Mac's attention. "That's Half Dome. Most famous rock in Yosemite."

The rock was as big as a mountain, but severed in half, like a baseball cut down the middle. From the lookout point, the dome was in profile, so the front appeared as a thousand-foot sheer wall, while the back side appeared rounded. The magnificent structure was five miles away but dominated the valley before him.

Buck figured there should have been busloads of tourists at the oversized parking lot next to the road, but there was only one vehicle there.

He shook his head. "Is the park closed for maintenance? Where'd all the tourists go?"

An ancient black Ford Model T sat by itself in the lot. The car looked like it had been refurbished and shined up. A man and woman, both dressed in black formalwear, stood next to their ride as they admired Half Dome.

Thank god. At least there's someone here.

He imagined they were getting married, as a viable explanation. Maybe waiting for the preacher to show up. What better place to tie the knot than before such a backdrop? He didn't stop the truck to ask what they were really doing.

"Good luck, people," he said, feeling better that he wasn't alone anymore. "I've got miles to make up."

Buck didn't look back for the next thirty miles. He hit nearly ten thousand feet going over Tioga Pass and then rode the Jakes down the other side. There were plenty of opportunities to leave more messages for Garth. The boy still didn't answer his phone, but it did help pass the time. As he approached the end of the road, the trees got smaller, the environment became desolate and rocky, and finally, the Sierra Nevada Mountains were behind him.

It was dinnertime when he finally saw the mirage-like surface of Mono Lake. Surrounded by squat hills and devoid of tree cover, it looked like sleeping giants napping at a swimming hole. More importantly, it was the gateway to Nevada.

"That was fun," he said tiredly to Mac.

The golden looked up at him from the front seat, but instantly put his head back down in a can't-be-bothered way.

"Fine, don't break out the champagne, but I'm glad to be back in civilization. That was a hundred miles of ghosts, if you ask me."

Big Mac blinked without any concern for Buck's ramblings.

He read the beat-down welcome sign. "Mono Lake. Population 22. This is a two-gear town, don't you think?" He laughed at his joke. The place was so small, it only took until second gear to get through it.

A few single-wide trailer homes made for bleak accommodations. They looked like they came in on the wind because they were randomly spaced in weedy plots and covered with varying layers of brown dust. A half-lit Subway logo announced the town's sole dining establishment, and a neon sign for 'motel and gas' was the other big draw.

"Oh yeah! Jackpot!" Buck used his steering wheel to straighten himself on his seat. "Look at the price of gas! Under two bucks."

Feeling it necessary to spread the joy, he reached into his secret stash of jerky treats above the windshield and handed one to Mac, who promptly scarfed it down.

The tension of the day evaporated with a pop when he realized how much money he would save. Fueling in Modesto cost him over four dollars a gallon. His wallet would barely notice him topping off the Peterbilt in the great metropolis of Mono Lake.

"We're staying here tonight."

Brooklyn Park Pier 5, New York

Dawson growled as he drove the boys across the three soccer fields.

"Don't kill us, dude!" Sam yelled.

They were on the last field when Dawson crushed the brakes.

"We'll never make it!" Garth exclaimed.

When they approached the far edge of the last field, the mad driver jammed the wheel and the cab spun sideways on the field's surface. The boys crashed into the front seat again. Garth waited for the freefall, but the car came to a stop while it was still upright and on four wheels.

His head rang from being tossed around, and his heart beat faster than it was ever designed to handle, but he kept his wits.

"Get out!" he screamed to Sam.

Each boy fell out his own door. Garth was on the passenger side, so when the door opened, he almost tumbled over the edge of the pier and into the fish-stench water.

"Shitballs!"

He hopped to his feet, brushed off the bits of turf from his knees, and ran behind the car to meet Sam. Garth's legs wobbled, and he tripped on the shredded turf as he came around back, but he caught himself on the bumper. The hard-braking cab driver had managed to tear up the turf in one long furrow and bunches of it were wedged underneath the vehicle like an old rug.

Soccer players and concerned parents ran for the exit, leaving Garth and Sam alone with the cab driver.

Dawson spoke from the front seat as if they were all in on the plan. "There it is! I had to get us close before stopping the car or it would have had time to run. Get ready to attack!"

Sam crawled behind the trunk.

"Are you all right?" Garth asked.

"No. I think I just shit my pants."

Garth snickered. "You did not."

"It's not funny, dude. I think I really did."

"We've got to get out of here," Garth replied without salting his friend's hurt pride any further. "This guy has lost it."

Dawson popped the trunk from inside and walked around to the back. He chewed on his nasty cigar as he reached into the dark space. Garth had it in his mind to run away until the man pulled out a revolver.

"I stole this cab and got these weapons together to stop this invasion. Now you'll see. This is how you kill a fucking *Tyrannosaurus Rex*."

"Hold on a sec," Sam whined.

Garth put up his hands. "We're cool."

Dawson carelessly flopped the gun around for a moment, giving Garth more of a scare, but then the gunslinger aimed it at the nearby construction crane.

The black crane was affixed to a floating barge parked against the pier. The metal machine was probably seventy-five feet and bent near the top, so it formed a shallow, sideways V. If Garth squinted and didn't think about it—and was crazy—he might imagine it was a dinosaur standing tall.

When the gun went off, Garth put his hands over his ears, but the concussion still rattled his brain. The acrid smell of each blast blew right in his face as if to mock his helplessness.

The insane cab driver cranked out six shots in quick succession, each one aimed at the big crane. Garth expected little explosions for ricochets, like you see in the movies, but his dad often reminded him real life wasn't like Hollywood, especially when it came to guns. He figured Dawson missed completely, and the bullets went across the bay to the tall buildings in the financial district.

Dawson dry-fired a few times. "Fuck! Empty!"

He cocked his arm back and threw the gun in a high arc. It soared for a couple of seconds and crashed through the window of the operator's compartment at the base of the crane's arm.

"No fucking way," Sam said with awe.

Dawson pulled out his cigar and cheered. "Score one for the good guys!" He leaned inside his trunk, puffing hard on the stogey. "Now we go hand-to-hand, boys. I've got hammers, shovels, and a guitar. Grab something to fight with. Let's go!"

The boys watched as Dawson tossed off his glasses, picked up a hammer, and charged the barge. He jumped off the pier and across the five-foot gap between the boat and its mooring. The guy rolled once on the deck like a superhero, ignored when his newsboy hat flipped off, then got up and charged the crane as he promised.

Garth and Sam looked at the odd weapons in the trunk, then at each other.

"Are you thinking what I'm thinking?" Sam asked.

"If you say anything besides getting in this cab and driving away, I'm going to leave you here with this fruitcake." He slammed the trunk lid.

"You read my mind," his buddy replied.

Garth ran to the open door and climbed into the driver's seat. Dawson had left the keys inside.

"Hey!" the cabbie yelled. "Where are you guys?"

Garth spoke, but there was no way for Dawson to hear him over the revving engine. "You stole the cab, so we're stealing it back."

"Just go," Sam advised.

"Nothing can stop us now," Garth said excitedly. "We're going home."

CHAPTER 28

Wollemi National Park, New South Wales, Australia

Destiny expected the two outback men to see they were boxed in by the fire and immediately get to work thinking of a way to escape it, so when they backed the truck down the road and hopped out, she followed with grim determination. Finally, they were doing what needed to be done to survive.

They went right to the loaded bed and tossed out some of the firewood, giving her confidence they had a plan, but when Stephen pulled out a pillow-sized silver bag of wine and saluted her with it, she became confused.

"What are you doing?" she wondered aloud. Smoke swirled around her and over the creek, like a stage prop from a film. The smell of the fire wafted in, too, as if it needed to remind her of the danger. Whatever the guys had in mind for the approaching menace, their plan should not have included alcohol.

The driver patted his prize. "We're gonna tackle this goon bag and be done with it."

"You-you're joking?" she stammered. Destiny looked at the men, the bag of wine, and then turned to the hill behind her. It was still clear of fire...

I don't owe them anything, she thought.

She looked at the remaining safe stretch of road and the flowing creek alongside it, working out how much time was left before the fire consumed everything.

"You are welcome to join us," Christian said wistfully. "You were a good sport sitting in that dog box with us."

"Yeah, you're a legend, miss," Stephen added as he opened the wine and took a swig from the spigot.

"Sure," she said as if they were distractions to her thought process. She couldn't believe two grown men were behaving this way, but she also didn't understand why she wasn't already running to safety.

"I'm going that way." She pointed up the steep hill. "We can all make it, I'm sure." It wasn't any worse than the escarpment she'd climbed earlier in the day. If they took it slow, she figured anyone could make it to the top.

Both men looked up the ridge and stroked their beards like that was a requirement for thought, but then they turned back to the liquor.

Christian took the bag. "I don't want to drink and walk. Might spill me drink." He faced Stephen before taking a long swig. "Let's get blind, mate. Cheers." He saluted his brother with the bag.

She glanced longingly up the hill once more, but then walked around the truck to stand by the bag of wine. "Damn you guys. My head hurts like hell. I think only one of my lungs is working. And you two are piss farting around, instead of trying to live. But fuck all, I can't just walk away and leave you here. I left my mates last night, and that led to disaster. I'm not leaving you as well."

"We do appreciate it, but look at us," Christian replied. "We never missed a meal in our lives. We'd make it ten yards onto that hill and pass out dead. That's why I was so keen to drive through this fire. It's the only way we'd have made it."

She became agitated. "You've got to try to hike it."

Christian handed the bag to Stephen.

Destiny looked for a way out. The truck couldn't go through the fire on the road, and it wasn't stout enough to go in the creek, and nothing on earth could drive up the remaining safe hillside.

The creek.

"I'm not leaving you guys," she said to reassure herself, "but I think I know how to get us all out of here. You've got to follow me right this second."

She trotted over to the creek and waded in until it was up to her hips. The cold water felt refreshing and comforting in the face of so much fire.

The two men watched her but didn't move.

"Come into the water," she said slowly to get them to understand. It was like coaxing a wounded animal.

The fire crackled in the trees on the far shore. The heat from the blaze beat on her back like the sun at the height of summer. There was no margin of error.

She waved frantically to get them to come in, but still they didn't move.

"We can't swim," Stephen finally admitted.

"I'm standing," she deadpanned. "It doesn't get deeper than this. We're going to get soaked as protection from the flames and then we'll float down this creek until we clear the fire."

All of them turned toward the fallen tree a hundred meters downstream. Most of the branches on the blocked road were aflame, but some were above the water. They would have to duck under the hotspots as they went.

To show them her plan, she dipped into the water and paddled with the current.

"Like this! Come on, what have you got to lose?"

Stephen took a few tentative steps. "Can we bring our wine?"

"Bring whatever you want," she muttered. "Yes!" she said louder.

The two giants walked with surprising haste to the edge of the rocky creek and then waded in. They dropped in behind her and got as low as possible. Soon, the guys motored forward in their own clumsy ways.

"Stick with me, boys. We're going to make it out of here. I promise."

Pole Line Motel and Gas Station, Mono Lake, CA

Buck sat inside his cab running the numbers on the miles he'd driven. He used that as a guide for how many gallons of diesel the Peterbilt had burned. Strictly speaking, it wasn't necessary, because he was going to top off the tank, but he liked to record every bit of data when he was hauling freight.

It also made him feel normal again.

"Two hundred and sixty divided by six miles per gallon? You got the answer, dog?" Buck glared at Big Mac like he expected a reply from his favorite student. "No? I'll tell you." He did some quick division. "Forty-three gallons, but we'll add another twenty to cover all the idling and speeding we did."

The big blocky numbers under the motel/gas sign said the price was $1.40 per gallon for diesel. He didn't need to write it down. "Even with all the extra we need, that's still less than a hundred bucks for sixty gallons of gas here. In California!"

It was a big payoff after a day of mayhem.

Mac sat inside and pawed at the driver's side window as Buck went through his fueling routine. He pulled out his Comdata credit card but halted in surprise to see that the pump didn't have a credit card reader.

"The readers must not have made it all the way out to bumfuck, California," he mumbled.

He wasn't going to complain, however, since he was saving a bucket of coins compared to buying it in the big city.

"Be back in a moment!" he shouted up to Mac.

There were only two pumps at the mom and pop station, the other unoccupied. A young man and woman smoked cigarettes while they leaned on a blue car parked at the little motel. Their bad habits assured him he was no longer alone.

Buck shuffled into the building to pay the cashier for his gas but found only one register for both the motel and the service station. One side of the room displayed a few sundries for motorists such as oil, snow scrapers, and soda pop, while the motel side had landscape oil paintings and little tourist knickknacks. A big window at the back of the room framed Mono Lake.

He went to the cooler of drinks, ever on the search for his Dr. Schnee. There were fifty cans of energy drinks, but no soda. He assumed truckers must have been the main clientele of the store.

An older gentleman in a sweaty white T-shirt and blue jeans stood behind the counter. "Paying for gas?"

Buck made his way to the register.

"Yes, sir. Give me a hundred on pump one." Buck handed him a hundred-dollar bill. He always carried a few with him in his wallet but kept five more in his hidey hole inside the sleeper. If he was ever pulled over and searched, he didn't know how he would explain that the only things he kept hidden in there were two guns, lots of ammo, and hundred-dollar bills.

The motel manager took the bill and held it up to the light. "Looks kinda funny. I've never seen one like this before."

Buck thought nothing of it. "Yeah, the government likes to play with our money. Is there a problem?"

The man took a few more seconds to examine the bill, then stuck it under his drawer. "Nope. You're good on pump one."

A minute later, he had the nozzle in the tank. Mac looked down on him from the driver's seat.

"We'll do better tomorrow, little buddy. We'll sleep here tonight and then get up to I-80 and burn this cheap gas away." He absently kicked the tires and did a visual inspection of the fifth wheel and pigtail connectors between the tractor and trailer. It was something he'd done a thousand times while the tank filled up.

He jumped a little when his phone vibrated in his pocket.

"Shit!"

He yanked it out and looked at the text message. "It's from Garth!"

It was short and sweet. "Hi dad. Home safe. Can you talk?"

He scrambled to dial the phone.

Please pick up this time.

Three Mile Island Nuclear Generating Station, Pennsylvania

Carl's team took ninety minutes to prepare the radio-controlled tortoise. After the lessons of other failed containment scenarios in the nuclear power industry, his own team had failed to keep the machine fully charged. *What a nut-punch.*

He thought he was due to have a heart attack for the time he lost, but Carl finally had the tortoise operating inside the airlock of the containment building. The small robot carried a wide array of sensors and crawled on two wide tracks, making it the ideal reconnaissance vehicle for investigating dangerous environments, such as the outside of a nuclear reactor.

"Seal the outer door," he advised what was left of his team. He'd already initiated a SCRAM shutdown, which was basically turning off the reactor and telling his non-essential people to scram. The nuclear fuel didn't just turn off, however; there was a long period where radioactive decay continued but at a much lower level. He needed to ensure that cooldown could be done safely.

The outer part of the airlock wheeled shut, leaving the mechanical turtle caught between the two cement vault doors.

"Now, open the inner one," Carl ordered.

"Roger," Ken replied. He continued after a short pause. "Door is open, sir. Radiation has flooded the airlock."

"What level are you getting?" Carl inquired evenly.

"It's off the scale," Ken replied with a wobble in his voice.

"Stay focused. We've already initiated the shutdown. Let's see what's happening in there to make sure it doesn't get any worse. Maybe we can save some lives, right?"

Ken stood next to his workstation as if he was going to leave, but then he rubbed his bald head with both hands, like he was forcing his brain to think. After a few seconds of consideration, he sat back down.

"Good," Carl went on. "Moving the tortoise inside."

A screen on the wall broadcast what the black and white camera recorded. The vehicle went inside the round containment chamber, which was about a hundred feet across and one-fifty high. The space was packed with piping, wires, and other equipment, giving it a cramped appearance. The fuel rods were under a heavy metal grating on the floor, but the camera zeroed in on a huge object that did not belong anywhere close to the reactor.

"Sir, are you seeing this?" Ken asked.

Carl nodded but didn't take his eyes from the old locomotive wedged inside the containment area. The tortoise sent an image that had to be a mistake. A distorted view. A flaw caused by the high radiation. He tried to make sense of it, but failed.

If they were going to die because of a meltdown, they were going to die. But the cause of this one was going to confuse the hell out of everyone if he didn't report it scientifically. He wanted to avoid sounding panicked or mad with the first signs of radiation sickness.

I'm writing my own epitaph, he reflected.

Carl spoke into a mic at his terminal while he watched the robot recording. "Despite the impossibility of what we're seeing, it appears as if the tortoise is providing one-hundred percent clear footage at this time. I can see the interior of the containment chamber, and I'm able to identify the metal floor on top of the pressurized unit." He waved to his co-worker. "And I'm including Ken Elfmann in this recording. Say hi, Ken. Show them your bald head."

"Hello," Ken replied. He waved glumly to the interior camera that was part of the recording apparatus throughout the plant.

"We are both observing the camera and we can both confirm there is an object lodged inside the containment chamber, and it appears to be big enough to have affected the pumps at the very least, and maybe the core itself."

He spoke to the other man. "Can you tell the recording what it is we're looking at inside the sealed concrete bunker of Unit 1 at Three Mile Island Generating Station?"

"Yes, sir. It appears to be a huge diesel locomotive. It is sticking straight up out of the floor as if it got buried there. I can easily identify Union Pacific on the side, and the engine itself is labeled as *Valkyrie*."

"Thank you, Ken. I confirm his observation. For those watching this later, we both have our full faculties. The film will prove what we are now seeing. By some miracle of time and space, a giant train engine has appeared in my reactor room. There's no telling what damage is down there, and for the record, I have no idea how it got there."

All at once, the video jerked, and a tremor shook the control room. The big wall clock fell with a crash. When the image came back, the diesel monster fell a few feet more through the containment floor. He imagined the weight crushing the pressurized system, which would blow coolant water all over the insides of the room, turning it to steam. That would expose the fuel rods—

"Radiation spike!" Ken screamed. He ran for the door and didn't look back. The few other employees who'd braved it out took that as their cue to follow him.

"Well, fuck." Carl sat back in his chair and did his best to maintain professionalism. As the old saying went—if he ran, he'd only die tired. There was no escaping what was coming out of that busted core: radiation-laced steam.

He leaned up to the microphone.

"I'll report this train wreck to the bitter end." He thought about it for a second, realizing he'd told an accidental joke. "May God have mercy on all our souls."

CHAPTER 29

Search for Nuclear, Astrophysical, and Kronometric Extremes (SNAKE). Red Mesa, Colorado

Faith's whole crazy day led up to her press conference. She'd scheduled it for 7:00 that night figuring only Benny from the *Denver Post* would show up. However, the word went out in the Front Range community, and several TV stations sent film crews with big-name reporters to stand in front of the cameras.

She looked out on the crowd from her place at the lectern, a little nervous but also excited. She had slides and videos lined up for after her introduction. "Ladies and gentlemen, thank you for coming this evening. I don't want to keep you long, so I'll get right to the facts."

The auditorium was another piece of the sprawling underground campus. It was designed to hold 2,000 people, but most of the seats were empty. About two hundred scientists and admin staff mixed in with the reporters.

"This place, as most of you know, is called Search for Nuclear, Astrophysical, and Kronometric Extremes, or as we lovingly call it, SNAKE. Put in simple terms, the name means we delve into the nature of reality. We hope to discover the true form of dark matter, and we expect to know more about the context of time itself."

After the opening, she scanned the crowd to make sure they were paying attention. It pleased her to see everyone's faces on her, not their phones.

"This facility was finished last year, having been built by a consortium of private enterprises in cooperation with the University of Colorado. It currently houses eight hundred and fifty-five personnel, but once all the offices and labs are in operation, it can hold three thousand."

She looked down on her staff. They were the people she'd been working with to solve the mystery of the shutdown. Dr. Stafford and the computing team sat on the left. Dr. Chandrasekhar and the physics group sat near the middle. A cluster of people in the back represented the facilities people. All flavors of engineers sat to the right. Mindy and the rest of the administrative group sat up front. She thought of them as five galaxies filled with stars.

Even Donald had made it, though he was a lone star in the last row.

"The science and materials community has come together at the SNAKE campus to push technology beyond limits thought impossible just three years ago. The Rocky Mountain Hadron Collider is the perfect synthesis of magnets, cryogenics, vacuum, and superconductors to explore the raw power of the universe. To house it, we've used the newest tools in engineering to burrow out a sixty-two-mile loop under the foothills and hogback of the greater Denver region."

It was boilerplate press material, but she'd done enough of these talks to know to always include background data. She looked at it as a way to build up to the main point of the night, which was going to be her revelation that SNAKE might have caused the world-wide blast of blue light. At least, that was the plan when she started talking.

Her mouth spoke the words on the printed page in front of her, but her brain went elsewhere. It focused on something Bob used against her as a joke, or an insult, during one of their heated exchanges earlier in the day.

Hell, maybe we caused all the world's problems. That would be the ultimate roundhouse kick to SNAKE's beanbags.

Bob jokingly blamed SNAKE and her leadership for the blue light. She was convinced he didn't know how right he was, but she couldn't let go of how it made her feel. To be described as the cause of the whole world's problems disturbed her on a fundamental level. They were doing science for the good of humanity, not to cause it harm.

That was why Bob made the biting implication in the first place. He knew even a harmless joke about it would drive her crazy. She was disappointed in herself for still thinking about it, even there on the stage, but the more she mulled over his words, the more it morphed into a dark presence in her thinking.

The press people spread out in front of her wouldn't care about nuance. She knew from hard experience that they would turn on her faster than a poked bear if they found out she was personally responsible. Had Bob's insult become a cautionary tale for her?

"One of our first experiments on the main supercollider was done in conjunction with Azurasia Heavy Industries." Her eyes surfed the crowd in search of Mr. Shinano, but he wasn't there. "Unfortunately, AHI was on the system when the worldwide blue light shut it down prematurely."

If she revealed to the world that SNAKE was responsible for the mysterious interference, would it really help solve the mysteries elsewhere in the world? Hours ago, she would have said yes. Now? It might slow the research down.

"The reason we brought you here tonight was to explain what we know about that shutdown..."

You can't tell them the truth. Not yet. Of all the messed-up things, Bob was right.

Her pause dragged on because she wasn't sure what to say next.

Don't be a hero after the battle is won. It was something her grandpa used to say. The first battle was figuring out SNAKE was responsible, but she didn't have to go any further and get the world involved. That would bring interference, and inevitable slowdowns. It was possible she'd be fired, even if she was hailed for revealing the truth. None of it would help her SNAKE team solve the mystery of the energy burst, and time could be a factor.

"We don't know what shut it down," she said in a businesslike voice.

"STOP THIS RIGHT NOW!" a man shouted from the back of the room.

Men in black business suits filed in through the rear doors and went down the side aisles. A handful of military men in blueish-camo uniforms came in through the middle door at the back and stood by their leader, probably a general—the man who shouted at her.

The gaggle of press stood up and looked at the cause of the disturbance. Cameras slewed to take in the interruption.

The military official continued talking. "You will stop this press conference and remain seated. Elements of the United States Air Force and agents from the Federal Bureau of Investigation are here to maintain security within SNAKE while we ascertain the validity of a possible terrorist threat."

Oh, shit.

She stood aside from the lectern and watched as the official came down the middle aisle and hopped up onto the stage with her.

He spoke quietly. "Ma'am. I'm General Smith from North American Aerospace Defense Command. Is there somewhere we can talk?"

The blood in her veins ran cold as she imagined all the trouble she was in. Not only was he a real general, as she guessed, but he had brought the entirety of the government with him. Whether true or not, that was all she could see.

"Yes," she croaked. Faith led him to a private reception area. He and some of his men followed her in. A female guard shut the door and stood next to it. The soldiers weren't toting rifles, but all of them had pistols hanging from their belts, even the general.

"Is my team in any danger?" she asked once everyone was inside.

General Smith's face was grim. "You are Faith Sinclair?"

"Yes, sir," she answered dutifully.

"Ms. Sinclair, did you tell anyone outside of this facility SNAKE was responsible for the worldwide energy pulse?"

It took her by surprise. "You mean the blue light?"

"Is that what you call it?" he asked. "Is that a scientific name?"

"No," she admitted, still off her guard. "It is what the news calls it."

He spoke like it was the most important meeting of his career. "We've tracked the blue light back to this facility and got here as quickly as we could. It is critical you tell us: Have you revealed the truth to anyone on the outside?"

She shook her head, not really thinking of the implications. "There isn't even anyone inside the lab who knows. I just found out a little while ago we were responsible. I had slides..."

General Smith appeared taken aback. He looked at his watch. "It has been almost eight hours since the event. No one in here knows you were the ones who blasted the world with...whatever it was?"

"No. We knew about the blue light right away, but it didn't happen here. We kept working on the assumption the light blew our link with the Denver power grid. It was what happened, but not in the order we first thought."

The general rubbed his chin as if considering a complicated chess move.

"Dr. Sinclair, this might be the most crucial action you ever make as a scientist. I'm asking you NOT to tell the world SNAKE is responsible for the blue light."

She couldn't contain her surprise, and she had a million questions, not the least of which was how he discovered her lab was the source, but he held up a hand to stop her from voicing those thoughts.

"Things are worse than you can imagine out there. Infrastructure has been knocked out. People are missing. Time itself has shifted certain, uh, assets of the U.S. military."

Time? That grabbed her attention.

"If the world finds out all their problems started at this laboratory, where do you think they'll go to exact a little revenge?"

"Here?" she responded.

"Here," he repeated with authority. "So, you see why I stopped your briefing?" The general stood ramrod straight. "Let me ask you again. Is there anyone you've told outside this facility?"

There is one person.

Sydney, New South Wales, Australia

It took Destiny and the two men ten minutes to float down the creek to safety. They did have to duck under a few fallen trees, but she kept the guys floating through the tight spots until they cleared the Wollemi Park fire and reached the blacktop.

Stephen even managed to salvage his bag of wine. While they sat next to the road and caught their breath, he offered her a drink. "Want to celebrate?"

"No," she admitted. "I just want to find out what happened to my team."

Stephen ran his fingers through his dirty beard and turned serious. "Miss. I have a confession to make."

"You aren't married, are you?" She figured he was going to try hitting on her. It was flattering, but not in a million years would it happen.

Stephen chuckled. "I wish that's all it was. We really are married. No, the thing is...me and me brother, here...we started your big fire." He pointed to the coal-black smoke behind them.

"I don't know what to say."

"Yeah, it's kind of a thing with us. We drive into the forest, you know, where no one will ever find us, then we drink a bunch of wine while we cut our limit on wood. We're usually so knackered afterward, we lay down and sleep it off. It was cold last night, so we burned some of the wood to keep warm, but..." He gritted his teeth. "It got away from us. We woke up to a rager."

None of it surprised her. She could almost sympathize. "I had the same rude awakening. That, plus the blue light."

"We're real sorry, miss," Christian added.

"It's all water under the burning fire," she joked.

Over the next several hours, she said good-bye to her two rescuers, hitched a ride to Sydney, and made it into her flat.

Before she did anything else, she used her landline to dial the Sydney Harbor Foundation and confirm her team was still alive.

The over-the-phone reunion lasted several minutes as numerous colleagues hopped on the line to say they were sorry for leaving her. They all had the same excuse: they thought she died when she fell into the fire. They attempted to fly the drone to confirm her status, but they lost contact with it as it got close to her prone body. The team's leader said there was no choice but to abandon her. The fire was rushing to cut off the entire valley and all their lives were in danger.

Destiny was too tired to be upset. She hung up the phone and promised to kick some asses another time.

"I'm alive. That's what matters. And I saved two lives doing it." It buoyed her spirits to know she helped the two men, but her emotions cratered again when she saw herself in the mirror.

"My god, who are you?" she asked the reflection. Her dip in the water had done a fair job of cleaning her shirt and shorts, but her face was smudged with soot as sure as if she worked in a coal mine.

She was keen to peel out of her clothes and take a nice, long shower, so she tossed her phone on the bed to get undressed. It landed face-side up and a message appeared on the lock screen.

"What the hell?" The text had come in a couple of hours ago but must not have triggered a notification. It was from her sister.

"Dez, please listen. I have terrible news. Have you seen the blue light? I'm sure you've heard of it. Well, it came from here. From SNAKE! I know. It's crazy. I've read the news. They say people and things appear to come back from the past. Planes are falling from the sky. Storms. Earthquakes. Everything in the news today was caused by us. I'm sure of it. Please. Please. Please. Stay in your flat. Stay safe. I'm going to make an announcement in two hours to help the world understand what we did. I love you, sis. Talk soon."

Her body was spent. The shower suddenly didn't seem important. She wanted to fall over in bed and go to sleep. Wake up tomorrow and have her life back.

Instead, she dialed her sister. She did the math in her head. It was one in the afternoon Sydney time, so it was eight in the evening in Denver. It didn't matter, though. She'd wake up her sister even if it was the middle of the night there.

A man answered. "Hello?"

She tensed up. Something was wrong.

"Is Dr. Sinclair there. I...uh, have an exciting offer for her concerning firewood." She bit her knuckles to keep from saying anything more. Her time with the wood hoarders had rubbed off on her.

The man was not amused. "Who is this?"

She hung up without saying another word.

The phone rang immediately. It was Faith's number, but she tossed the device on the bed.

"This is all wrong. The whole day has been wrong." Faith's message spooked her. She backed from the bed like the phone was going to jump up and make her answer.

"People and things from the past?" Stephen and Christian acted like throwbacks, with their old Commodore, complete with tape deck. But they weren't *from* the past. They were just backward.

The Tasmanian tiger.

Her breath caught as she put that piece into the puzzle.

The phone rang again.

Destiny flung around to put her back to the person trying to contact her. She required some time to think of how it all fit together. Standing near the window, she grabbed one of the drapes and made like she was going to close it, but she stopped immediately when something didn't look right.

"Drop me on my ass and call me Humpty."

Her apartment came with a wonderful view of the Sydney Harbor. But it wasn't the view she had grown accustomed to.

The familiar white half-moons of the iconic opera house were gone. The wall of the foundation below it was gone as well. The dock attached to it disappeared, too. In fact, the entire complex had been returned to a natural rocky point, trees and all.

The Sydney Harbor Bridge stood tall over the empty shore, but it appeared lonely without its famous friend.

"Faith, what have you done?"

Staten Island, NY

Garth and Sam made it home, but it took several hours of sitting in traffic to do it. With Dawson far behind, they didn't worry about being attacked by the maniac again, but it wasn't exactly smooth sailing. Since Garth was driving a cab, several pedestrians tried to flag him down and get inside, especially when he was stopped at lights. Garth solved the problem by having Sam sit in the back and pretend to be a paying customer.

It was ten o'clock by the time he pulled the cab around the back of his house and turned off the engine.

"At least we'll have an easy ride to the airport, tomorrow," Sam suggested as he got out of the back.

"Yeah, great idea," Garth replied. As soon as the engine was off, he pulled out his phone. "I've got to let Dad know I'm home. I'll leave out the middle part where we got into a batch of bad cologne." He laughed, finally letting air out of the stress he'd built up while driving the stolen cab.

"You can tell him. Just don't mention I almost crapped my pants."

Garth taunted his bud. "Hey, why bother talking at all if I don't mention that?"

Sam socked him on the arm through the driver's open window.

"Dude! That one hurt."

Sam laughed at his usual obnoxious volume. "I know. It's a thanks for driving award."

"For future reference, cash is appreciated." He pointed to the fare meter, which had been running the whole time. It was well over two hundred dollars. "Give me a second to text Dad, okay? Then I'm gonna kick your ass."

"Bring it," Sam replied, his cockiness returning in the safety of Garth's home.

Garth typed on his virtual keyboard. "Hi dad. Home safe. Can you talk?" There was more he wanted to say, but he'd save it for the call. Before he put it back in his pocket, he scanned for voice messages, but there were none. He felt a little let down, like his dad couldn't be bothered, but he knew it was unfair. Dad had to drive all day—a fact he now appreciated a lot more after his own time behind the wheel.

The phone rang the instant it returned to his pocket. The ringtone was a "Nyuk, nyuk, nyuk" laugh from Curly of the Three Stooges. It was Dad's ringtone.

He got it back out and picked up immediately. "Dad!"

"Hi, son," Dad replied. "So, you're safe back at home? Did you get my messages?"

"I just checked. I don't have any messages from you today."

"Hmm. I sent...a few. Look, I'm in nowhere California. A place called the Pole Line Motel near Mono Lake." Dad sounded tired. "It's been a strange day, to say the least, since the blue light went overhead."

"I saw it, too!" Garth replied. "Sam and I watched it go by while we were at the airport waiting for his parents. After it left, a plane crashed right in front of us. We were almost hit by flying debris. It was crazy." Garth went right to fifth gear and talked a mile a minute. "Then we almost died in a subway crash, we were chased by a woman with a broom, and we..."

He slowed down when he thought of Dawson. His dad would think it was irresponsible for staying with the mad driver for as long as they did, and it would be hard to explain the finer points.

"And we found a cab with its door open and the keys inside, so we borrowed it to get home in the fastest way possible."

Dad switched to interrogator mode. "You stole a cab, son?"

"The subways got shut down. It was our best bet to avoid walking, and I knew you'd want me home without delay."

"That's true. I saw cars with their doors open, too," Dad said as if he'd struck on an important fact. "It can't be a coincidence. Something is wrong with society. I know it now."

Sam chose that moment to knock over some trash cans.

Dad heard the noise. "What's wrong? Is someone attacking you?"

Garth laughed. "No, it's just Sam being Sam. It's dark here."

"Dammit, son. Listen, I'm not on the highway right now, but tomorrow, I'm going to get back onto Interstate 80 and then I'm going to drive the 80 all the way to White Plains. Then I'm getting in my pickup truck and coming straight there. Do you understand?"

"I do, but what do you mean by something is wrong?" It had been a messed up day, but he figured it was only him. If his Dad was experiencing similar issues... "What have you seen?"

Buck sighed on the other end of the line. "The news is all over the place. Plane crashes, yes, but also weird shit like that Malaysian airliner coming in for a nice landing like it hadn't been gone a day. I ran into a giant storm here the weather service said formed because several storms appeared on top of each other at the same time. There's another storm on the East Coast, too. Have you heard of it?"

"Audrey?" Garth answered. "Yeah, we heard some guy talking about it in the city. Said it's kind of a lame rainstorm coming up the coast."

"It's not lame, son. Listen..." Dad sounded unsure what to say next. "If the storm is like the one I survived, you'll have to go in the basement and hunker down. I think that's the best thing."

"I have a cab," Garth said hopefully. "I could drive west on highway 80 and meet you in the middle. It would get me away from the storm."

Sam heard those words and replied, "I'm not leaving. My parents are coming home!"

"Sam's not leaving," Garth repeated to Dad.

"Son, look. That's not a bad idea, except you are fifteen and don't have a driver's license yet. I—"

"Hey, I drove across the city without any problems," he said a little too defensively.

Dad laughed in a friendly way. "I have no doubt you can do it, son. I've seen you drive. You've got a good eye for the road. But if you get pulled over in a stolen cab, you may get tossed in jail until I could come get you out. Jail is no place to be when the shit smacks the fan, if you catch my meaning."

Garth spun the whole conversation on its butt. "Dad, I'm sorry for what I said to you last week. I really didn't mean any of it. I want you to come back."

"Man, I'm glad to hear you say that. I've been thinking the same thing, and I'm sorry for how our last visit went down. I even bought you something as a peace offering." The phone went silent for a few seconds before Dad spoke to someone on his side. "Say hi, Mac."

A dog barked through Dad's handset.

"That's my good buddy, Mac," Dad said proudly. The dog barked again.

"You got me a dog? What kind is it?" Garth was excited now. They'd talked about it for a long time, but he'd never expected it to happen.

"It's going to be a surprise for when I get home," Dad teased. "But I promise you'll love him, like I do. Listen, now. I need to tell you something."

Garth concentrated as his dad outlined how to get into his gun safe. His stomach clenched as he heard words like rifles, handguns, ammunition boxes, and self-defense. Over the years, Garth had watched his dad clean numerous firearms in the basement, and they'd been shooting in the pine barrens lots of times, but Dad was talking like bad guys would soon be knocking at the door. It changed everything.

"I understand," he replied after several minutes of description.

"Son, I love you more than anything in the world. Whatever happens, use the good head God put on your shoulders and remember the things I've taught you. The blue light has people freaked out. When people get scared, they do stupid things. I'm not saying it will get bad there, but I want you to be ready if it does. That's all."

Dad didn't want him scared, so he tried to breathe deeply and stay calm.

"I'm good, Dad. We're going to get Sam's parents in the morning, then we'll stay here until you get back."

"Am I on speakerphone?" Dad replied.

"No."

"You're a grown man, Garth, so I won't tell you what to do, but I would think long and hard about going out again. Sam's parents can catch a cab home on their own, you know?"

"Uh huh."

"And I love Sam like a distant son, but he has a tendency to, uh, how should I say this..."

"Find trouble?" Garth suggested.

"Yeah," Dad chuckled. "Just don't let him cause any problems for you when things are so serious, okay?"

Too late.

"I hear you," Garth answered. "I won't."

"Good. I'm hoping I've eaten a bad hamburger and everything will go back to normal tomorrow. Then we can laugh about this in a few days when we're out fishing together."

"Sounds cool, Dad."

Dad cussed under his breath before speaking into his phone.

"I've got to go, the motel guy is yelling at me. Talk to you tomorrow, okay? I love you, and I'm coming home for you. Bye, son."

The line clicked off.

"I love you, too," he said a few seconds later.

Garth was home safe and snug for the night, but he had a lot to think about. His mind reeled with the information his dad had unloaded on him about how to secure the house. It was almost too much.

Sam showed up a second later, as if he'd been waiting for him to hang up. "I bet I can drink a whole two-liter of Mountain Dew tonight."

Garth smiled at his best friend, but shook his head slowly, as if seeing Sam through new eyes. His phone call had been about cracking into gun safes and preparing for doomsday. Sam wanted to spend the night doing the usual—playing games, drinking soda, and watching funny videos.

Somehow, he needed to find a middle ground between the two extremes.

"I'm sure you can," he said in a friendly voice. "But let's get inside before you get us into any more trouble."

I'll see what tomorrow brings.

Pole Line Motel and Gas Station, Mono Lake, CA

"I've got to go, the motel guy is yelling at me. Talk to you tomorrow, okay? I love you, and I'm coming home for you. Bye, son." Buck clicked off the line while the motel proprietor came storming at him.

For a fleeting second, he considered pulling out his pistol to stop the apparent threat, but the man wasn't armed with a proper weapon. He was, however, waving a hundred-dollar bill.

"You! Stop filling your tank!"

Buck put up his hands in mock surrender because he'd finished up while on the call with Garth. "I can't take the gas out, Mr. Jenkins."

Fred stopped near the front corner of his Peterbilt. "You swindled me. This bill is counterfeit."

"No, I got it from the ATM at my bank just this morning. It's good money, sir."

"How can it be good money? Ben Franklin is too big, and it says it was printed in 2019." The man held the bill so Buck could see the date. Sure enough, it was printed last year.

Buck laughed. "And here I thought you were serious. That's a great joke."

"What's so funny?" Fred pushed back. "It is..." He paused to do the math in his head. "Twenty-nine years off. Tell your counterfeit guy he really blew it."

Mac's nails scratched the window above him, so Buck gave the pup a little wave. That seemed to catch Mr. Jenkins' eye.

"Don't you dare leave. I'm calling the police."

This guy is nuts. What did I do wrong to deserve a whole day of crazy people?

"Okay, hold up. Do you have the internet? I can show you online Ben Franklin is the correct size. Easy."

"Internet?" the motel worker asked. "We don't have anything like that here. We ain't like your fancy cities, or wherever you came from."

Buck didn't take it personally. He lived in the city but wasn't a city boy. "I have other money. I can give you smaller bills if it would make you feel better." He reached for the wallet in his back pocket.

"No," Fred snapped. "I don't trust you with phony cash."

Buck became worried. He'd gotten off the phone with Garth and advised him to stay out of jail. Now he was in danger of breaking his own good advice. "Sir, this is really a huge misunderstanding. I'm a professional trucker. I'd get fired from my job if I went around passing bad bills. Please let me pay with a credit card."

"I only take checks and cash."

Buck kept some checks in the logbook with all his other paperwork. Since he traveled all over the country, it paid to be prepared for every type of payment method. If he ran out of cash, and phone lines for credit cards were down, he'd have his checkbook as a final fallback. It had happened two other times over the years.

"I have a checkbook. How about I pay for the gas and a room, and I'll give you a nice tip to pay for your time out here talking to me. I'm telling you the truth. This isn't anything illegal."

Fred Jenkins appeared poised to run back into the motel, but Buck spoke before he left. "I'll pay the check before I park my truck. That way you'll see I'm serious about staying. What kind of idiot would stick around if he was paying with fake currency?"

The motel operator became more relaxed.

"You can even keep the bill as collateral until I leave."

It was the kill shot he needed. Fred finally showed his crooked teeth with his smile. "I can do that, I guess. Tomorrow, I might have to call my brother, though. He works at a casino in Reno. You can imagine, he knows everything about fake money." It wasn't meant as a threat; the man sounded curious about the new bills.

"Sounds good," Buck answered in a noncommittal voice. He didn't plan to stick around for extra scrutiny. He'd write off the hundred as a business expense if it meant he could leave at sunrise tomorrow without ever talking to Mr. Jenkins again.

Buck took care of the payment and parked the truck. He spent some outdoor time with Mac by walking him around the trailer during one of his inspections. When satisfied his tractor-trailer would hold together for the next day, he fed the pup his kibble and took a short break to breathe in the fresh air and admire Mono Lake. The round lake was a hundred square miles of blue in the drab, arid desert of the California-Nevada border region.

Not a bad place to visit.

As dusk fell, he used the key to get into his room. He didn't bother asking Fred if his motel was pet friendly. It wasn't in the best shape anyway, so a little pet fur wasn't going to ruin the place.

"Ask for forgiveness, not permission, right, Mac?"

The Golden Retriever ran into the room and jumped on the first of the two beds, just like he did in the sleeper.

"Oh, you want this bed? I think you got the best one." He playfully pushed the dog over on his side, which made him spring back up, ready for another push. Buck repeated it many times until Mac barked.

"Whoa! We have to keep it down." He flopped down on the bed next to his pal and scooted his way up to the pillow. Mac laid down next to him, leaving a microscopic amount of room between them. When he was able, Buck pulled out a jerky treat and put it in front of Mac's nose.

"You did good today. Enjoy."

True to form, the puppy needed only three bites to inhale it.

Minutes later, the soft bed and warm dog made him sleepy. His bad leg was still sore from his frantic run to catch Mac, but it was better. He spoke with his eyes closed, but his hand and arm on Mac's coat.

"What a weird day, huh? First the blue light, then the storm. Walmart fell apart while I was inside... Be glad you stayed in the sleeper. And the checkpoint was the cake topper, don't you think?"

Mac let out a noisy sigh, as if Buck was keeping him awake.

"We did see some cool cars, though. The '65 'stang was really something, wasn't it? And how about the driver?" In the comfort and safety of his room, he let his mind drift back to the woman's impressively small skirt. "And then we saw that Model T up in the park. I wish we could have looked under her hood. Those motors look silly compared to today's engines. I'll show you someday."

Buck was a gearhead when he was back home with Garth. He was always fixing up old cars and selling them on the side to make a little extra cash. It was no accident he noticed interesting hotrods, no matter how attractive the drivers.

"I promise," he added as if Mac was about to argue with him.

It wasn't even dark yet, but he'd had a long day. The sooner he got some shuteye, the sooner he could get up and do it all over again. Mac's even breathing suggested he valued the same thing.

His last thought of the day was the same as his first. Reconnecting with his son on their brief call hammered the point in.

"I'm coming home, Garth."

Telling his son he was bringing Mac to him as a gift, and hearing how much Garth anticipated meeting him, unleashed a new sentiment in Buck's consciousness. It was a feeling he embraced willingly, especially after the close-calls of the day.

"This time, I think it will be for good."

To Be Continued in End Days, Book 2

If you like this book, please leave a review. This is a new series, so the only way I can decide whether to commit more time to it is by getting feedback from you, the readers. Your opinion matters to me. Continue or not? I have only so much time to craft new stories. Help me invest that time wisely. Plus, reviews buoy my spirits and stoke the fires of creativity.

Don't stop now! Keep turning the pages as there's a little more insight and such from the authors.

AUTHOR NOTES – E.E. ISHERWOOD

Written January 10, 2019

Thank you for joining us on our new post-apocalyptic series, *End Days*. I'm humbled you would reach this point and still have the energy to read my author notes. I'll keep it short.

I'd like to thank Craig Martelle for partnering with me on this endeavor. He saw the potential for this story and shared his creativity to make it shine. As a writer used to working alone in a dark room, it was fantastic to have someone as invested in these words as I was myself. His directives were simple. Write about great characters. Keep it hopeful, not oppressive and dark. And finally, tear the world down to the foundation.

Book 1 peeled off that first layer. I can't wait to show you what's at the bottom.

Speaking of characters, I knew from that first day I wanted to write about a father and son having a grand adventure. My son is a few years younger than Garth, and I'm a few years older than Buck, but I found both characters easy to write using my own experiences with my son.

I love road trips, which is another key element of this story. With each interaction along Buck's journey, he must consider if it will help or hurt his chances of making it back to Garth. If you've ever taken a cross-country trip, you know how minor things can have a big impact on your journey. You forgot your driving music. You didn't dress for the weather. You never imagined how a taco salad in Amarillo could ruin your trip across Oklahoma...

This is the second post-apocalyptic series I've done. My other seven novels (*Sirens of the Zombie Apocalypse* series) also feature a tight-knit family engaging in heroic adventures to save the people they love in a dying world. I'm drawn to the desperation of major biological and technological disasters, perhaps because it strips life down to bare frame. I can walk away from writing these books and look at my own life while thinking, "Buck had to escape a riot at Walmart, and I'm complaining about needing a light jacket while walking to the mailbox. Suck it up!"

Finally, a lot of my other author notes mention the coincidences I experienced during the process of writing. This book has one, too.

When I was a kid in the 80s, my parents took me on lots of vacations to the western part of the United States. No, not flights to Disneyland or relaxing on the beaches of Malibu. We piled in the family Suburban and then sat for what felt like years as we drove 2000 miles across the country. It was debatable if those trips were vacations or punishments for us kids.

While I was writing about Buck's journey in the Central Valley of California, I needed to get him over the Sierra Nevada mountains. I used Google Maps and picked the road I thought was most efficient. It turns out it went through Yosemite National Park, and it was one of the places I'd visited as a young adult. I even have a photo of the same valley where Buck looks down from Olmstead Point.

Now that my son has seen photos of California, he wants to go there, too. I'm secretly excited to see how well he'll do on the same 4000-mile round-trip. Maybe he'll write a book one day featuring the places I've taken him.

That's all I have in this short note. Join me on Facebook or my website. I'll post some pictures of the beautiful country Buck is driving through. I love to talk about travel, survival preparation, and the end of the world.

Thank you again for heading out on this first *End Days* adventure.

EE

E.E. Isherwood's other books

End Days (co-written with E.E. Craig Martelle) – a post-apocalyptic adventure

Sirens of the Zombie Apocalypse – What if the only people immune are those over 100? A teen boy must keep his great-grandma alive to find the cure to the zombie plague.

Eternal Apocalypse – Set 70 years after the zombies came, a group of survivors manipulates aging to endure their time in survival bunkers, but it all falls apart when a young girl feels sunlight for the first time.

Undead Worlds Volume 1 – Short story. "On the Rocks"

Undead Worlds Volume 2 – Short story. "Picking it Up in the Middle"

Descent into Darkness – Short story. "The Nine Lives of Captain Osborne"

The Expanding Universe Vol 1. – Sci-fi short story.

Metamorphosis Alpha Vol 2. – A short story set the world's first science fiction RPG

Amazon – amazon.com/author/eeisherwood
Facebook – www.facebook.com/sincethesirens
My web page – **www.sincethesirens.com**

Once you've signed up for Craig's **newsletter**, I would be thrilled to have you also join **mine**.

That's all the time I have. The next book calls to me!

AUTHOR NOTES - CRAIG MARTELLE

Written January 10, 2019

You are still reading! Thank you so much. It doesn't get much better than that. E.E. Isherwood approached me about six months ago about writing a post-apocalyptic series together.

We talked about a plot and a way ahead then E.E. dug deep into it.

We regrouped every couple chapters to make sure we were still on track and through it all, we never lost sight of Buck's sense of urgency in getting back to his son while his nature of helping others continues to compete with his primary goal.

We have book two ready, but will wait 28 days before publishing it so that we can make sure book three is ready 28 days after that. Why? I like publishing on Mondays. Simple as that. I think it kicks off the week right. Also, if there are any issues, Amazon's day shift is on board to fix them. Publishing on Friday through Sunday carries the challenge only if something goes wrong when I have to wait until Monday to get it fixed anyway. So there we are.

This book is a bit longer than most post-apocalyptic stories, weighing in at 80,000 words. That's okay. This is an epic adventure that will span three (four) books. We hope you can relate to Buck & Garth as much as I do. Now that I have grandchildren, I want them to be self-sustaining, too. I know that my son will teach them well.

We went somewhere warm for Christmas and New Year's, finally getting back home on January 7th after traveling all day and then some. When we left Bali, it was 85 degrees. When we landed in Fairbanks, it was -38F. That's only a 123 degree difference in the span of one day. It was a bit of a shock on these old lungs so I'm doing everything I can to remain indoors. My wife has been taking Phyllis for her walks and I'm limited to just letting her run outside for a kick potty call. She doesn't want to be out there any more than I do.

Onward and upward. I have a great number of books in the queue, ready to be delivered every Monday for the next couple months. I think you'll like what you see. Monster Case Files is a great deal of fun and excitement. It is Scooby Doo meets Nancy Drew in the modern age. I'm not sure there's anything else like it.

That's it, now. I'm off to keep writing and working with my co-authors to bring these incredible stories to you.

Peace, fellow humans.

Craig Martelle's other books (listed by series)

Terry Henry Walton Chronicles (co-written with Michael Anderle) – a post-apocalyptic paranormal adventure

Gateway to the Universe (co-written with Justin Sloan & Michael Anderle) – this book transitions the characters from the Terry Henry Walton Chronicles to The Bad Company

The Bad Company (co-written with Michael Anderle) – a military science fiction space opera

End Times Alaska (also available in audio) – a Permuted Press publication – a post-apocalyptic survivalist adventure

The Free Trader – a Young Adult Science Fiction Action Adventure

Cygnus Space Opera – A Young Adult Space Opera (set in the Free Trader universe)

Darklanding (co-written with Scott Moon) – a Space Western

Judge, Jury, & Executioner – a space opera adventure legal thriller

Rick Banik – Spy & Terrorism Action Adventure

Become a Successful Indie Author – a non-fiction work

Metamorphosis Alpha – stories from the world's first science fiction RPG

The Expanding Universe – science fiction anthologies

Shadow Vanguard – a Tom Dublin series

Enemy of my Enemy (co-written with Tim Marquitz) – A galactic alien military space opera

Superdreadnought (co-written with Tim Marquitz) – an AI military space opera

Metal Legion (co-written with Caleb Wachter) – a galactic military sci-fi with mechs

End Days (co-written with E.E. Isherwood) – a post-apocalyptic adventure

Mystically Engineered (co-written with Valerie Emerson) – dragons in space (coming Jan 2019)

Monster Case Files (co-written with Kathryn Hearst) – a young-adult cozy mystery series (coming Mar 2019)

If you liked the story, please write a short review for me on Amazon. I greatly appreciate any kind words, even one or two sentences go a long way. The number of reviews an ebook receives greatly improves how well an ebook does on Amazon.

If you liked this story, you might like some of my other books. You can join my mailing list by dropping by my website **www.craigmartelle.com** where you'll always be the first to hear when I put my books on sale. Or if you have any comments, shoot me a note at craig@craigmartelle.com. I am always happy to hear from people who've read my work. I try to answer every email I receive.

Amazon –
www.amazon.com/author/craigmartelle
BookBub –
https://www.bookbub.com/authors/craig-martelle

Facebook –
www.facebook.com/authorcraigmartelle
My web page – **www.craigmartelle.com**

That's it—break's over, back to writing the next book.

Made in the USA
Las Vegas, NV
24 April 2025